Love and Other Risky Business

Over The Top Love Book One

Sarah Brenton

Contents

Content Notes

While this book is a romantic comedy, it does contain an on-page traumatic brain injury, as well as discussions around painful periods, a elective hysterectomy, and infertility (there are no miracle babies). There is also mention of parental death when the heroine was a small child. Like all my books, this one contains explicit sex scenes as well as strong language. Full content notes can be found on my website, www.sarahbrenton.com. Please take care of yourself when reading. xx

To everyone who feels like a little too much.

Chapter One

Mina

Sometimes, a good man *does* fall out of the sky.

Five years ago, on the worst day of my life, Timothy Foley landed at my feet after a jump from a second-story balcony. Tonight, he drops into the limo via the sunroof, landing—through some impressive contortions—on my lap to the utter amazement of the friends sitting across from me.

"Why yes, Mina," he drawls with a diabolical grin, eyes crinkling at the corners, dimples popping. "It *did* hurt when I fell out of heaven."

"You're an overgrown lapdog," I complain, digging my fingers into his ticklish ribs to dislodge him from my lap. He howls, spilling into the seat next to me—all two-hundred-some muscled pounds of him.

He might fall out of the sky all the damn time—for *fun*—but that's not me. My heart is banging around my chest and if the cold sweat I'm now sporting ruins this beautiful midnight blue Mioe dress, I will kill him. That he gave it to me for my birthday two hours ago will not save him from my wrath.

This dress is everything I am not. It's freedom and luxury and wild nights. Wearing it, I could be someone who'd jump through the sunroof of a limo.

"You love me," Timothy teases, and I do. He's my best friend, though we're cut from a very different cloth. I'm the calm he craves, he's the thrill that inspires me—from a safe distance. It sounds like a bunch of bullshit, but it's woven into us in a way that's hard to put into words.

We just…work.

It used to terrify me, the idea of Timothy let loose in my life. Like the Tasmanian Devil, he'd whirl through, tossing my careful existence into the air and leaving me precariously perched in his wake. But something about him drew me in and I've never had cause to regret it. He never pushes my boundaries.

He's my person.

"Do I though?" I ask in response to his certainty of my love, side-eyeing him as the limo slinks through LA traffic.

"Yes." He pulls me into a hug, enveloping me in the fresh citrusy scent of his cologne. I wrap my arms around him and squeeze him back. He gives the best hugs. The kind that takes all the nearly severed pieces and pushes them back into place. This week has been hell and I'm hanging on by a thread, but five seconds in his arms and I'm whole again.

He nuzzles my hair, his chest expanding as he takes a deep breath. With a barely audible sigh, he lets me go, turning to the two women sitting across from us. "He wasn't there. One more place?"

We're kidnapping a movie star.

Honestly, this night is on par with most friendiversary nights, but to Charlotte and Lexi, who flew to LA to surprise me for my birthday, this is bonkers. They've met Timothy a few times via video chat, but they have no idea what a night out with him is like. Thankfully, they're on board, dying of curiosity because he won't tell them who our target is.

"We're coming in this time," I say. I'm not spending my birthday- friendiversary sitting in a limo while Timothy ducks in and out of clubs looking for his wayward other bestie. I want to dance.

Timothy grins, dipping his chin in agreement. The beauty of our yearly celebration is that, while there might be a plan, no one ever sticks to it. Anything can happen.

The day we'd met, I'd walked in on my boyfriend balls deep in another woman. On my *birthday*. Timothy saved me that night. He let me be a mess, then he took me on one of the craziest nights of my life. Every year since, we celebrate my birthday and our friendship, and he does everything in his power to make sure I have the best day since he met me on one of my worst.

It's the one day of the year I allow myself to let loose and pretend I can live as he does—fearlessly, impulsively, but also risk-free, because Timothy's got my back.

It's become my favorite day of the year.

Charlotte pushes her coppery hair back, letting out an excited squeal when the limo stops in front of LA's hottest new club. A line stretches outside the entrance and a cluster of paparazzi mill about, hoping to catch a shot of a celebrity. Possibly the celebrity we're here to kidnap.

Timothy exits via the door this time, holding it open and helping us out. A smattering of flashes goes off at the sight of a well-dressed man stepping out of a limo before the photogs realize none of us are famous. Still, I smooth down the slinky dark blue dress and pray no one got a puss shot.

This dress *is* criminally short, held on to my body by the grace of god. The back dips low, nearly to the top of my ass crack, while the front is a narrow halter loose enough that a stiff breeze could have me tits out if not for judicious use of boob tape. The designer behind Mioe hit it big last year when Kate Van Sandt, America's Sweetheart, wore one of her dresses to the Oscars. Now only celebrities and rich people get their hands on a Mioe dress. Timothy's a stunt performer, not exactly a celebrity or someone making obscene money, but he does know everyone, so it's not surprising he managed to get this dress.

We bypass the line, Timothy greeting the bouncer by name and engaging in a complicated handshake, then we're inside with the top tier of LA's party scene.

My friends immediately point out a few celebrities, speculating who our target might be. Charlotte's pale skin is already rosy with excitement, and Lexi's brown eyes are sparkling.

I know who we're here for, but even if I didn't, I'm used to celebrities. I've worked various wardrobe jobs in movies and TV. Seen a lot of famous butts.

The club is swanky and dark, awash in neon blues and pinks, and filled with sexy bodies in motion. The thumping EDM isn't half bad. More tension slips off me. Tonight, I'm not going to worry about my job, my bills, or my side hustle. My inner party girl is coming out to play.

"Happy Birthday, Mina!" Timothy snags us all shots and we clink the glasses together and tip back the blue drink. It burns on the way down, setting my blood on fire. I love it.

He grips my elbow, leaning close enough I can almost taste the sweet alcohol on his breath. "I'd better find Nic."

Our kidnappee. Dominic Fontana is Timothy's best friend from childhood and the star of the massive Warwick superhero franchise. I've only met him a handful of times, but he's going through an acrimonious divorce and Timothy's worried about him. I don't know a lot about it, but routinely being photographed at clubs getting up close with other women isn't helping him counter the claims that he cheated on his wife.

Timothy will be checking the dark corners, and this club has a few. It could take a while.

"We'll be on the dance floor," I say, smoothing my hands over my hips. The dark blue charmeuse of this dress picks up the lighting beautifully. I'm obsessed.

When I look up, Timothy's still standing there, staring at my hands, which are still stroking the short skirt. I immediately stop. "Timothy?"

His eyes snap up to mine. "Nic can wait for a bit."

Um...okay.

"Come on." Lexi squeezes my arm and takes off for the dance floor, Charlotte shooting me an excited grin before following her.

Timothy places his hand on the small of my back as he follows us, the little touch raising goose bumps everywhere despite the heat of the club.

I shake it off. Timothy's attractive. He's tall and well-muscled in a lithe way with a body that frequently defies the laws of physics. His dimpled smile and light brown puppy eyes can incinerate panties—not mine—and the energy he brings to a room draws people to him. He has this way of making every person in his orbit feel special.

I love how he makes me feel.

Conversely, I hate his job. Hate his hobbies. Hate the heart versus cheese grater feeling that comes from loving an adrenaline junkie.

I'm not attracted to Timothy—I'm seldom attracted to anyone—but if I were? If I wanted more than friendship with him? It would end me.

So these goose bumps? They have to be unrelated to his touch.

The dance floor is crowded, and within minutes Timothy is pushed close to me, or maybe I'm pushed closer to him. He gives a little self-conscious laugh, which is a lie because nothing about this man is self-conscious. I roll my eyes at him, but the man can dance, and all of a sudden, he's dancing *with* me, not next to me.

Every brush of his body on mine tugs the silky fabric of my dress over my skin, filling me with this achy, inconvenient *need*.

The dress. Of course. It *has to be* the dress. It's so sexy it's tricked the dormant parts of me into waking up. A perfect storm of music, alcohol, and the energy of the club. It's not Timothy.

I turn, putting my back to his front, so I can't see the way the lights make his eyes look hungry. Tonight is my night to get wild—whatever I'm feeling, it's temporary. I'm going to enjoy it, not overthink it.

I'm drifting away to the music and the rhythm of the crowd when Timothy's hands slip around my waist. My breath hitches at the press of his fingers. Something pulls tight, low in my stomach. His chest is firm against my back as we sway. We haven't danced like this before. It's sensual. It's...*good*.

This is a bad idea, but it's friendiversary night. It doesn't count. I relax, sinking into him. Enjoying the way he feels, the way he touches me.

Maybe it's the bass reverberating through our bodies, but I could swear he groans, and the achy need he's inspired in me narrows to a sharp longing.

"Have I told you how beautiful you look tonight?" His lips brush my ear, his breath cool against my too-warm, too-tight skin, and I suppress a shiver.

He has, several times. Why do butterflies explode in my stomach *this* time?

"I'll get Nic, then we'll go," he says reluctantly, his hands slipping to my hips as I struggle to breathe.

I nod but he holds on to me for another ten whole seconds, during which I inch closer to spontaneous combustion, before he lets go and is swallowed by the crowd. My back feels cold without the heat of his body and that shiver finally runs free.

Charlotte grabs my arms. "What was that?"

"Nothing." I shake it off and suck in a deep breath. It's too hot in here.

"That was something," Lexi yells over the music. She blows a strand of lavender hair out of her face. "You two need to bang it out."

I dismiss that with a laugh. "We're just friends."

He asks me out at the end of every friendiversary night, and for the first time, I wonder if he actually means it. A little buzz of anticipation thrums through me and I tamp it down. This is a silly tradition he keeps up because he gets a kick knocking me off-kilter. That's all.

Even if Timothy was interested in more—and he's not—and if we were willing to risk our friendship—and we're not—he's always after someone new and exciting. He's got a new boyfriend or girlfriend every week. They don't even last long enough to meet me.

Dating Timothy isn't an option. He wouldn't mean to, but he'd end up hurting me and I'll never put myself in a position where I find my heart smashed into the floor again. We are perfect as friends, unsuitable as more. These little sparks of attraction can't change that.

When he asks me out tonight, I'll say no. We'll stay friends.

The music bleeds one song into another—they all sound the same—and everything except tonight drains away as I dance.

Through a break in the swaying bodies, I catch sight of Timothy at the bar, his hand on Nic's shoulder as he leans in to say something over the loud music.

We need to go before Timothy and I end up dancing again, so I grab Charlotte and Lexi and we make our way over.

Timothy grins at us, and when he holds his arm out, I slot myself underneath, for science. Just to see if his touch does anything to me.

It doesn't. No weird horny feelings—until his drink touches me right above my elbow. The glass is cold and wet with condensation, and I inhale sharply. I want him to hold the glass against my neck. Slide it down my spine. Chase it with his hot tongue.

I want him.

Panic slides over me, because what the hell? Tonight, of all nights? And

Timothy? He's my best friend. I'm not going to be his adventure of the week.

Thank god Timothy's busy introducing Lexi and Charlotte to Nic. He doesn't notice when I steal the drink out of his hand. My friends are too busy staring at Nic with wide-eyed wonder to witness the unfurling disaster that is my physical attraction to Timothy.

I slowly drain his entire drink. It's delicious, which helps.

Maybe this is a transitory thing that will go away tomorrow. I cross my fingers and force myself to pay attention to the conversation happening around me.

My friends are pretty and Nic's eyes turn predatory for two seconds until Timothy steps on his foot and shakes his head. With a heavy sigh, Nic slips into a more pleasant, less casual-sex-is-how-I-handle-my-problems-can-I-introduce-you-to-my-dick personality.

Timothy takes his empty glass from me, one brow raised like he's on to me, and sets it on the bar. It's an act. He's completely unaware of my crisis. If he knew what was going on in my head, he'd overdramatically faint from shock.

"Let's go bowling," he says brightly.

Oblivious. Just the way I like him.

We pour into the bowling alley half an hour later, discarding heels and dress shoes for bowling shoes and ordering cheap beer from the bar. My night is safely back on track—any little sparks I feel for Timothy will take a back seat to kicking his ass.

This place exists in some bizarre world where everyone could be a competitor from the movie Dodgeball. We're sandwiched between some metalheads and furries bowling with bumpers and ramps. There's also a group dressed like 1920s gangsters a few lanes down, and a bachelorette party decked out in sashes and penis hats at the other end. A random gorilla wearing a fedora walks by several times, apparently unattached to any of the groups here.

Once we're in our lane, I turn to Timothy, jabbing him in the chest. "You're a cheater."

His smile is impossibly adorable—and guilty. He knows what he's done.

"Bowling? In this dress?" I motion down my body and the way his eyes follow makes my stomach flutter. "Is that the only way you can beat me?"

His grin turns wolfish as his eyes return to my face. "Maybe."

"I'm going to beat you if I have to flash my ass to everyone here." I slip my thumbs under the halter top near my collarbone and give it a gentle tug. "Also, boob tape. Do you think I'm an amateur?"

He laughs, his eyes crinkling softly. "I never underestimate you."

Dammit. Why did he have to say that? I can't afford to swoon, I have asses to kick. I pluck my ball off the rack and step up to play.

Five frames in and I'm barely ahead of Timothy. Nic and Lexi aren't far behind either. Charlotte's struck up a conversation with a guy a few lanes down, so we skip her turns.

"My evil plan might be working." Timothy gives me a diabolical grin, pointing at the scores as I step up to take my turn. I flip him off.

A wolf in the next lane lets rip a—you guessed it—wolf whistle as I'm about to release my ball. It doesn't leave my hand as it should and something in my finger pulls and snaps.

Pain shoots up my arm, my finger throbbing.

"Dammit!" I cradle my hand and watch my ball veer into the gutter, inches away from a pin. Icy panic competes with the pain. A sprain is the last thing I need. I've seen the pile waiting for me at work—alterations to hide a pregnant actress's growing baby bump and a ton of beadwork on a wedding dress for the finale. The wardrobe supervisor is the worst I've ever worked with and I need this job to pay the bills. I also need to start on the autumn release of my side hustle Wild Things, and I can't sew hundreds of pairs of underwear with a sprain.

Timothy skids to a stop in front of me, sweeps me up into his arms, and carries me away from the lane.

"Timothy!" I shriek, squirming in his arms. My whole ass is probably hanging out of this short dress and that's a different story than the little peek I may or may not have flashed while bowling.

He figures it out, shifting me in his arms and tugging at the dress. Too hard. Hard enough to pull the tape off. One of my tits pops out.

I squeal, he looks down, his eyes going wide, his hands squeezing me tighter—and he trips.

Chapter Two

Timothy

Physical prowess and muscle memory save the day—I don't drop Mina Andrei, the woman I've loved for five years. Instead, I catch myself, rolling her in my arms, hiding her with my body while she covers herself. I don't look. I can't get distracted and trip again. Her safety is more important than a peek.

Jackie Chan holds up a hand to give me a high five, but my hands are full and he isn't the real Jackie Chan. No, this is the invisible manifestation of my unrequited love, created at the suggestion of my therapist. In theory, making my feelings the third person in our friendship is supposed to help me do…something. I don't know, I don't remember and it doesn't matter because my "therapist" is an old hippie who gets stoned and spends all day on the beach waxing a surfboard I've never seen him use.

Five years. I've pined so hard I could give every household in California a Christmas tree, and this little strategy of naming my feelings? It isn't working. Jackie kicks my heart around daily and now we both know what shade of pink Mina's nipples are.

Dusky rose.

Our lives are never going to be the same.

I set her carefully on her feet at the bar. My face is hot and I'm not sure if I'm struggling to contain my laughter or if I'm hyperventilating because I saw her breast.

"Ice in a towel," I manage to say to the bartender. "And two slippery nipples."

The love of my life smacks my chest with her good hand, her dark eyes sparkling as she tries not to laugh. "Smartass."

"How's your hand?"

Mina ignores my question and her injured hand, fussing with her dress instead. "You are lucky you didn't rip this masterpiece."

She's worried about her dress, and I tripped because I saw a nipple. I bite my lip, but I can't keep it inside any longer. My head drops to her shoulder as I shake with laughter.

Mina laughs, probably because I'm laughing, then she hits me again, on the arm this time. "Rude."

"I'm sorry about the nip slip," I say when I get it under control. I suck in a deep breath because her scent is intoxicating—a little floral, a lot spicy. Like candlelit nights, luxurious bedding, and scattered petals.

"Tit slip," she corrects wryly. "It was all out there."

Sure was, and what a glorious sight. Pity I had to share it with half the weirdos in LA.

The bartender comes back with the towel-wrapped ice and I pull my face off Mina's shoulder, gently taking her right hand. She can't afford to miss work, so I watch her face closely for any sign of pain as I spend a long minute moving her elegant fingers. She's humoring me, but I always take what I can get from her.

I love her hands. I love when she touches me, those innocent little platonic touches that are never enough. My dreams are filled with her hands. I want to suck each fingertip. I want to feel them flick over the barbell in my right nipple. In the best dreams, her fingers are wrapped tight in my hair, guiding my mouth back to—

"Nothing broken," I announce, ending my examination abruptly and placing the ice in her hand before she can figure out where my thoughts have gone. I'm not a doctor—never stunt-doubled for one on TV—but I've broken a lot of bones. I've sprained and strained just about everything. If she'd done some damage to her hand, there's no way she'd be staring up at me, her eyes wide and dark like—whoa.

My breath catches. She's never looked at me like this before. Like she wants to climb me. I wet my lips and her eyes track the movement. Shit...am I imagining this? Did I want it so hard that I manifested it?

"Does it hurt?" I ask, my voice unexpectedly coming out too deep, too growly.

She blinks at me, her brow furrowing. "What?"

Inside, I'm doing backflips across the bar. With a huge grin, I grab her wrist and raise her hand in front of her face. "Your hand?"

Her cheeks turn an adorable pink. "Oh. No, I must have tweaked it. It's fine now." She's frowning as she turns to put the ice on the bar, and Jackie Chan gives me a solid shove. I take a step closer to her. When she turns back, her eyes go wide.

My hand lifts to her waist and Mina glances down in surprise. I do, too, because I didn't tell my hand to do that, or to slip the tips of my fingers under her dress where the halter meets the skirt—Jackie's pulling my strings. We watch as I pinch the silky fabric between my finger and thumb, adjusting it with a little pull.

My heart and brain catch up to what my body is already doing. The result is an old-school cartoon fight, a squiggly mess of oomphs and ows and eeks, before all three pause at the realization my hand is in her dress and she hasn't murdered me.

Mina boxes. Not competitively, but she can kick my ass. I need to proceed with caution. Except I'm so starved for her touch I don't mind if she kicks my ass.

She doesn't kick my ass. She swallows.

I swallow, too, and slowly, from the bottom up, I tug her dress over half an inch, putting it back in place.

Her nipples pebble as my fingers brush around the edge of one small breast and I forget how to breathe. Dusky pink. Her nipples are small dusky pink beads. I want to see them slick from my mouth. Her breath is coming short and fast, the rise and fall of her chest dragging the silky fabric over those pebbled nubs. I bite back a moan as the erection I managed to avoid in the thick of the moment comes roaring to life.

My fingers keep moving, continuing to adjust her dress, over her collarbone, until I reach her neck. Her eyes are on my face now, but I keep mine on my hand as I slip my fingers into her hair, my thumb brushing the lobe of her ear, making her little dangling earrings tinkle.

When I back her against the bar, she sucks in a breath, but she's still looking at me like she wants to devour me.

I'm so down with that.

I've dreamed about kissing her a thousand different ways in a thousand different situations, but it's never felt like the right time and this? It's time.

God, I've *ached* for this moment so I draw it out, letting it breathe while our hearts race and—

"Two slippery nipples," a loud voice says, accompanied by the slam of two shot glasses. Mina jumps, looking away and blushing hard.

Jackie Chan kicks a barstool clear across the room.

I grab the shots, giving the bartender a look that goes unnoticed. I hand one to Mina, we clink the glasses, and down the drink. Maybe I can salvage this? Bring us back to the brink of something amazing.

"So," I start to say, placing our empty glasses on the bar as an excuse to lean into her space again.

Mina's eyes go wide, but not at me. It's all the warning I get before I'm pushed out of the way and my freaking boss scoops her into a bear hug.

For fuck's sake. The first time that it's felt like the right time, and I've lost the moment. My shoulders sag as I deflate.

"Great timing, Danny," I grumble, elbowing him in the kidney while he continues to hug the woman I love.

He responds by blindly shoving me aside before releasing Mina and turning a big grin my way. "Oh, hey, Timbo. Didn't see you."

Then it's my turn. I'm not a little guy at all, but Danny is like The Rock. But bigger. He lets me go with a slap to the back that would dislodge a lung on anyone else. "Didn't think you'd be so happy to see me." He smirks.

I adjust my pants, annoyed but not embarrassed. "I'm not."

Danny laughs. "First round is on Timbo," he announces, and shit—the whole stunt crew is here.

I give Mina an apologetic smile. She knows what's coming. She nods and turns to order a beer, perfectly calm like we weren't five seconds away from making out at the bar.

Frustrating, but okay.

Turning back to Danny, I invite the crew to join us. The invitation is a formality. This group was joining us whether we asked them to or not.

Everything's fine. I'm still spending tonight with the love of my life. She's special, and if I have to share her with everyone, well...they're damn lucky.

The pins crash behind me and I turn around, awaiting applause that doesn't come.

Seriously? No one is watching me? A more perfect strike than the one I just bowled doesn't exist—at least not until my next turn—and not a single person saw it? What the hell is happening tonight?

I want to scream. Maybe roar is more accurate. Nothing is going to plan, which isn't uncommon, but *come on!*

I was this close to kissing Mina and instead of her at my side or on my lap between turns, she's ignoring me. Every time our eyes meet, her face turns pink before she looks away. Like she's embarrassed. With everyone else, she's laughing, chatting, and having fun.

Maybe it's a sign. She's not ready, and the universe is telling me to hold tight for another year, but goddammit I don't think I can survive another year in Jackie Chan's headlock.

Mina looks up at me suddenly and claps. That's more like it. I kick aside all the shitty feelings taking over my chest tand beckon for more. She lets a loud whistle rip. I'll take it. I curtsy to Danny—who I'm playing against—and Danny graciously takes off his shirt since he only took down six pins.

Mina wolf whistles for him. Dammit, I wish I'd bowled a gutter. *That* whistle should be mine, but I had her attention for a few seconds. Better than nothing.

The night is still young. I'll find time to tell her how I feel.

There's a fine balance between protecting a friendship and trying to turn it into more. I've been erring on the side of caution, asking her out on friendiversary night while spending the rest of the year trying to stuff Jackie Chan into a box so he doesn't embarrass us. Three hundred and sixty-four days trying to stuff the greatest stuntman, athlete, and actor of all time into a box is exhausting. Not to mention spending each of those days dissecting what went wrong every other year I've asked her.

I think I finally know what I'm doing wrong.

I've been cool and casual about it. She doesn't think I'm serious. That has to be it, right?

So tonight, nothing is going to stop me from making it clear I have feelings for her. Especially after what almost happened at the bar. Maybe I have a chance.

"Hey, America's *second* Sexiest Man!" I shout because Nic—who got knocked from the top by Gabriel Sinclair last year—is talking to a woman at the back of our group. "You're up!"

Considering I sent his whiskey-hued ball down the lane, he's going to be waiting for that turn. Sucka.

Nic grabs my arm on his way up. "You've got an admirer." His eyes drift to a woman with rose gold hair standing not too far from the woman he'd been talking to.

"Always have a few," I scoff at him. I'm not oblivious, even when I pretend I am. The woman he pointed out has been undressing me with her eyes for the last twenty minutes. There's also a wolf furry who sniffed me—I'm taking that as a compliment—and a lanky guy covered in tattoos with the metalheads who keeps sending sly glances my way.

"So go have some fun," Nic says, slapping my arm.

What does he think this is, the old days when we first came to LA? I don't need a wingman, I'm not interested in anyone other than Mina. Even if I were, tonight would not be the night for that.

"I am having fun." I lie. Well, it's sort of a lie. I'm not having the fun I want to have, but Timbo's Bowling "Death by Match Play" is the best and also the reason why this place makes me put up a massive deposit. It's impossible not to have fun.

"No," Nic says, "you're pining over a woman who wants to be friends. It's weird. Move on."

My anger is back and Jackie Chan is ready to throw. "Know what's weird?" I lean closer. "Screwing around to make what Addison did hurt less."

Nic's gray eyes harden. "You don't have a—"

"No, *you* don't have a clue and you're messing up your life. Keep your dick in your pants and call my therapist so the next Mrs. Fontana doesn't have to worry about antibiotic-resistant Syphilamydia. Except my therapist doesn't have a phone. You can find him on the beach. When you're done, get tested."

I've been trying to limit the damage from Nic's ho phase but finding a balance where he doesn't realize I'm micro-managing his life like the evil genius I am is exhausting. My cockblocking skills are ninja-level—ask my parents—but if I have to pull him away from one more twenty-one-year-old model, I swear to god...

Nic's handsome face darkens. "There's never going to be another Mrs. Fontana."

Oh, the smell of that bullshit. "I'm going to laugh you back down the wedding aisle." I hum a wedding march because it will drive him nuts and it does. His shoulders hitch, his scowl deepening. "Goats at the reception," I say before he opens his mouth.

Nic rolls his eyes and goes to wait for his ball.

It isn't lost on me that I'm getting up in his business while getting mad at him for getting in mine. The difference is I'm right, and he's wrong.

I drop into the chair next to the most beautiful woman on the planet. It's unfair how badly I want to touch her. Wrap my hands in her silky chestnut brown hair. Look into her soul-devouring dark eyes for hours. Kiss her lush mouth and her lush everything and lose myself so entirely inside her search and rescue will have to find me.

Nic's words roll around in my head anyway. I'm not wrong...but what if I am?

I'm still not convinced what almost happened at the bar wasn't my overactive and very graphic imagination. Maybe I'm too busy feeding my ego with the idea she has feelings for me.

Which would make me the biggest self-entitled dick in the world.

I lean into Mina and ask quietly, "Am I the biggest self-entitled dick in the world?"

Mina sizes me up. "I wouldn't say the biggest."

I grin at her because she's joking, which means I'm not acting like a self-entitled dick. "Oh, no, I am though. The biggest."

"Above average. By a bit."

"You're mean," I complain as Mina stands to take her turn. She laughs and walks over to find her ball.

She's up against a barely-legal-to-drink stuntman named Dex and the good-natured jabs the two of them have been trading might be verging on flirty now.

Grumble.

Timbo's Bowling "Death by Match Play" isn't any match play. There's a rolling penalty for whoever gets the lower score. Curtis got to toss Nic's ball down the gutter when Nic didn't make it back from the bar in time a few frames ago. Danny had to lose his shirt when I got a strike to his spare. If Mina loses to Dex, she has to finish her drink and his before their next turn, or she'll be bowling the rest of the game in her underwear.

Considering she's braless and we're all treated to a peek at her lacy thong every time she bowls, I have a vested interest in helping her cheat if it comes down to it—namely, I don't want to share.

The moment she steps up, we all go silent as we watch like the perverts we are. Mina gives no fucks—she models the underwear she sews, so her ass is already online and yes I have every image bookmarked and saved—and she flips off anyone who whistles. Including a fox furry earlier—though she cuddled the fox after they dropped their ball on their foot.

Dex motions for her to go first. He's a nice guy. Handsome and tan, with floppy ash-blond hair. I had to cut my hair short and dye it darker to stunt double for Nic, so I'm a little jealous of Dex's locks. Honestly, I just want hair long enough to be pulled in the heat of the moment.

Not that I'm having any "heat of the moment" moments these days.

I mentally revoke my opinion of Dex being a nice guy when it becomes apparent he's standing back for the view up Mina's short dress. Jackie Chan kicks me for not clocking Dex, but really, Jackie, who can blame the kid?

Mina beats him, so he has to drink her beer and his before his next turn or strip.

"Sorry, Dex," she says with a laugh. "No clue where my drink went. Might as well strip now."

I hand Dex Mina's beer, giving her a stern look.

She ducks her head, blushing, but she doesn't sit next to me again. She stays standing with Dex.

I frown and stare at my bowling shoes. Maybe I'm reading too much into the incident at the bar. Maybe she's into Dex. She's never really been into anyone, so would I even know?

Asking her out is a jump I've face-planted every year. I'm sick of landing on my face. I need to know if this year I can make it. I need a sign.

I stand, grabbing Mina's hand and twirling her into my arms. She looks surprised, but she's going with it. Probably because she's tipsy.

"Let's get out of here. We'll go dancing, just you and me." I want to touch that silky dress again, so I pull her close. The fabric catches on the rough pads of my fingers as I slide them up and down a few inches. My eyes practically roll into the back of my head, but I don't break my stride, swaying her like we're at a middle school dance.

Only my thoughts are very grown up.

Mina laughs, but I can feel the little shiver that slips down her spine. I pull her tighter against me and her laugh stops.

The rest of the bowling alley fades away. Nic could be juggling bowling balls. The furries and the metalheads could be having an orgy. I wouldn't see any of it.

Look at me. See me. My heart is yours. Hope is too raw to let me say it out loud, so I tell her with a look, with a squeeze of her hand, her waist. Five years of longing pulled tight into this moment and all I need is one sign she wants this as bad as I do. Something to keep me from giving up.

Mina glances over her shoulder. "I can't leave my friends."

My heart takes the body slam. *Thanks, universe. Wrong fucking sign.*

Her friends have left her. Charlotte's chatting with Curtis, who is not only a dead-ringer for Regé-Jean Page, but also has an Irish accent, tells the best stories, and fosters kittens. Charlotte, who looks a bit like Isla Fisher but taller and somehow less potentially stabby, has forgotten Mina exists.

It's been driving me nuts all evening, but I don't know who in the world of celebrity Lexi resembles. Whatever. She's talking to a woman at the bar. I don't know the woman, but she's from the group dressed like 1920s gangsters, and Lexi appears very interested.

Her friends are happy. The look in Mina's dark eyes tells me she knows. She just doesn't want to leave with me.

"Okay," I say quietly, releasing her.

The beer is flowing and the next two hours pass in a whirl of laughter and the occasional bit of nudity as I pretend my world isn't crumbling. The amount of shit-talking has everyone clutching their sides. Nic spills some beer on a beaver and we're seconds away from a brawl until I manage to separate them. And pull Nic away when the beaver whips him with their tail.

Although Dominic Fontana getting his ass kicked by a beaver would be worth the lifetime ban from my favorite bowling alley.

I turn and somewhere in the background the clatter of pins as someone gets a strike provides the perfect soundtrack to my heart breaking.

Mina's got her hand on Dex's forearm, a big smile on her face. They laugh at something he says, but her hand lingers before falling away.

How is Dex doing this?

Watching her tease him as they take their turns is worse than being set on fire and I was set on fire yesterday, so I know this for an absolute fact.

It's time for me to face reality. She's never loved me as anything more than a friend, and I'm an egotistical asshole for feeling entitled to her heart.

Nic's fucking the ghost of his demonic ex-wife out of his system...maybe I need to try that strategy again. Maybe it'll work this time.

The woman with the rose gold hair drops into the seat next to me, flashing me a smile, and I know exactly where the look in her eyes leads.

Chapter Three

Mina

My team won. I didn't have to strip to my undies, and I got the phone number of a hot twenty-five-year-old who might be Timothy-lite. Instead of feeling on top of the world as I prop a drunk Lexi against the limo and cover a drunker Charlotte's head as she stumbles into the back, I'm miserable.

Tonight is not supposed to be like this. I'm supposed to be letting go and having fun, and this is neither.

Screw Timothy for disappearing with some random woman on our friendiversary night. He's supposed to be with me, making me laugh, helping me forget the past and the tedium of my day-to-day life. Maybe I've been trying to get a little space from him tonight because I'm freaking out, but he wasn't supposed to give me more. He wasn't supposed to go off with someone else.

He danced with me, made me feel things I haven't felt in years, and I don't know what that means or what almost happened at the bar before Danny showed up, but Jesus, how fast he forgot about me when another woman came along is insulting. It meant nothing to him.

Not that I want it to mean anything, right?

I don't know...maybe?

God, I'm a mess.

The party's still going at the bar, but Lexi's about to drop, and if Charlotte has one more drink, things are going to turn ugly, so we're going home because

I won't be able to manage both of them alone.

And I am alone. It's better this way. I want to scream at the night sky "I am perfectly happy." Tomorrow I'm going to my boxing gym and spending an hour pummeling imaginary Timothies and I will be fine.

Just. Fucking. Fine.

"Mina!"

My heart rockets to my throat as Timothy bursts out of the bowling alley. I press a hand against my chest, taking a deep breath. I am not made for adrenaline.

Timothy makes it to me in about four long strides.

"You're leaving without saying goodbye?" The lights from the bowling alley behind him cast his face in shadow, but I can still see the hurt in his eyes.

I turn away to help Lexi into the limo and lie. "I was going to find you once I got them in the limo."

"Oh." He runs a hand through his hair, glancing around. "I'll grab Nic and we'll go."

Nic left an hour ago with a pretty brunette, which Timothy would know if he hadn't disappeared with the woman with rose gold hair. "Stay." I don't sound half as bitter as I feel. "You were having fun."

Timothy looks away. "Yeah," he says absently before turning back to me. "Sorry, nothing went to plan."

"Nothing ever does," I say.

The grin that slips over his lips erases all the tension he's been holding. "Let me make it up to you. Let's do this night over. How about Friday?"

I cross my arms, irritated he'd ask for a do-over after abandoning me for a hookup. Irritated I already have plans. And of course, irritated at myself for having complicated feelings about a man I can never have. "I can't."

"Hot date?" he jokes, knowing full well I haven't been on a date since my cheating ex.

My face flames. "Actually, yeah," I say because I'm pissed off he left me on our night.

Something flashes in his eyes. Jealousy, maybe. Hurt.

Instead of feeling like I won this round, it feels like I took a punch to the chest. "Dex?" he asks quietly.

I agreed to meet Dex for a drink after watching Timothy walk away with that woman, but I've already decided I'll cancel. Dex flirted with me, and I flirted back because tonight is supposed to be about having fun and forgetting cheating ex-boyfriends who ruin my birthday, but there was no spark, no need to see Dex again.

I drop my arms to my sides. I don't want to talk about this now that it feels shitty, so I downplay it. "It's just a drink."

Timothy is silent for a moment as he kicks at a few loose pebbles. "He's a good kid."

Emphasis on *kid*. My face goes hotter. Dex is twenty-five, hardly a kid, but I'm thirty-five.

He's a kid.

Timothy's face scrunches, and for a moment, I think he's going to say something else. I don't know, I don't want to know, but I give him a moment to tell me. If he wants to.

He doesn't.

The sick feeling in my stomach stops when Timothy steps forward, wrapping me in one of his amazing hugs. I rest my cheek against his chest and squeeze my eyes shut. I want to enjoy the tiny slice of this man that's always mine, but I can smell her perfume on his shirt and I want to cry.

He kisses my forehead, soft and sweet like I'm something fragile. His lips linger for a few heartbeats and my whole body buzzes, my lips aching for the press of his. I keep my eyes closed, waiting, wanting. Dreading.

He kisses my cheek. "Happy Friendiversary." My other cheek. "Happy Birthday." He pulls back and squeezes my arms. "You know I love you, right?"

I swallow the lump in my throat. "I know."

Here it is. He's going to ask me out. What would it be like if I were the kind of person who could say yes to him?

But even this dress on this night can't make me into that person. It can't give me courage or take away my fear. I can't say yes, ever, because I will never be enough for him and he'll never be what I need.

Squaring my shoulders, I'm as ready as I'll ever be to keep him friend-zoned for another year. I'll snuff out this attraction and everything will be fine again.

He smiles, but his smile is off. Sad. "Good night, Mina."

My "no" dissolves on my lips as he turns and jogs back to the bowling alley, leaving me standing alone beside the limo in the dark. He looks over his shoulder once and waves, then he's gone.

He didn't ask.

Chapter Four

Timothy

After last night, one thing is crystal clear: I am a chicken.

I've jumped out of planes and hung from helicopters. I've been set on fire, yanked around on wires, and dropped onto trains, cars, and buses. I've fallen off buildings and leaped between them. I've broken bones and been stitched up...not a problem.

Last night, I stood on the edge of confessing my feelings for my best friend, and I choked.

I choked again with the woman with rose gold hair because her name was Nina—because of course it was—and almost kissing her felt like a betrayal. I don't know how to get over Mina, but that ain't it.

Even Nic's yogurt tastes like defeat this morning. It's his last one but I like this brand better than the one I've got and I figure after he put those doubts in my head last night, he owes me. He's still asleep. Chiara left an hour ago. We've met a few times over the years through mutual friends, so it was nice catching up over coffee. She didn't ask me to put a shirt on. Or pants, since I'm sitting at the table in my boxer briefs, this being my house and all. She didn't even ask about the Nerf gun lying on the table next to my orange juice.

She's a good woman and lucky for Nic she looked satisfied. She's not going to run to the tabloids or brag on social media about her night with him, so he won't be getting any calls from his management whining that his image can't take another hit while he's in the middle of this divorce.

It sucks watching him sleep around when I know he's in love with my sister. Not that he'll admit it.

That's a whole mess I don't know how to fix.

Irritated, I push the yogurt away. I'm grumpy. I hate being grumpy.

I couldn't sleep last night—my brain wouldn't shut up and I was a giant ball of pent-up frustration. When jerking off didn't help, I swam a billion laps in my not-very-large pool. Looked at the photos I'd taken of the evening on my phone—which didn't help, because there was Mina in that hot as fuck dress, so of course I had to get myself off again. Somewhere around 3 a.m., I had the bright idea to see how many times I could come before sleep took me.

Five times total. My dick hurts despite ample lube use and I'm pretty sure I won't be rising to any occasion anytime soon, but I did manage to claw out two hours of sleep after that. Didn't improve my mood.

Going on like I have the last five years isn't an option anymore. I need to smother Jackie Chan and move on.

I sigh and go back to pushing a couple of raspberries around Nic's yogurt with my spoon. I don't want to move on. I want Mina.

"Morning," Nic mumbles with a yawn as he comes up the stairs. I reach for the Nerf gun—yes, I've been waiting for hours to ambush him solely because it will make me feel better—and nail him with no less than ten darts before he disappears back into his lair, a.k.a. my basement, shouting curses at me.

"Thanks for the yogurt," I call after him.

I get a solid minute to enjoy his yogurt in peace before a Nerf dart pings off my orange juice. Instinct kicks in and I grab my Nerf gun, dive rolling behind the not-great protection of chair legs. Nic's cautious, though. I have ample time to scramble behind the kitchen island.

Nic takes the high ground, dashing up to the next platform on my open staircase, where he can rain darts into every room on this floor while mostly shielded by the metal railings.

My heart is pounding, but I fire a few off at him, grab the pre-loaded second Nerf gun from the kitchen drawer, and book it outside. Nic doesn't follow me.

At least not yet. Wise, since I've had enough time this morning to fill and stash numerous high-powered water guns.

I'm crouched along the side of the house when I hear it. The slide of the glass door, followed by the click of the lock.

Bastard!

He'll be sitting comfy at the front door, waiting for me to walk in.

Not today, Warwick.

I pull the homemade bungee Nerf gun strap over my head and haul myself up the smooth concrete retaining wall that elevates my privacy hedge. From there, it's a five-foot jump to the ledge jutting out from the house. It's tricky. I have to grab on to the smooth-ish surface and if I go too hard, my momentum will carry me too far. But I've made this jump hundreds of times. I easily make it.

From here, I have to make my way hand over hand along the ledge to my balcony, where I can pull myself up. I left the door to my room open, so as long as Nic doesn't look over his shoulder from his position near the front door, he shouldn't see my legs dangling through the patio door as I hustle along.

If he does, I'll be in serious danger of a nut shot.

My arms aren't even burning when I reach the balcony. The smooth glass is useless, but between each pane is a gap I can easily wiggle my fingers through. I climb up and I'm about to swing myself over the balustrade when I see him. Sitting in the lounger on my balcony, a glass of orange juice in his hands. *My* orange juice.

"Morning, asshole," Nic says casually, bringing the glass to his lips as he raises the Nerf gun like some real Godfather shit.

I backflip off the balcony, a smile on my face at the shocked look on Nic's. My pool's not deep enough for a headfirst dive so I bring my feet around. I'm not on top of my game this morning. Instead of being tucked into a ball when I hit the water, I belly flop.

It's like hitting concrete dick first.

I'm screaming internally under the cool water, and when I break the surface, I let it out in a roar.

Nic must have raced through the house. He skids to a stop at the edge of the pool. "Jesus fuck Timbo!"

"I think I broke my dick." I gasp, swimming a couple of feet to the edge and pulling myself up. Carefully, because if my dick brushes the edge of the pool I'm going to scream. I rubbed myself too raw last night for this.

"You're lucky you didn't break your head," he snaps, arms crossed. The look on his face says he's two seconds from calling my mom.

"I've done that a hundred times." Sure, my pool is narrow-ish, but it's right below my balcony. As long as I don't push out too far, I'll land in the water. I don't usually belly flop, but I'm tired and heartbroken.

I get to my feet, plucking my wet undies away. My dick twitches, and not in its death throes.

Huh.

Guess I learned something about myself.

I shake the water from my hair and grab a towel off a lounge chair, shaking it out before wrapping it around my hips. I don't need to walk around with a semi in wet boxer briefs while Nic's here. He'll think it's him and his ego doesn't need that.

He follows me inside. "How'd last night go? When I left, you were getting friendly with a woman who hadn't relegated you to the friend zone."

I open the fridge and pull out one of his smoothies. "Nothing happened." One mouthful and I know why he didn't take the drink away from me. I spit it back into the container with a gag. "Stop worrying about my dick and start worrying about food poisoning."

"I'm worried about *you*, not your dick." He takes the smoothie to the sink and hands me a glass of water, which I drain. "Are you suffering from a sudden attack of celibacy?" he asks. "Do you need to see a doctor?"

"I'm fine." I'm not and there's nothing sudden about my celibacy, but he hasn't been around to notice until Addison kicked him out. Anyway, Nic's more of a mess than I am. "You're the one approaching sex like it will solve all your problems. Tell me, you feel good after?"

"After getting laid? Yeah, fucking fantastic."

"Nic."

He stares at me for ages. I stare back. His face is giving nothing away, and Nic's not good at acting, despite the Warwick role.

"For a little while, yes," he says eventually, and the mask cracks. He sags against the counter.

"And then it doesn't," I prod. I fell in love with Mina before I meant to. The first few months, I wasn't happy about it. I tried to fuck her out of my system. It didn't feel good—outside of the thirty seconds on either side of climaxing—so I stopped.

Nic's situation isn't all that different. Using sex to forget or cover feelings isn't the answer.

He scrubs a hand over his face. "I try not to think about it."

This is as close as I've gotten him to that big scary thing he doesn't want to acknowledge. We're in the same hemisphere now. "Maybe your heart wants something else." Like my twin sister.

His face darkens into a scowl. "I'm not in love with Addison."

Nope, still not even on the same planet. I open the fridge and hand him one of my yogurts to replace the one of his I ate. "I don't think you ever were."

Nic doesn't say anything, looking away as he peels the top off the yogurt. "You're right. I can't remember ever loving her. And I asked her to marry me anyway. What is wrong with me?"

"Do you really want me to answer that?"

He shakes his head and opens a drawer to pull out a spoon.

I study him for a long moment as he leans against the counter, eating the yogurt, his gaze a million miles away. Some introspection would be good for him.

He clears his throat. "Thanks for taking The Bus for me, by the way."

Okay, guess we're talking shop instead of feelings. I'll allow it. Don't want to push him and have him shut down.

"The choreo is tough." The Bus is what it sounds like—a bus but on a hydraulic rig that allows it to tilt, swerve, and buck. Nic does a lot of his stunts, but he's never mastered the trickier fight sequences. He's also a bit freaked out about heights and the bus is a good ten or fifteen feet above the ground depending on the position it's in. So, I get to do it. Which is great, because I love it.

Right now, I need the clarity of mind that comes from focusing on movement. For about ninety seconds this morning, from the moment I jumped to the balcony to the moment the pain of hitting the water receded, I forgot about Mina and Dex, my stupid broken heart, and Jackie Chan squeezing my nuts.

I can't fuck myself out of love, but I can work my heart back to whole.

Nope. That won't work either. Can't even fool myself. But this pent-up frustration, this rage and sadness, has to go somewhere, so it's Take Your Broken Heart to Work Day for the foreseeable future.

After barely making it through the rest of the weekend, Monday morning rolls around and I am itching to throw myself into work. The real heroes of the film transform me into the character Warwick, which means black leather pants and a corset-like vest that makes everything I have to do uncomfortable but does wonderful things to my ass. I get the wardrobe guy to take a shot of my butt before I realize I can't—shouldn't—send it to Mina. I send it to my family group chat instead.

I'm prepared, but Danny opts to run through the scene a few times before we start filming. What I'm not prepared for is Dex.

"She's so fucking hot," I overhear him talking to Curtis.

My hands clench. He's not being disrespectful or gross. Mina is fucking hot and Dex has hearts in his eyes.

Same, kid.

Danny runs me through the scene, but I can hear Dex still talking about his date, asking where he should take her like a goddamn puppy and I know he's going to ask me because she's my best friend. I'm going to have to give him an honest answer because I don't want him taking her somewhere she'll hate.

Not that I want her to have a great time with him.

Except I do, I want her to be happy.

Jackie Chan smacks the back of my head.

"Got it?" Danny asks, oblivious to my inattention.

"I can do this in my sleep," I say, climbing onto the rig. There's a complicated series of brief interactions with six other stunt guys as I move through the bus, but I've been doing this for fifteen years. I've trained for the sequence but haven't done it in the rig yet, since Nic planned to do it, but that doesn't matter. Muscle memory and instinct will fill in the gaps.

I run through it by myself a few times, the whole rig moving, tossing me about as I swing from handrails and smash into the walls. Easy.

When Danny's happy, the other guys clamber on. We'll do a few more run-throughs because this is a little tricky with tight quarters and a moving set. I'm confident we could film now, but Danny's the boss.

I wait for everyone to take their positions, my thoughts drifting to Mina. I don't like how we left things the other night.

Danny's voice cuts through the noise and immediately I step up to Curtis. We exchange a few blows, never touching, before the bus lurches, throwing us into the wall.

I haven't called her yet. Or messaged her. I've wanted to, but I don't know what to say.

Curtis falls, defeated, and Luis promptly runs me up a wall so I can flip over his head then feign bashing him into that same wall.

Sam is next. I dodge a punch from them.

Saturday night was the closest Mina and I have come to fighting. Maybe I should give her some space.

Sam goes down and I swing from a handrail, "knocking" another guy out of the fight.

I should give her at least a week. I don't want to know how her date goes. Probably I'll find out at work. Shit.

I fake taking a punch from Andrew while the bus lifts, slamming hard enough to rattle my teeth.

If the date goes well...

I barely dodge the next punch from Andrew, and the bus tilts.

Mina doesn't date. I've never seen her with someone else. I'll have to.

Finishing Andrew off, I spin, catching myself as the rig tosses me into a seat. Then I'm up and moving and—

Dex is in my face.

There's nothing in his expression beyond the job, but even that irritates me.

The punch I throw should pass by his face a couple of inches. I graze him instead.

Surprise crosses his face, but we're professionals. We keep going.

Mina hasn't dated anyone the entire time I've known her, so for her to say yes to Dex...she must have connected with him.

I let my next punch tap him because seriously, fuck this kid. What does he have that I don't? The bus tilts and for a split second, my mind blanks. I dodge Dex's punch by instinct alone, but his kick connects with my stomach, throwing me back as the bus swerves.

There's a loud crack as I smack into a pole, lightning exploding in my head.

Danny's voice rings out and everything stops.

I take a deep breath, running my hand over my head, checking my fingers for blood. Nothing. Anger burns off the pain when Dex reaches a hand down to me.

How'd I get on the floor?

"The fuck was that?" I demand, slapping his hand away and struggling to my feet.

"You forget the choreography or something?" he says, trying to laugh it off. "How's the head?"

Usually, I would laugh it off too. I've been punched and kicked by accident before. It happens. Instead, I snap at him. "I don't forget choreography. You were sloppy."

His eyes narrow in irritation. "You nearly took my head off."

Danny strides down the aisle of the bus and everyone ducks out of his way. He grabs me around the shoulders and marches me off, calling out for someone to get some water.

Off the bus, a poor mirror image of myself—same costume, slightly taller—hands me a bottle of water someone else handed him. "You okay?" Nic asks, his face pinched.

I scowl at his question. "When did you get on set?"

He frowns at me.

"Sit," Danny barks, pointing at a chair. "Drink that."

"You don't have to yell," I grumble, twisting the cap off the water bottle. I'm not thirsty, but I take a long drink. Pressure is building behind my eyes and honestly, I want to go home, crawl into bed, and admit defeat. Life is kicking my ass right now.

Danny disappears and reappears with a...first aid person? First responder? Para...something?

"Do you know where you are?" she asks calmly.

"At work." I hand the water bottle back to Nic, rising to my feet. The world tilts like I'm still on the bus. That happens sometimes, though it doesn't usually make my head pound. It'll go away in a minute. "I'm ready, let's do it again." This time I'll keep my cool when I reach Dex. Getting pulled off has put my tail between my legs and I'm ready to be professional.

Nic grabs my arm and I shake him off, but my stomach's not sitting right. "I don't have a concussion, I'm fine."

The first aid lady is already on the phone when I pitch forward, emptying my stomach.

Wow. That was unexpected. What did I eat? Probably Nic's smoothie from...the other day? Or, this morning? God, when was that?

I'm exhausted. I don't put up a fight when Danny sits me back in the chair.

Nic grabs my arm and squeezes so tight it hurts, pulling me back from...somewhere. "Hey. Stay awake. Can I call your mom? Jessie?"

I blink. Jessie? Shit, he must think this is serious if he's willing to call my twin. It's not. It won't be. If I'm going out in a stunt, it's not going to be some easy little fight sequence on a bus. "I'm fine." I feel off, but fine. I can do this. I can do anything except make Mina love me. "I need to stop drinking your old-ass smoothies."

"The ambulance will be here soon," some woman with a phone says. I can't see her—the lights are too bright and squinting hurts.

They're calling an ambulance? Something cold prickles over my skin. I grab Nic's hand. "Get Mina."

CHAPTER FIVE

Mina

"WORK IS KILLING ME today," I complain, sipping at my iced coffee. I'm in the parking lot, the back of my hatchback open so I can sit in the pathetic shade it provides. It's my lunch break and I'm video chatting with Charlotte and Lexi, who flew home yesterday. I already miss them. "I've got at least a million more seed pearls to sew onto this silk evening gown, my hands hurt, I'm pretty sure I'm going cross-eyed, and Cruella de Vil has been on me all day. I want to go home and sleep for a hundred years."

I don't really want to go home. I can't afford my apartment without a roommate, and my current one is a yoga instructor named Chantal who is going to cost me my deposit if she keeps burning sage. Also, I don't have time to sleep. I need to make a decision so I can start cutting fabric—all of it rescued from a fate in the landfill—if I want to stay ahead of schedule with my autumn release of Wild Things.

"Get a new job," Lexi says with her usual bluntness. Charlotte looks sympathetic as she nods.

I try to ignore the way that makes my chest tighten. I need the pay and this show has high ratings into it's third season. When I first came to LA, I struggled to find steady work, picking up bartending jobs and tailoring gigs to make ends meet because shows get canceled and movies don't film forever. Sewing was what I knew, what I grew up with, and wanted to do, but the reality of trying to make a career out of it was hard as hell.

The job I have now is safe, even if it's mind-numbingly dull and the supervisor is a nightmare.

"Maybe it's *time*," Charlotte whisper shouts at me. "Wild Things."

Lexi nods enthusiastically.

It's not time. My side hustle is doing well, but it's still a baby, and as much as I dream of running my little business as my full-time job and making enough to live comfortably off it, that's not possible yet.

I started Wild Things out of necessity, making comfortable period panties out of scrap fabric because my flow was heavy and relentless. I made some for a few friends. Then their friends. Then a few pairs of cute, comfortable regular panties. Since I used scraps, I kept my costs low and the extra income added a layer of security.

When it got out of control, I turned it into a subscription service. Four times a year, my subscribers get a package containing two pairs of regular panties of their choosing, in styles ranging from thongs to boy shorts, and one pair of period panties. I source the fabric from the big boys of the LA fashion industry—stuff that would otherwise end up in a landfill—so every package is a little different and my overhead is low. Streamlining my workflow into quarterly releases helped my productivity, and I'm making pretty good money these days, but I have to keep on schedule. If I fall behind, I'll have angry customers and Wild Things won't be strong enough as a brand for me to expand.

Hence my call to Charlotte and Lexi. My deadline for choosing the colors for the autumn line is today.

"So which do you think?" I ask again, propping my phone against my handbag so I can hold the two cards up at the same time. Each one contains five swatches and a couple of sketches for a little embroidered embellishment.

"The one on the left," Lexi says, predictably going for the bolder, darker colors.

Charlotte moves closer to the screen, squinting. "The right." Of course, she picks the softer jewel tones.

Dammit. I knew this would happen. I should just call Timothy. He's my usual sounding board for Wild Things. He has a way of talking me through things until I figure out what I want. His encouragement got me through that first rocky year when I was still figuring things out. Plus, he makes me laugh at myself, and right now, I really, really need a laugh. And a hug.

We haven't spoken since Saturday night. We don't speak every day anyway, but this feels wrong, like unfinished business hanging over me.

He didn't ask me out. I sigh for what has to be the eight-hundred and twenty-third time today. It's like he closed a door I thought would remain open forever. I liked it open, with its fresh air and possibilities. I want to bang on it and demand he open it again.

Which makes me a selfish asshole, since I have no intention of ever taking a risk and walking through that door.

No, I want him to ask me out every year, whether he means it or not because I like the idea of being someone Timothy wants.

I'm not happy about this. I need to be a better friend. God, if he had real feelings for me—and I still don't think he does—then I've been a real asshole to him.

I should text him.

"Lunch is almost over," I say to Charlotte and Lexi, tossing my cards into the back seat of my car. "I need to get back. Thanks, ladies."

"When's your date with the twenty-five-year-old hottie?" Lexi asks.

That shouldn't make me feel guilty, but it does. "I'm not going."

"Why not?" Lexi demands.

"Because she's holding out for Timothy," Charlotte answers.

"I'm not holding out for Timothy," I say, rolling my eyes and sipping my iced coffee. "There's no spark with Dex. Plus, he's a stuntman."

Lexi blinks at me.

"I like guys who keep their feet on the ground," I say to her, shutting the hatchback. I lock my car and head back across the parking lot. Nan said some variation of that—*surround yourself with people who keep their feet on the ground and their heads out of the clouds.* She meant it literally. My parents died in a climbing accident when I was four. Nan wanted to protect me from experiencing that kind of heartache again.

"Sooner or later someone is going to come along and make you take a chance," Lexi warns.

"Yeah, well, it won't be a stunt guy." I down the last of my iced coffee and toss the cup in the garbage as I walk by. It won't be Timothy. So what if I haven't felt the slightest attraction to another man since Matthew McCheating-Asshole? I can handle the loneliness.

We end the call, and I have just enough time to send a quick text to Dex.

> I'm sorry, I can't make our date this Friday. I'm not in a good place for relationships or dating. Hope we can be friends.

ME

There. At least that's done. I turn my phone off as I step into the wardrobe department, and when I reach my workstation, I stuff it into a drawer.

I crack my knuckles, pick up my needle, and bend back to my task. My life is fine. I don't need to chase heartbreak or financial insecurity. I'll keep my feet on the ground and work toward my goals and one day my life will no longer be this lonely slog through day-to-day existence. My caution will pay off with a hot, faithful, kind accountant boyfriend who will make sure that when I'm ready to jump and turn Wild Things into something bigger, I can do it.

The wardrobe supervisor, who everyone refers to as Cruella, walks about the room, but I ignore her, even when she hovers over my shoulder.

"This needs to be redone. It's sloppy." She points to two inches along the neckline with a bony finger, waiting for me to nod before she moves on.

When she leaves the room, I let out a string of obscenities.

Mariko, the wardrobe coordinator, laughs and comes over. "Apparently," she says in a hushed voice, "Cruella overheard Selena complaining about the vermilion gown last week."

Selena is the director, so that will have stung Cruella's pride.

"They only got one take of the alley scene before the dress snagged something and tore. It happened three more times and Julien had to sew it up quick each time so they could keep going."

Poor Julien. At least he works well under pressure. I'll take my hours of slow beadwork over the cast and crew breathing down my neck.

Mariko is called away and I sigh at the silk dress. The beadwork is fine, but Cruella will know if I don't redo it.

A door crashes open somewhere to a collective hiss—Cruella demands serenity and whoever barged in is going to cop it from her.

Not my concern, I tell myself as I spend a handful of seconds undoing hours of work.

"Mina!" a deep voice calls out, edged in a panic that slices through my calm corner of the workroom.

I jump, scattering seed pearls everywhere as I spin around, heart in my throat.

Nic's eyes lock with mine. His skin is pale, and he's out of breath as he pushes toward me. He's still in costume, I note, but the rest of my brain has gone fuzzy because there's only one reason Nic would ever visit me at work. It's my nightmare.

Everything slows in the worst way.

"No," I tell Nic, tears burning behind my eyes. Don't. *Don't say it.*

He doesn't hear me. His voice is strangled, holding back emotion. "There was an accident on set. Timothy—"

My heart stops beating.

He can't be gone. No. Not Timothy. He's unstoppable.

Mariko shoves my handbag and phone at me. Nic pulls me to my feet, yanking me toward the exit. My phone slips from my numb fingers, smashing onto the floor. He curses, bending to pick it up, and shoves it back into my hand. Strong hands grab my shoulders and Nic's gray eyes are suddenly in my face. "Do I need to carry you or can you walk? We've got to go, the driver's waiting."

Timothy's alive. There'd be no reason to rush if he were...if he were...

"Go!" I shove Nic and that's all he needs to take off through the warren that is this particular corner of the studio. "How bad?" I ask, matching his pace.

Nic looks at me and the terror in his eyes says *bad*. After that, I lose myself so all that registers are flashes. Nic barking at me to buckle my seat belt. Nic's muffled voice as he speaks on the phone. The wait is agony, the traffic thick like honey, my head buzzing with bees.

I turn my phone on, half expecting a message from Timothy, explaining this is a mistake.

My screen is cracked and there's nothing from him.

Chapter Six

Mina

Somehow, we make it to the hospital. My broken phone rings as we hurry through a corridor. It takes me a few tries to answer it thanks to the cracked screen. I'm desperate for it to be Timothy, calling to tell me it's all a mistake, he's fine—it was someone else. Or he's pranking me and he'll jump out yelling *Gotcha!* Even though he would never do that to me.

"Mrs. Foley?"

I don't know the voice on the phone. I don't know the number. It's not Timothy. My heart sinks and bile rises into my throat. I must say something as Nic leads me down the corridor because the voice on the phone keeps talking.

"Your husband was involved in an accident today. As his emergency contact—"

Husband. Mrs. Foley.

My brain turns these words over, but everything is molasses. I'm not married. I'm not Mrs. Foley. Mrs. Foley is Timothy's mother. His older sister who's married—I don't know if she took her wife's name, so maybe not. It's definitely not me.

Nic takes my phone. "She knows," he snaps, ending the call.

This doesn't make sense. But neither do the words *Timothy* and *accident* in the same sentence. He does risky shit all the time, but his luck is legendary.

Anger surges up in me and I turn on Nic. "What happened?" My voice is barely working, but he hears me. His face is dripping with sweat and he's visibly shaking. He looks seconds from vomiting.

My panic snowballs.

Nic swallows. "He took a kick and it knocked him into a pole. Hit his head. He was…" His voice trails off as his eyes lose focus.

"He was *what*?"

He tugs at the collar of his shirt and swallows. "Different. A-angry. He threw up. I'm sorry, Mina—I can't do this. I have to go."

"No." I lunge for him but he slips out of my grasp.

His eyes are wide and terrified, darting wildly over everything in the corridor. "Call me, let me know."

I make one last attempt at grabbing him as he turns, but he evades me.

"Don't leave me alone," I shout after him, but he's already gone.

"Mrs. Foley?"

I whirl at the voice behind me. A nurse is standing calmly, looking directly at me. My mouth opens to correct him, but if the hospital thinks I'm Timothy's wife, they'll tell me how he is and I'll commit fraud to find out. "That's me. I'm his"—I have to swallow before I can push the word out—"wife."

"Your husband is in surgery," he explains. "He had a bleed on his brain and they need to drain it to reduce the swelling. It's a fairly straightforward procedure."

I suck in a breath. Straightforward? It's brain surgery!

The nurse keeps talking about the procedure, but I'm not following. I can't think about how Timothy's having *brain surgery*, so I get hung up on the one thing that doesn't matter.

My husband.

Why do they think we're married?

When the nurse pauses, I nod again because my words are stuck in my throat. They're nothing more than a scream anyway.

"He was conscious when he came in, which is good. He was asking for you and you'll be able to see him when he's out of recovery. The doctors will want to talk to you after, but your husband was lucky to get here when he did."

The nurse promises to update me and has me sign some paperwork. I remember to sign Mina Foley, but my hand shakes so much that it wouldn't matter if I wrote Andrei instead. "Can I call someone for you?" he asks as he takes me to a waiting room.

I shake my head. I don't want anyone—I want Timothy.

The waiting room is bland and I stare at an impressionist-style painting of a beach, clinging to my cracked phone like a lifeline. Time must pass, but my world is standing still. My heart is standing still. I'm waiting to find out if it will ever beat again.

My phone rings and I'm surprised and dismayed to find twenty minutes have passed. I perform some finger gymnastics to answer the call through the cracked screen—Timothy owes me a new phone if he makes it out of this.

That *if* makes my voice crack when I answer. "Yeah?"

"Hey. How...how is he?"

Nic's voice is rough, on the verge of breaking. I pinch the bridge of my nose and close my eyes for two seconds. "In surgery, you coward. Why did you leave?"

He takes a deep breath and lets it out right into the phone, a loud *whoosh* in my ear. "I haven't been in a hospital since my parents died."

He had a panic attack. I can see that now, but I don't care. "You're his best friend. He needs you."

"I called his mom, she's going to call you. She's going to fly to LA tonight. Will you keep me posted?"

"Yeah." I open my eyes and stare at the wall. I didn't want the nurse to call anyone, but I want Nic here. He loves Timothy like a brother and we could support each other, if...

I can't think about that. I drop my voice to an angry whisper, glancing around for anyone in scrubs. "They think I'm his wife."

"Yeah." He doesn't sound surprised. "Shit, someone spotted me—I'm in the parking lot. I've got to go. Call me the moment you hear anything."

The call ends and I stare at my phone in irritation.

If he'd have done his own goddamn stunts...

That's not fair, and it's not how this works. Nic's not trained. He's not as replaceable. I understand it, but it doesn't stop me from wishing it was someone else who got hurt.

My anger at Nic burns out quickly. I curl in on myself and try to focus on something, anything. I don't want to fall apart here, surrounded by strangers.

My phone rings again, but I can't see the number through the tears in my eyes. I think it might be Danny or one of the other guys on the crew checking in. I manage to accept the call through the cracked screen. "He's still in surgery." My voice breaks and I sniff, rubbing at my eyes with my free hand.

There's a moment of silence before a woman says, "Shit, honey. He's going to be all right. Promise. You know that stuff bouncy balls are made out of?"

Dammit. It's not Danny. Her voice sounds vaguely familiar, but it doesn't matter. She could be a cold call scammer and I'm going to talk to her because, for a hot minute, I'm not alone.

"Some kind of plastic or polymer?" I guess.

"Oh." She sounds stunned, then laughs. "I was going for rubber. Anyway, that boy is made of the same stuff. He'll bounce back. He always does."

I stare at my worn Chuck Taylors, frowning. Who is this woman, and how does she know Timothy? Should I know her? How do I recognize her voice?

"Balls stop bouncing eventually," I say, but there's muffled noise on the other end like she's talking to someone else with her hand over the phone. Timothy might not make it. He might make it but be a different person when he wakes up. What if he...stops?

"It's a head injury." She's back, sounding a little confused. "I don't think you need to worry about his balls, sweetie."

I choke. "Who are you?"

"Oh! Timothy's mother. Celia." She laughs, and it's a nervous laugh. "Nic gave me your number—he told you I'd be calling?"

Oh. My. God.

The hospital is going to have to stuff me in an elevator and take me down to the morgue. A tiny laugh bubbles up from my lungs despite the humiliation that has my face on fire. I clamp my hand over my mouth, but it's too late. She must have heard that.

She did. She laughs too, but I can hear the edge in it, where she's holding on.

"That's it, honey," she says with another laugh. "Let it out. Do you feel a little better?"

I nod before I remember she can't see me. "Yeah, but he's in surgery, and I—"

"Did the doctors tell you anything? They should've since you're his *wife*." The way she says that last word makes it clear she is not happy about this. Timothy, at least, is in trouble. Maybe me too. Shit.

"I'm not. He's not. We're—" Not.

"Oh." She pauses. "It's not important right now," she adds gently.

Of course not.

But if Timothy lied and told his parents we're married...he wouldn't do that, would he?

It's not important but I can't focus on what is.

"What happened?" his mom asks. "Start there."

I press my hand to my forehead and take a deep breath before telling her everything I can remember. What Nic told me. What the nurse told me. I'm shaking by the time I finish, fighting the tears.

There's a pause long enough for a deep breath before her reassuring voice comes back. "He's going to be okay, honey. Do you have anyone with you?"

"No."

"Dammit. I hoped Nic would make it." She sighs. "He doesn't like hospitals. His dad died at the scene of the car crash, but his mom was in the hospital for a while. Nic had to make the decision to take her off life support. This will be hard for him."

My stomach turns. He belongs to the same shitty Dead Parents Club as I do and I called him a coward. I'll need to apologize.

"We're about to take off," Celia says abruptly, "so I've got to go, but we'll be there real quick, honey. Promise."

Until Timothy's parents arrive, I'm here for him. He's not going to be alone.

We say goodbye and I stare at the wall again. My thoughts are a jumbled mess of prayers screamed in my head for Timothy to be okay. I make every bargain with every deity and universal force I've ever heard of. Anything they want, if he survives.

I jump when the nurse touches my arm, but the smile on his face is reassuring.

"Your husband is out of surgery," he says quietly. "Everything went well. He's awake and asking for you."

Relief hits me like a wave, and I slump against my chair. "Oh thank god," I murmur as a tear breaks free. It's followed by another. The nurse wordlessly hands me a tissue. Somehow I catch myself, shoving my emotions back into place before I can become a blubbering mess.

When I'm ready, the nurse leads me down the corridor. It's quiet. Late. A memory nudges me. Nan passed away at night after a short stay in the hospital. She'd had pneumonia. I was nineteen, not ready to be alone.

Timothy is going to be okay. He has to because I don't want to be alone again. If anyone can survive a massive blow to the head, it's him. His thick skull is the stuff of legends.

"I understand this is a lot for you," the nurse says quietly when he stops outside a room, "but if he's asleep, please let him rest. It's important for his recovery. We also put him in a neck brace. He doesn't have any injuries to his spine, but when he came in, he was complaining about some pain. He's strained a muscle, and the brace will only be on for tonight, so he doesn't aggravate it in his sleep."

Taking a deep breath, I nod, and we enter the room.

Timothy's asleep, but the sight of him, the rise and fall of his chest, makes my heart squeeze hard.

"He's doing great." The nurse pats my arm before leaving us alone.

Oh, god. Timothy.

I don't expect my heart to reach for him the way it does, for it to take me to his bedside, but I could've lost him today. I could still lose him. So for one blessedly private minute, I allow myself to feel it. To acknowledge it and name it.

I love him.

I love this motherfucking asshole so much it hurts every day, but right now, when he's lying in this bed, in a hospital gown with bandages around his stupid head, the pain in my chest is excruciating.

His face is slack from the drugs they're pumping into him through an IV. I've never seen him asleep. Never seen him this motionless. He takes up most of the bed, but he looks so helpless right now. This isn't the Timothy I know. My Timothy is larger than life. A goddamn puppy—barely house-trained, easily excitable, and if left without sufficient attention, will destroy your shit. Chaos in a six-foot-three mass of muscle and mischief, with a panty-meltingly good smile.

I love him. It isn't something easily contained in a box labeled "friend." It's big and scary and I hate how strong it is. Overpowering. I'm caught in his undertow and I can't handle it.

I push the tears from my eyes, and taking a deep breath, I count to sixty, slowly pulling myself back together. I can never, ever allow myself to love him as anything more than a friend. This, right here, is all the reason I need.

My parents didn't make it to the hospital. By the time the rescue helicopter got to them, it was too late, though they'd likely died on impact. I was four. I barely remember them, barely had them in my life, and I still feel the hole their loss left in me.

Timothy's just like them, wide-ranging instead of focused on one activity, but chasing after adrenaline all the same. He's lucky today, but the next time?

Brushing my fingers over the flat, stiff hospital sheet, I lock my feelings down. It's not easy, but I'm determined. When I'm back in control, I let myself really look at him.

It's hard to look closely at the man when he never sits still, so I drink him in. I want to memorize every feature of his face. His light brown eyelashes lie against his cheekbones, unexpectedly long. His lips are full, parted slightly, and already chapped from the dry hospital air. His skin should be golden, but he's pale and his hair, dyed darker and cut short for his work on Warwick, is stark in contrast. I miss his unruly honey-blond curls.

I could be missing him. I could have lost him. Tears prick my eyes again.

He stirs when I place my hand over his. I lean closer, holding my breath as I anxiously watch for any sign he might be waking. I need him to wake up. I need to know he's still my Timothy.

His hand captures mine, squeezing weakly as his brown eyes flutter open, slowly focusing on me. They're hazy with sleep and drugs, but when they meet mine, they go impossibly warm. "Mina." His voice is rough, barely a whisper. Weak.

My voice cracks in half and I rub at my eyes with my free hand. "You asshole."

The corner of his mouth turns up like he's caught me. I'm pinned open. He can see right through to my heart.

He wets his lips, his eyes fluttering closed again. "Marry me."

Chapter Seven

Timothy

"Marry me."

My head hurts, but the pain feels distant like I'm touching it through a wall, so I don't really care. I breathe in the faint scent of Mina's jasmine perfume. I'm in a hospital and I'm hurt, but she's holding my hand and I'm not scared anymore. I love her and I'm done wasting time.

My throat is parched, but I ask again. "Marry me."

"Timothy." Her voice is soft anguish and I don't know if that's a yes or a no. *Please be a yes.*

Dark brown eyes glare back at me, framed with thick black lashes and the prettiest face to ever scowl at me. So it's not a yes. Not yet.

"Why does everyone think we're married?" she asks the ceiling, her voice thick with frustration.

It's too hard to explain now and I need to make her smile.

"Mina..." My throat is dry and sore as hell. I swallow before I try again.

She reaches for something out of my field of vision, but whatever she's doing brings her closer to me. I breathe in her scent and goddamn, I want to hold her right now.

Well, I want her to hold me. I'm not sure I can move yet, even to wrap my arms around her. My entire body feels impossibly heavy.

She holds a straw to my lips. I greedily pull a sip. The cool water soothes my throat and I continue to sip slowly. I can keep her this close forever if I sip as slowly as possible. It's science.

Mina proves this to be untrue when she deems I've had enough and pulls the straw from my lips, setting the water down.

I shift, but I can't move my neck. Panic, dulled by the drugs, hits. A neck brace. Shit. "Did I break my neck?"

"Nope. Your brain. Or that thing passing as your brain."

Oh, thank god. I manage a weak grin. "RIP my cock. Why the neck brace?"

She's holding herself so tense a stiff breeze would shatter her.

"Because," she grits out, "they don't have a Cone of Shame big enough at the nearest veterinary clinic to fit over your thick neck."

Oh, she is pissed. She loves me and she's scared. Maybe I should be, too, but I'm not. "What happened?" I don't remember, so it must be bad.

"You hit your head and bled into your brain—you could've died!"

Oh.

That's...not great.

The tears in her eyes, the anguish in her voice—it has to mean something. I reach for her hand. "Marry me."

"Stop it." She sniffs and pulls her hand away.

I'm exhausted. My eyelids flutter, but fighting it isn't working. So. Tired. "You're trying to blow me. Off," I add, having forgotten that part. Which was probably important. *Let me love you. You can blow me if you want. Marry me, though.*

Did I say that out loud?

Her brown eyes go to the window and yeah, I think I said that out loud.

"Timothy." Her voice is tight. Pained. "They cut into your thick skull. Drained blood out of your brain. Don't make me kick your ass."

I can't stop grinning. Maybe it's the drugs, but I think it might be because she loves me and I know it for sure now. Words are getting hard, though. "You are *so* mad at me."

Her hand closes over mine again, gently. "No more stunts."

"For you." Sleep is tugging me under and fighting it is impossible. "I'll retire."

She places her other hand on my chest, right over my heart. "Timothy—"

Somewhere in me, I find the words I need just before I go under. "It's already yours."

Chapter Eight

Mina

Timothy is out like a light. I talk to the doctors when they come in, then sink into the chair next to his bed to update everyone. Starting with his mom.

> He's out of surgery. He woke up and talked to me. Sleeping now. Doctors are happy.

ME

I won't mention any of the nonsense he said to me. That had to be the drugs or the brain injury talking.

> <smiling face emoji> How are you doing?

CELIA

I'm wrecked. I take a deep breath and look at Timothy. I need his arms around me, holding me until everything's better.

> Honestly, I could use a drink.

ME

> Go get some water.

CELIA

> I think I need something harder than water.

ME

Maybe I shouldn't say that to his mom, but Christ, it's been a day.

> I got you. <winking face emoji>

CELIA

> Get something to eat too. You don't need to hold a vigil by his bedside while he sleeps.

CELIA

How does she know?

> Are you spying on me?

ME

> <eyes emoji>

CELIA

> I'm kidding.

CELIA

I'm not sure she's kidding. I get up and peer out the door, but everyone is going about their business. No one is watching me.

> I'm fine. I'd rather stay with him.

ME

> Okay, honey. I'll see you in a few hours.

CELIA

Nic's next on my update list. Texting on my broken phone takes all my concentration, so I blink twice when a cup of coffee, a bottle of water, a muffin, and a candy bar are placed on Timothy's empty tray table.

"Sorry, best I can do this time of the night," the nurse says with a smile, disappearing before I can ask.

When I ignore the food, I get another text from Timothy's mom.

> Eat. Drink. You need to take care of yourself, too, sweetie.

CELIA

She has spies in this hospital. The food and drink came from her via the nurse, I bet.

I've never met any of Timothy's family, but he talks about them a lot. I've heard stories of wild holidays and childhood adventures. The general chaos of a family as eccentric as Timothy. I could probably tell the story of The Great

Crème Brule kitchen fire like I was there, but for the life of me, I don't know what his mother does for a living. Or his father. Until tonight, I didn't know their names.

Half of Timothy's stories are full of tangents and a good 60 percent have to be hyperbole. It can be a little hard to follow. Maybe I missed those details. Or Timothy left them out.

The muffin looks a bit dry so I eat the candy bar and sip the coffee to distract myself from the aching loneliness that settles over me.

I watch Timothy sleep for hours, rapt by the rise and fall of his chest. I've been crushed into hundreds of his bear hugs, but my cheek tingles with how badly I want to press it there to listen to the heartbeat I've watched and memorized on the monitor.

Marry me.

He didn't mean it. He's drugged out of his mind, he just had brain surgery. It shouldn't surprise me how easily he can throw out something ridiculous like that.

If Timothy ever gets married, it will probably be on a whim. A whirlwind wedding in Vegas twenty minutes after he pops the question.

Quick footsteps and a nurse's quiet voice outside the room catch my attention. A woman rushes into the room. I rise from my chair and she wraps me into a tight hug before I can register anything beyond *Timothy's mother.*

The soft smell of her perfume sticks in my nose as I sniff back the sudden tears burning in my eyes. I haven't had a mom hug since Nan died and I cling to her, the touch-starved orphan I am. Her hands are reassuring, stroking my hair, dredging up a longing for the family I don't have.

"I hope you're Mina," she whispers, "or this is going to be awkward."

My laugh sounds half-mad. She pulls away, holding tight to my arms as we stare at each other.

Holy. Shit.

I know her, though I've only seen her heart-shaped face, brown eyes, and neatly swept-up auburn hair on TV or the cover of a cookbook.

Timothy's mother is *Celia Foley.*

Why didn't I know? Why didn't he tell me sometime in the last five years his mother is the goddamned face of the Home Cooking Network? I don't watch a lot of TV, but Celia is *everywhere*.

"How's he doing?" she peers around me at her son, keeping her voice low as she releases me.

"He was up, for a little while, talking." Asking me to marry him, talking about his dick, the usual. "He's going to be fine."

"Bounces back like rubber. Or a polymer or whatever." Celia smiles, reaching into her designer handbag and pulling out a small flask. She presses the smooth metal into my hand. "Timothy's favorite whiskey. I don't know what you drink, but I figured there was a chance you liked it too. How are you doing?"

I stare at the flask clapped in my hands. "Um, you know Timothy and I aren't married, right? We're just friends."

Celia waves that off. "Nic filled me in. I was a little surprised Timothy gave you power of attorney and made you the sole beneficiary of his will, considering he never told us about you, but—" Her eyes go wide. "No! I mean—shit."

My eyes must be mirroring hers. "He *what*?"

Her brows furrow. "I'm exhausted. It's been a day. Please forget I said that. Timothy talks a lot, but it's not always anything of substance, you know? He's probably mentioned you, and I wasn't listening."

The hurt look on her face will have to wait—the part about him not mentioning me isn't what's freaking me out. "He...gave me power of attorney?"

Celia frowns. "Sweetie, you would've had to sign some papers in front of a notary or two witnesses. He couldn't just give it to you. Though he can with the will. And he did." Her tone shift tells me she's not happy about that. Neither am I.

"But I've never—" oh.

That bastard.

Last year I lost a bet over a Lakers game. I had to sign a few papers without reading them. He assured me I had nothing to lose financially—and I trusted him against my better judgment—so I'd signed. Danny was there, and Curtis. He had them witness. Dammit.

Celia rubs her eyes. "He has a lot to explain tomorrow."

"In that case"—Timothy's quiet voice makes us both jump—"be quiet so I can sleep."

We both turn to the hospital bed. Timothy's smiling that drugged-out smile at us.

Celia bustles over, hugging him gently while he mutters a slew of sleepy complaints and calls her a nag.

I hit my limit.

Timothy's not alone. He doesn't need me, so I grab my broken phone and leave, edging past the softly spoken, Mr. Rodgers-esque man who must be Timothy's father talking to the nurse outside.

I'm nearly out of the hospital when Danny walks in, his expression torn up. He spots me immediately and I'm swept into another hug, this one bone-crushing. It's Timothy's arms I need, though. God, if I'd lost him...

"I'm so sorry," Danny says, squeezing me tighter. "How is he?"

I catch Danny up. The whole time he stares at the elevators, his eyes brimming. I've known Danny for close to a decade. We box at the same gym, and I was close to his ex-wife before she moved away.

Danny and Timothy have been friends just as long, though it was years before Timothy and I met. I was with Matthew McCheating-Asshole, so Danny, Linnea, and I didn't hang out that much outside of the gym and Timothy's more of a martial arts guy than a boxer. Our paths never crossed.

When I caught my asshole boyfriend cheating, I had nowhere to go and a strong desire to hit something, so I went to the gym. When several rounds with a punching bag failed to make me feel better, Linnea suggested I stay with them and tag along to a party at some producer's house in the hills. Alcohol, she insisted, solves all problems.

Why not?

We were barely there for five minutes when Timothy landed at my feet, took one look at my puffy but stunned eyes, and claimed my friendship.

I knew him by reputation—word had gotten around set of some of his exploits and only three-quarters of the gossip was about his sex life, plus Danny and Linnea spoke warmly of him. They waved me off with a "go, forget Dick-weasel, and have some fun."

Timothy wasn't after *that* kind of fun, thank god. He found us a quiet spot and a bottle of vodka and pried the hurt out of me piece by piece, easing the grip it held on my heart with the best bear hug. When my tears dried, he took me on a wild night out that ended in the best brunch overlooking the Pacific. And when I friend-zoned him, he accepted it.

"Visiting hours are long over," I say to Danny when I'm done.

He winks. "I know a nurse who can get me in. Let me give you a ride home, first. I've got an extra helmet."

"No." I can't even hide the shudder at the thought of getting on a motorcycle, let alone with someone like Danny who probably drives too fast and weaves in and out of traffic, and possibly wouldn't hesitate to jump a curb. "I'll get an Uber. Thanks anyway."

Danny gives me another hug and we go our separate ways.

The hospital's not too far from my place. I drink the whiskey in the back seat, watching the city lights go by.

A text comes through from Celia.

> Get some rest. See you tomorrow?

CELIA

The thought of seeing Timothy twists my stomach, but the thought of not seeing him twists it harder.

> I'll come by after work.

ME

> Timothy's lucky to have you.

CELIA

I cap the flask and tuck it into my pocket, queasy as hell. Timothy's lucky to still be alive.

My apartment is small and dark, reeking of stale sage smoke thanks to my yoga instructor roommate. I stumble into the kitchen, tossing my bag onto the counter, when three Post-it notes catch my eye. Chantal's preferred method of communication. Hearts dot her i's.

I didn't want to do this by Post-it Note.

You've been mostly really nice, but

I'm moving in with Brent—this weekend.

Shit. I crumple them, tossing them into the garbage. Chantal and her damn sage are a risk to my deposit, but I need her share of the rent to afford this place and save money. I'll need to find another roommate, and for all her woo-woo shit, Chantal at least didn't eat my food or steal my stuff.

I can't deal with this tonight, not after the emotional wringer of today. I fall across my bed fully clothed, passing out hard.

I wake in a puddle of sunlight. Late morning sunlight.

SHIT.

I scramble up.

The cracked screen on my phone doesn't like my pin.

Oh, no. Oh, no, no no, please, don't be...

There are half a dozen text messages and four voice mails when I finally unlock my phone. Celia's text says Timothy is awake and has been asking about me. I don't read the others. The voice mails are all from work. Mariko, informing me I'm thirty minutes late and Cruella is pissed, especially after I left work early and didn't tidy my workspace. Another message when I'm an hour late.

The final one Cruella leaves herself—don't come in.

Chapter Nine

Timothy

"Timothy Alexander Foley."

My eyes are already closed against a raging headache and if I don't open them or move, maybe my mother will think I'm sleeping and go away.

She's not a T. rex. It doesn't work.

Through mostly closed eyelids, I watch as she pulls the chair up to my bed and sits. Her feathers are ruffled. She's not going anywhere. Worse, she knows I'm faking it.

"I got what you asked for from your house," she says, sounding annoyed, "and I packed you a bag, and for fuck's sake, Timothy, how many different kinds of lube does one man need?"

That makes me smile. She loves me. I'm her favorite child—not counting Nic, who shouldn't count because he isn't hers.

Opening my eyes all the way sucks. The curtains are drawn against the bright morning sun, but my headache doubles down anyway. "I should've warned you about the lube."

"You should've warned me about the lube," she agrees, irritation thick in her voice. "And the wife."

Mina. I miss her. She slipped out last night without saying goodbye. Without saying anything.

"We aren't married," I say as a nurse walks in with yet another flower arrangement—bright yellow daisies this time. Since I woke up, my hospital room has bloomed into an enchanted garden. Low-pollen flowers in bright colors, shiny Mylar balloons, and teddy bears crowd every surface allowed. I make a promise to every single *Get Well Soon* that I'll be back to full strength in no time, better than ever.

My mother stares at me. She looks exhausted. Can't blame her, since she spent most of the night watching me sleep. "Why, Timothy?" she asks, sighing.

I close my eyes and explain as best I can with a throbbing head. If something bad happened to me, I wanted Mina by my side, taking care of me. If something *really bad* happened, I wanted to leave her everything, so she'd be taken care of.

"You never told us about her." There's pain in my mother's voice and no real way to erase it.

I kept her a secret from my family because I was afraid they'd be able to tell from the moment I said her name that I was hopelessly in love with her. I was terrified they'd see she didn't feel the same, and they'd pressure me to let her go so I could find someone ready to give me their whole heart.

But I don't want someone else's whole heart. I want the tiny pieces of Mina's that slip through her fingers when she isn't looking.

I've wasted too many days, thrown away years of happiness we could've had. She's a cautious person and I've approached her carefully. It hasn't worked.

"Do you like her?" I ask.

My mother's eyes narrow on me and she sighs again. "I do. She was so freaked out last night. She cares deeply for you."

She loves me. I could see it in her eyes last night too. I could see everything.

"Did you find it?" The reason I asked my mom to dig through my lube and sex toy collection. I'd laugh about that, but I'm not in the mood and it would only make my headache worse.

She pulls a small red box out of her purse, holding it up. "We need to talk about this."

I extend my hand and she reluctantly places the box in it. "I already asked her to marry me. She thought it was the drugs." It *was* the drugs—I was out of my mind. I think I even told her I'd retire. But wanting to marry her was real and I'm going to tell her how I feel and ask her again. We've been friends for long enough, and I don't think a world exists where we wouldn't be sexually compatible. We can date as long as she wants before I take her down the aisle, so long as she says yes.

Mom's already shaking her head. "Oh, Timothy. Honey, no. Not like that. She said you're just friends, you can't...propose out of nowhere. From your hospital bed!"

"I love her." Can't she see? None of the rest of it matters.

"But you haven't even—"

"I'm tired of waiting and getting my ass kicked by Jackie—"

My mother stiffens. "Who's Jackie?"

"Jackie Chan." Obviously.

We stare at each other for a long, long moment.

"Okay, honey," she says, getting slowly to her feet, and taking a few steps toward the door. "You sit tight for a minute, I'm going to step out to find the nearest—Doctor! Perfect timing!" She grabs the doctor's arm when she walks into the room, but releases it almost immediately. "Oh! I'm sorry. Um...he's a little...confused."

"I'm fine." Apart from the massive headache. "My therapist had me name my unrequited love—"

"The old hippie on the beach? *That* therapist?" My mother puts her hands on her hips as she narrows her eyes at me and I immediately regret telling her about him.

"He's qualified," I protest. I mean, I think he is. He has a PhD from the School of Living an Awesome Fucking Life.

The doctor barely blinks, walking up to the bed to shine a light in my eyes before flipping through my chart.

My mother sighs, closing the door and rounding the bed. "I'm his mother." She says it like the burden it is, staking her claim to stay in the room.

The doctor nods, still looking over my chart. "How does your head feel?" she asks me.

"Like someone drilled a hole in it," I respond. My mother's eyes widen at me—her way of full naming me without uttering a sound.

"Imagine that." The doctor looks up at me as she puts the chart back. "You're a stunt performer?" She turns to the laptop on her mobile workstation.

"Yeah. You've probably seen me in…" my voice trails off when she stares at me. She doesn't give a fuck, but I do. "I'm good at my job."

"Obviously not that good." The doctor clicks through something on the laptop.

My phone isn't close at hand or I'd show this doctor a few of the stunts I've done. I'm damn good at my job. One of the best. I will be the best one day.

The doctor reads something—possibly my medical history given how long she's silent—before stating, "You need a new job."

An anvil lands on my chest. "What?" I manage to choke out.

"You've had a couple of mild concussions in the past, and now a subdural hematoma. Maybe you could do stunt work for another twenty years and take a dozen more hits to the head and be fine, but if I were your insurance company, I wouldn't bet on you."

I open my mouth but the doctor is already onto my excuses and cuts me off.

"Maybe you'll hit your head slipping in the shower, or doing something mundane, and yes, that could kill you too. It's about managing your risks. No one expects you to wrap yourself in Bubble Wrap—"

"I do." My mother raises her hand, but the doctor ignores her.

"—and go through life scared of every little bump. But you don't have to run toward the big risks *you do not have to take*. Find a less dangerous job."

"And new hobbies." My mother crosses her arms.

The doctor's eyes narrow. "Those too."

I tip my head back and close my eyes. "Just ruin my life."

"For the moment, you have a life," the doc says. "You're looking to make a full recovery. Next time, that might not be the case. Make an appointment with that therapist. Or better yet, a real one."

The doctor stands and promises to check in on me tomorrow, vaguely mentioning if I'm doing well in a few days, they'll talk about discharging me. Then she's gone and Mom is standing next to my bed looking triumphant.

I look away, my eyes landing on a cheery orange and yellow Mylar balloon with the words "get well soon" across the front. If getting up didn't make my headache worse, I'd pop it with my bare hands. Every balloon in here. I'd rip the flowers to shreds and...okay, I couldn't hurt the stuffed animals—I'm crushed under the weight of my broken ego, but I'm not a monster.

"It's for the best, sweetie," my mom says softly.

It's my fucking life. It's who I am, and suddenly, just like that, I'm not? No, it's not *for the best*.

It's how I channel my energy. Without it, I'm scattered, pulled in twenty directions. I'm out of control and impulsive. Mom should understand—I know she hasn't forgotten my teenage years. I rigged a zip line from the second floor of our house to a tree in the yard, for fuck's sake. Took the car for a joyride before I had my license. Skied off the roof, once. It didn't matter how many activities they enrolled me in—martial arts and gymnastics and soccer and track—it wasn't enough.

And now what? I'm thirty-three and I'm supposed to get a normal nine-to-five? Sit at a desk all day? Just thinking about it makes me itch all over.

A balloon bobs in a current of air I can't feel in this stifling room. All these people believe in me, they'll be waiting for me to recover, and I'm supposed to let them down?

Fuck that. Fuck all of it. That's not who I am.

"My head hurts." It does, but mostly I want Mom to go away. "Can you do me a favor on your way out? Get rid of all this shit?" I wave my arm at the flowers, balloons, and stuffed animals.

Mom's face softens. She still doesn't understand, but she must feel my pain. "Yeah, honey. I'll take care of it. Get some sleep."

I hold the little red box tighter in my hand. I still have this. If Mina says yes, I can deal with the rest later, and I won't have to face it alone. But right now—headache. I need to sleep.

My dream is slow to let me go and I cling to it as long as I can, but pain edges into my awareness.

Someone is sitting on my bed, holding my hand, feather-light touches tracing over the back of it. Mina's perfume floats around me. "Come here," I murmur. I can barely open my eyes or move beyond holding out my arm.

I think she's going to say no, but after a moment, she slips off her shoes and climbs into my bed, tucking herself under my arm. She curls into me, warm and soft in the best places. Sometimes, when we watch movies at her place, we end up cuddled on her couch like this. Okay, so it only happens if I manage to sneak a scary movie on, but I get away with it more often than I should.

I kiss the top of her head and fall asleep.

A nurse comes in to check on my bandages. Mina's asleep, her head on my chest, her hand over my heart, exactly where it belongs. The nurse smiles, and I smile back. I get a thumbs up. The nurse leaves and I notice, before I fall asleep again, the balloons and flowers are gone. The stuffed animals too.

Mina's not in bed with me when I wake next. She's sitting in the chair, staring out the window and tapping the ring box on her leg. Guess she found it in my bed. Not exactly how I wanted to do this, but I'm not waiting for the right time anymore.

"I was dreaming about you," I say.

Her eyes move slowly toward me, over my sheet-clad body. Her eyebrows go up slightly when she reaches my hips and I glance down because there is no way—

Huh. Massive tent. I'm impressed, considering the headache and the drugs still in my system. Pretty sure I couldn't get it up intentionally right now.

"It was a good dream," I add weakly. My throat's dry again.

"You're such a dick." There's a rueful little smile on Mina's lips, though, as she stands to hand me the water I could easily reach myself. I hope it means *Oh, Timothy, you're ridiculously handsome, and as soon as the doctor clears you for sex—*

Best not to follow that train of thought or the next doctor or nurse to walk in will whisk me off to the medical marvels ward. Not a real thing? Well, it would be. Named after me. The Timothy Foley Massive Dick Ward.

I snort a laugh. It hurts like hell and the laugh transforms into a wince.

Mina looks doubtfully at me. "How are you feeling?"

"Not great." I take a drink of the water and set it back myself, patting the bed next to my hip. After a long moment, Mina sits. "I'm sorry. For not asking before giving you power of attorney. Are you mad?"

She sighs, but shakes her head. "No. Yes. I don't know. Last night, they told me everything and let me see you. But what if I'd had to decide on life support?" Her voice cracks. "We've never talked about it. That's not fair to either of us."

"I trust you to make decisions for me."

Mina shudders. I take her hand and squeeze. "And the will?" she asks softly. "What am I going to do with a motorcycle, Timothy?"

"Forget the motorcycle." I run my thumb over her knuckles. "I have a trust fund, a house, and good life insurance. I want you to be taken care of."

"I'm not your responsibility." She pauses, frowning. "You never told me...I thought you were just a stuntman. You have a trust fund? And how is your mother Celia Foley?"

"I think she asks how I'm her son at least twice as often," I joke.

Mina gives me a look.

"I like being Timothy Foley, Handsome Stuntman. Not Timothy, Celia Foley's Son with the Trust Fund. Besides, you weren't impressed with Nic, I didn't think you'd be impressed by my mom."

"*Your mom is Celia Foley!*"

My head is pounding now. "Yeah, but have you seen Nic's abs?"

Mina rubs her forehead like she's the one with the headache. "Jesus, Timothy."

I shrug. After a moment, she smiles and shakes her head.

Now. It has to be now before she finds something else to be mad at me about. I gently take the ring box out of her hand and Jackie Chan raises his fists in the air.

She has to know what's coming—her initials are embossed on the box—but I don't like the way the smile drops from her face.

"Mina." My heart is pounding, the hills and valleys on the monitor narrowing. Her hand trembles in mine. "I love you. I've been in love with you since the day we met. I know this is fast, we haven't even dated, but that doesn't matter. We know each other so well, better than a lot of married couples." I flip the box open. Her eyes snap to the ring. "I can't get on my knees right now, but as soon as I can, I will. If you'll say yes. Marry me?"

I wait. Jackie waits. Only one of us needs to breathe and I'm not sure either of us is.

The breath Mina draws is shaky as she reaches out, closing the box. All the light goes out of the room, all the air out of my lungs. It's a miracle the machine monitoring my vital signs doesn't blare out an alarm.

There's so much sadness in her eyes. So much heartbreak and I don't think it's all mine. When she speaks, her voice is gentle but certain. "No."

Jackie Chan clutches his heart and falls to the floor.

Okay, no, we can come back from this. Mom was right. Wrong time, wrong place.

I tuck the box under the blankets. "Sorry. I screwed this up. I'll wait until I'm out of here. Take you somewhere nice. Do it again without the morphine."

Mina gets to her feet, and she's pale. "You've been in this hospital bed barely conscious for the last twelve hours—how do you have a Cartier engagement ring?"

"I've had it for a while." Don't ask. Please, don't ask.

"How. Long."

"Eight months."

Her eyes go wide.

I'm already wincing because I know how this is going to sound. "And four years."

Mina drops into the chair, staring at me. Her mouth opens several times and closes, no sound coming out.

I went with Nic when he bought Addison's ring, intent on talking him out of it. Then I saw this ring. Two carats. Emerald cut. At that moment, I knew trying to fuck away my feelings for her wasn't going to work. I'd had a scorching hot threesome the night before, and here I was, staring at a ring, wanting only her for the rest of my life. The thought of slipping this ring onto those long, talented fingers is more exciting than anything I've done in my life—threesomes and stunts combined.

I had the money, so I returned later that day without Nic, and bought the ring, planning on proposing one day. But even if I didn't have the money, I would've sold a kidney to buy it. It's perfect for her.

"Are you fucking kidding me?" Her voice is threatening, and I'm pretty sure she wouldn't smack a man in a hospital bed for being a presumptuous prick. Not 100 percent sure. More like 92 percent. "You bought this for me four months after we met?"

"I love you."

She looks ready to cry. When I beckon for her to come to me, she shakes her head. "You don't love me. I don't know where this is coming from, but you can't."

"I do."

Mina takes a deep breath and I can see the moment she becomes unreachable to me. "Timothy. You date a new person every week, right?"

Oh, no. She's got it all wrong. Those aren't *date* dates. "You don't—"

"Fine, nearly every week. Let's say forty people a year. We've known each other for five years."

Shit. Math. My head is splitting now. "Well, that's not really—"

"Two hundred people, Timothy. You've 'dated' at least that, probably more. If you loved me, you wouldn't want to be with anyone else. Not two hundred other people. You'd only want me."

"But I—"

"You don't love me, Timothy."

Down the hall, a wheel squeaks on a cart, rolling closer as little pinpricks of uncertainty dance up my spine. She doesn't believe me. I didn't expect Mina, of all people, to think me incapable of love and commitment.

"I do," I insist. She's not going to believe the truth about my supposedly busy love life. I need to change the subject. The past doesn't matter if she feels the same. "Do you love me? Is that why you haven't dated anyone in the last five years?"

"I haven't met anyone worth breaking my heart over." She looks out the window as she says it.

My heart squeezes at that, an extra blip on the monitor. Or there should be, anyway. "Give it to me and I won't ever break it. You can trust me."

She shakes her head. "We're better as friends, Timothy."

"We'd be even better as more. Give me a chance."

The squeaky wheel stops outside my room as Mina and I stare at each other, waiting for the intrusion to go away (me) or anticipating the interruption (Mina, probably).

"Lunchtime," a woman announces, stepping into the room, tray in hand. She sets it on my table.

"Join me for lunch?" I ask Mina, waving at the covered mystery food while the woman refills my water.

Wait a second. It's lunchtime? I frown. "Shouldn't you be at work?"

"They fired me," she says, making a weak attempt at jazz hands. "I left early yesterday and overslept this morning."

Anger fires me up enough to push the headache away. "Nope. Give me your phone. Cruella has gone too far this time."

Seriously, the way that woman treats her team is despicable. She's had Mina on the phone with me, so angry I could hear the tears in her eyes, more times than I should have ever let happen. It ends today.

Mina holds up her phone, raising an eyebrow. The whole thing is cracked to hell. "It barely works, and I don't need you making things worse."

Okay, right. Probably me ripping Cruella a new one won't reflect well on Mina in the industry. My phone is charging, just out of reach. I motion to it with gimme hands. "I'll find you a better job." With better pay. Better hours.

"Timothy." The tone in her voice is exasperated. Tears of frustration are filling her eyes. "Stop."

"There's a historical for this streaming service starting—"

"Don't."

No, I need to fix this. I have a better option and I should've thought of it first. The panic tightening my chest eases. "Okay, move in with me. I can support you until you find another job. Or however long you'd like. You can work on Wild Things."

I reach my hand toward her, letting it fall to the bed when she doesn't take it.

Mina gets to her feet, and after a moment, she steps up to the bed, bending to give me a quick peck on the cheek. "Get some rest, Timothy. I'll be fine."

I'm too tired to fight her right now, but *fine* isn't good enough. I need her to thrive. I need her to be happy.

Chapter Ten

Mina

Where is all this shit with Timothy coming from? It has to be the near-death experience and all the drugs he's on. I expected him to forget about yesterday's proposal, or at least to laugh about it. *Isn't that funny? What if you'd said yes?*

He has a ring. A big-ass beautiful diamond ring he bought for me years ago—

"Mina Andrei?"

I look up from my seat in the empty waiting room, where I've spent the last two hours on the hospital's free Wi-Fi, trying to search for a job. Trying, because the cracked screen on my phone makes it as frustrating as that conversation with Timothy.

A courier locks eyes with me, and the next thing I know, I'm holding a small box.

Goddammit, Timothy. Now what?

Well, I might as well take a break. Not like I can concentrate anyway. At least this won't be an engagement ring. Could be chocolate.

My stomach grumbles. I wouldn't mind if it's chocolate. Timothy knows all my favorite snacks, and from time to time surprises me with them.

It's not a snack. It's a new phone. An expensive one. With a little note that says sorry.

For a long moment, I stare at the shiny, perfect screen, sliding my thumb along the smooth edge. I should return it. Except it's his fault my screen cracked in the first place.

I lost my job. My roommate is moving out so making rent is going to be difficult. I can't rely on my side hustle yet. There's no way I can afford a new phone right now.

Okay, I'm keeping it. But I'm not going to rush into his room and thank him just yet.

I need some fresh air, but as I rise, Celia drops into the chair across from me, saying hello and quickly introducing me to Timothy's dad, William. He's a tall, lanky man with a quiet, professorial demeanor. The exact opposite of Timothy, except for the kind eyes with laugh lines.

"Timothy told us you lost your job." Celia cuts to the chase, leaning forward in her chair. "I'm terribly sorry."

Shit. What else has he told her—does she know he asked me to marry him? How embarrassing. For me. Timothy exists on some plane where embarrassment isn't a thing. "I'll find another one."

Celia glances at William and turns her TV-ready smile on me. "I'd like to hire you."

Why am I friends with Timothy? I told him I'd find a job myself and I meant it. "No thanks, Mrs. Foley. I can't cook."

She laughs. "Not to work with me. To...god, there is no good way to say this. William?"

He looks like he wants nothing to do with this conversation, but he leans forward, elbows on his knees, and does what he's told. "We'd like to hire you to provide a little home help for Timothy until he's fully recovered."

Hell. No. "I'd murder him."

Celia nudges William. "She's perfect."

Timothy must get his inability to listen to anything he doesn't want to hear from his mother. "I'm not going to cook and clean for him, and I think he'd rather I didn't." If he knew what was good for him.

Celia draws herself up straighter. "My son knows how to cook and clean for himself."

Dammit, I've insulted her.

"And he's not half bad at it," she adds with a little wince, "though in Timothy's case, having a fire extinguisher on hand isn't a bad idea. We just need someone to keep an eye on him."

"Nic's living with him."

"Nic is on set a lot," Celia says flatly.

"Among other things," William mutters, huffing when his wife elbows him.

"We need a babysitter," Celia says as she lets out a long breath. "We spoke with Timothy and he's happy to have you. The house is big enough—you'd have a bedroom with an ensuite, you can stay rent-free, and we'll pay you to keep an eye on him. That's all."

I laugh. Keeping Timothy out of trouble is a six-figure job better left to a dominatrix. "What makes you think he'd listen to me?"

She raises an eyebrow.

Oh-dear-god-no. He told her about the proposal. I can see it in her eyes, in the tightening of her lips. My face heats.

"Look, you need a job and we need someone who can keep him in line. You're our best bet. We'll pay you forty grand to keep him out of trouble for ten weeks."

Good thing I'm already sitting, because my legs go weak.

Forty grand.

That's a lot of money. It's more than I make in a year, and with forty grand, I could buy a new embroidery machine. Upgrade my website. Put something in my very empty savings account.

Celia might believe Timothy will listen to me, but what if he doesn't?

I'm resourceful. For forty grand, I could figure something out.

"Would I have to be in the house with him twenty-four seven?" Timothy will drive me insane. I'm pretty sure. Probably.

Celia shakes her head. "No, sweetie. If you need a break or you have something to do, go do it. Use your judgment. You know him, and he's desperate not to mess things up with you."

Yeah...speaking of that...

"I need to set some ground rules with Timothy before I agree to this." Who am I kidding? I'm agreeing to this anyway, even if it means turning down offers of marriage every single day. Which it probably does.

When I walk into his room, Timothy's eyes are half-closed, but he smiles at me like I didn't shoot him down two hours ago. "Did you get it?" he asks with a grin.

I roll my eyes and hold up the new phone. "Yeah. You shouldn't have, but I'm keeping it."

His grin widens, and he scoots over a bit, patting the bed next to his thigh. I sit in the chair instead. His grin dims.

"Your parents want me to move in with you while you recover."

"We could make it permanent," he suggests.

"Timothy."

"I'm going to need a lot of help. Not sure I can manage a shower on my own." That grin is back, heating my blood.

"They want me to babysit you, not give you sponge baths," I snap.

His eyebrows waggle. "They won't care if you want to give me a sponge bath."

"No." I shake my head with a frustrated laugh as I stand. "I'm not going to do this. I'll tell them no. What was I thinking?"

"I'm joking, Mina. No sponge baths. Unless you want to. I'm always open to that—"

"Everything is a joke to you!" I roar. "Could you be serious for two minutes and talk to me about this? I lost my job. I lost my roommate, so I'm going to lose my apartment when I can't make rent. I almost lost *you*. This isn't funny to me."

His lips press tight and he nods slowly, wincing. Shit. I shouldn't yell at him.

"I'm sorry," he says. "Sit, please. Tell me what you need."

I pace instead, too angry to sit, while he watches me. The effort it takes for him to keep his mouth shut must be monumental.

What do I need?

A new life, for one.

"I'm going to do it, so long as you want me to—" I hold up my hand, cutting off whatever stupid thing he's about to say about wanting me. "But only if you promise to accept we are just friends."

"No."

I whirl on him. "What do you mean 'no'?"

"I love you." He says it with a shrug like it's the most obvious thing. News-flash: The Sun Rises in the East. "I can't turn it off."

God, I want to cry. I sink into the chair and rub my temple. "Why do you have to make this so hard?"

"I'm telling you how I feel about you. I'm not trying to make anything hard for you."

Shit. He's serious. He didn't make the obvious dick joke.

"I want to help you. I need the money and a place to stay, but I need you to stop talking about this." The pain in his eyes makes me swear under my breath. "I love you, Timothy," I say softer. "But as a friend. Can you accept that?"

He closes his eyes, rubbing at them as he draws a ragged breath.

Shit. I've never seen him cry before—other than tears of laughter. I don't want to hurt him, but it's better this way. He has to see that.

His hand falls away, his eyes soft as they meet mine. "If that's what you want."

It is. It's definitely what I want.

The relief I feel isn't as strong as I expected. Instead, I feel oddly broken.

"If you change your mind"—Timothy's sad puppy dog eyes shred my heart to bits, his small smile stomping all over the pieces—"let me know, okay? Because I'm never going to stop loving you."

There are tears in my eyes again, and I don't know why. Today has been too much.

He holds his arms out. "Come here. Friend hug. Promise."

I need one of his hugs.

I sit on his bed, hip to hip, leaning forward to wrap my arms around him. His arms wind around me, holding me perfectly. The familiar scent of him is there but faded. I listen to his heartbeat, to each breath he takes. I'm so grateful his heart is still pumping and his lungs are still breathing, but I'm also angry and scared.

I need to get out of here. I escape the hug, rising to my feet. "I'll be back in a couple of hours, okay?"

"Going to the gym?" he asks, a soft smile on his face.

Hitting shit is good for the soul. He knows me so well. "Yeah."

"Wish I could come with," he says quietly, his eyes dropping to his feet, sticking up from under the hospital sheet.

"Soon enough," I say, and he brightens a little. "I'll tell everyone you say hi."

I manage to leave the hospital without running into his parents. Soon enough, I'm walking into my boxing gym, inhaling the familiar scent of leather, Lysol, and stale sweat. It's always hot in this gym, and the heat eases some tension out of my body before I've reached my locker.

Nan would've killed me if I'd taken up boxing before she passed away. She wrapped me in crushed velvet and kept me close growing up. The only thing she had left of her darling son.

I moved to LA after Nan died to get away from how suffocating my life had become. It was a huge deal, the scariest thing I've ever done, but I did it. Didn't take long to discover LA was just as suffocating. I needed an outlet. A coworker took me to her boxing gym, and that was it. I fell in love with the sport. I seldom get in the ring unless it's with someone I know won't knock my head off, but hitting a punching bag? Any day.

It helps me find space to breathe and the post-workout bliss lends clarity to life.

Not today.

Timothy's words ring through my head and I can't punch hard enough to knock them loose. *I love you. I can't turn it off.*

All those men and women he's dated. Slept with. He must have been able to turn it off with them.

It hurts. If I loved him the way he wants me to? I wouldn't survive the heartbreak.

The next ten weeks are going to be hard, but all I have to do is keep an eye on him. Keep him out of trouble. Live with him. Guard my heart against him. I have five years of practice at that.

So why does it feel like I'm creeping to the edge of a cliff to see how far the drop is?

For the first time in a long time, hitting stuff doesn't help. It tires my body, but that's about it.

When I get back to my locker, I grab my phone.

I'll do it.

ME

Her response is immediate.

<smiling face emoji>

CELIA

So is Timothy's, when I tell him.

You won't regret it!

TIMOTHY

I already do.

Chapter Eleven

Mina

I have never been to Timothy's house, entirely by design.

I assumed it would look like the unholy love child of a frat house and a shrine to adrenaline, and I didn't need the reminder that my best friend lived for doing dangerous things, so I declined all invitations until he stopped giving them. We hung out at my place or went out somewhere.

His house is nothing like I'd expected.

From the outside, it looks unassuming. Modern, in that boxes stacked offset on boxes style. It's gated, with a couple of trees in the front yard giving a little extra privacy. The inside, though...wow.

It's light and airy with an open floor plan and warm wood floors, but my eyes narrow almost immediately onto the L-shaped couch. It's white leather.

My jaw might be on the floor. Timothy owns white furniture. And it's *pristine*.

"Your room is on the second floor, first door," Celia says, closing the door behind me. She insisted I move in immediately, so I can be settled before Timothy comes home in a few days. "Bring your stuff in, have a look around while I make us some lunch. Then we'll talk."

The staircase is U-shaped and opens to the high-ceilinged living area. I carry my suitcases up the first flight to the landing and peer over the metal railing to the white couch below.

It's spotless, all right. Even the decorative pillows—coral and turquoise—are perfectly placed.

I continue to the second floor, pushing open the first door.

Like the rest of the house, the room is light and airy. Floor-to-ceiling closets line the wall next to the door. The queen-size bed is simply made, the blankets matching the blue accents of the room. A comfy chair sits in the corner, a reading lamp overhanging it. A large watercolor hangs on the wall—cheery sunflowers that brighten the room—and a door next to a mirror leads into a small ensuite with a shower nicer than the one I've left behind.

On my way out for the next load, I catch a glimpse of a *ficus* in Timothy's bedroom. His open door is up a half flight of stairs from my room and easily takes up most of the second floor.

Peering down the stairwell into the kitchen below, I can see Celia, her back to me as she chops something. Now's my chance to snoop.

I don't know what I expected, exactly, but this room isn't it. It's clean, for one. The vibe, for two, is chilled and relaxed. The hardwood floor is covered by a massive cream-colored rug, which is in turn covered by a massive king bed that looks to have been professionally made.

Timothy has a balcony, with a table, some wicker furniture, and a lounge chair. I'd step outside, but I'm afraid sliding the doors open might give me away.

A small sofa sits against the other wall, underneath a large watercolor painting of Timothy. The artist captured him perfectly. His form is picked out of the white background in lime green lines and he's standing in a wide stance on top of a building, fisted hands on his hips, chest puffed out. Bright orange splotches give him a laser-eyed effect, and the world's tiniest cape flutters behind him. It's clear the artist was making fun of him, but in a way that laughs with him rather than at him. The name in the corner is Jessie Foley—his twin—and the year indicates they were still in high school.

I think I'd like her.

Timothy has a walk-in wardrobe, so I stick my head in.

Okay, this is clearly a stockroom for an adult fun shop. One entire section is devoted to sex toys and every kind of lube on the planet. The bulk of the sex toys are still in their packaging, a large number of them designed for anatomy Timothy doesn't possess. Seriously, why does he have so many clitoral stimulators? Maybe he uses them when he's entertaining, and the lucky clitoris owner gets to take one home after? There are a couple of drawers in this section of the closet. I bet they contain his personal collection.

I know what I'm about to do is wrong, but I can't help myself so I pull open the top drawer quickly like that makes it better.

Immediately I slam it. I can't violate his privacy when I'd kick his ass if he did it to me. I'll just pretend I didn't catch a glimpse of cock rings and dildos.

Yeah right. I want to know all about them and what Timothy likes, and that's going to be a problem.

A section of a wall is devoted to designer suits and since high-quality, expensive fabric is my weakness, I turn to leave before I can succumb to the temptation of touching them. Then I see it.

A snowboard, sans bindings, sits propped in the corner.

I wander over. The shelves are packed with gear and protective clothing. I raise the sleeve of a bright orange jumpsuit. It's a wingsuit. He's jumped out of airplanes wearing this. My stomach roils and I want to ball it up and stick it in the trash, so I move on.

My fingers skim along an orange rope coiled perfectly on a shelf before my eyes land on a carabiner. I yank my hand back like it burns.

I forgot he climbs sometimes. Not like my parents did. He's not that good or devoted to it. But it's something he does.

That's enough exploring Timothy's room.

When I carry all my sewing gear into the garage—for now—I find all the rest. Surfboards, mountain bikes, skateboards, kayaks...his motorcycle. Other stuff that I'm clueless about.

His house might not be a shrine to adrenaline, but it's definitely adrenaline's storage space.

I leave my plastic tubs full of sewing stuff among it all and go into the kitchen, where the warm, sunny space dries the cold sweat off my skin.

The large island is lined with stools and the kitchen counter holds a cluster of potted plants. A closer inspection reveals they're real. Succulents, but still.

Timothy keeps houseplants alive.

Yes, his awful hobbies are tucked away in this house, but they're out of sight and this place is lovely. There's this whole other side to my best friend I haven't seen before because I was too scared to look.

Celia waves off my offer to help, so I wander into the living room, tracing my fingers over the arm of the couch. There are mirrors on the wall, two of them, reflecting the image of Celia opening the fridge.

The living room looks familiar. The pool and the lounge chairs outside, along with a low concrete wall topped with plants and a wooden fence screening the neighbor's house, ring a bell too.

"Was this house used as the set for a movie?" I ask.

Celia makes a choked sound and stuffs the Tupperware back in the fridge. "Oh. No, honey, let's not."

I frown, but she's already opening cupboards, sticking her head in.

Too late, I realize her shoulders are shaking with laughter.

Oh.

If a movie was shot here, it must have been big enough that I should know it. Racking my brain isn't coming up with anything, so I let it go.

We sit at the table and for a moment I stare at my plate. Timothy has dinnerware. Real dinnerware that's not paper or plastic or cheap melamine. Yet another surprise.

Celia is one of the best-known TV chefs in the country, so the lunch she cooked is delicious. Chicken, bacon, and brie on homemade bread with a side salad coated in a tangy-sweet raspberry vinaigrette. She lays out her expectations of me while we eat, and sitting here, in Timothy's house, the reality of my new job settles heavily on my shoulders. If he does something—no clue what, but it could be anything—under my watch and gets hurt, or worse, I'll share responsibility for it.

"What if I can't talk him out of something?" Timothy might, like Celia believes, be on his best behavior, but I'm not sure his feelings for me are enough. I don't even know if I believe they're real.

"If you can bodily prevent him, without putting either of you in danger, I'd be okay with that," she says, sipping her sparkling water. "Do what you need to, apologize for it later."

I nod, although Timothy could pick me up and remove me as an obstacle. The only bodily way to prevent him from doing something dangerous would be to kiss him. Which would put me in danger.

I guess that's an option, in an emergency. Then I'll apologize later because it won't be happening again. Destroy a friendship, ruin his trust in me, save his life.

Jesus Christ, what have I gotten myself into?

Celia sighs. "If you're worried about what he might do, and you feel you're losing control, call me. You might not be willing to play dirty, honey, but I will."

Celia has big fuck-around-and-find-out energy, but honestly, I don't know that she could do anything to stop Timothy from doing what he wants either. "Can I ask you a question?"

"Of course."

"Did you try to stop him from becoming a stunt performer?" I ask, taking another bite of my sandwich.

She sighs, pushing her salad around on her plate. "Here's the thing, honey. He's been like this since he could walk. Always climbing trees, racing anything with wheels down any slope, trying to fly. Becoming a professional stunt performer gave him an environment with at least some safety considerations in place, and that's better than nothing. So no, I didn't try to stop him. But things are different now. His level of background risk has changed. Everything has changed. And that's where you come in. You're sensible, and he's head over heels for you. He'll keep himself safe to keep you happy."

I drop my sandwich on my plate, no longer hungry.

"One other thing," she says as I take a drink of my water. "You and Timothy are adults. If you decide to enter into a sexual relationship, I'm not going to consider it a workplace issue."

My water goes down wrong and I thump the glass on the table, eyes watering as I cough. Celia laughs, delighted with herself.

"But honey, if he acts inappropriately or makes you uncomfortable, let me know, and I'll sort him out."

"I can handle him," I say when I can breathe again, but I'm not so sure.

Chapter Twelve

Timothy

I couldn't wait to get out of the hospital, but I didn't consider what it would feel like walking into my house. Everything looks just like I left it when I went to work six days ago, but I'm different. Broken. Frozen in the doorway. The scream I've kept inside is pushing against the back of my throat and I don't think I can keep it in.

Mina brushes my arm, her touch jolting me. I barely take in the concerned look on her face before I nope out.

"I'm going to take a shower," I mumble, walking quickly to the stairs and taking them two at a time.

"Timothy, slow down," my mother admonishes. Since I'm already on the second flight, I listen to her and take each step one at a time. Probably a good idea, since the sudden burst of activity sets my head to a dull throb.

"Don't forget to put a shower cap on," she calls after me. Like the headaches let me forget there are staples in my head.

Closing the door to my room, I let the pieces of me that are breaking off fall a little more. This is the first time I've had privacy since the accident, but a closed door won't stop my mother, so I head to the safety of my shower.

They want me to retire.

No matter how many times I turn the words around in my head, they never feel real. There has to be a way out. Something I can do to get back to my old life.

I peppered the doctor with questions and hypotheticals when she discharged me, but I'm struggling to see any open doors.

You could have died.

I want to scream at every person who has said that to me. I know I could've died. I know what the risks would be returning to stunt work. But it's my life.

I yank the tap on and dig around for the shower cap my mother will have tucked into a drawer somewhere. My anger hasn't burned out because my head hurts too much most of the time to process it, and yet it's all I can think about.

Mina's my escape, but that's not without pain either. She doesn't love me the way I love her and as much as I crave having her near, it hurts too much right now. I didn't fully think through the implications of having her in my house for the next ten weeks. It's not like I can magically stop loving her.

I don't want to face her. Or my parents. I stand under the spray of the shower longer than I should, letting the hot water carry my angry tears down the drain.

Eventually, I turn the water off and wrap a thick white towel around my waist. I can't wait until the staples come out of my head and I can shampoo my disgusting hair. Until then, it's dry shampoo for the win. I spray some well away from the staples, combing it through my short hair, and wincing when my fingers get too close.

I shave to kill more time before I have to pretend everything is okay. I even put on cologne because if I smell like myself, maybe I'll feel like myself, not this damaged impostor.

Doesn't work.

Balling up my old clothes, I drop them in the hamper on the way to my walk-in and stop dead in my tracks.

My snowboard is propped in a corner. At least a quarter of my walk-in wardrobe is stuff I'll never use again if I do the sensible thing and listen to Mom and the doctors.

The crack running through me barely has time to widen when there's a knock at my door. Before I can tell my mother I'll be down soon, it opens and Mina sticks her head in.

Her eyes go wide when she sees me, her gaze dropping over my body.

Disappointment sours on my tongue. Instead of puffing up my chest like a rooster, I deflate. She always looks. The problem is she *only* looks. Like I'm some piece of art she's scared to touch.

I'm not art, I'm Play-Doh, and I don't want her to look anymore if she isn't going to touch.

"Are you okay?" Mina asks, looking away, her cheeks going rosy under my glare.

"Fine." My voice is tight. I am not fine.

Mina…I can't let myself go there. I could tolerate the rest of it if I had her. But I don't.

Shit is bleak.

Mina walks over to stand next to my bed, her fingers smoothing over the creamy blankets. It irritates me, the familiar way she's touching the place where I sleep.

Because I've lost all sense of self-preservation, I imagine her dark hair spilling over the blankets, my face buried between her thighs. The sweet sounds she'd make, the musky taste of her, the feel of her fingers tugging my hair and holding me close. The way she'd move under me. Over me.

I can't breathe with how badly I want all the things I'll never have.

"Liar," she says, sitting and patting a spot, wanting me to sit next to her.

On the bed I'm picturing her naked in.

She's right—I am not okay. I'm pissed off I've spent the last five years pining for her, that she's become someone I can't live without.

"Get. Out." It's not me gritting those words through clenched teeth. It's not Jackie, either—he didn't make it. Died on the hospital floor when Mina said no. This is some splinter that's a part of me, made from me, and lodged deeply inside me.

Mina gets to her feet, her gaze narrowed. She's not going to cower and run because I growled at her. She's probably going to kick my ass. I deserve it, but I can't deal with her right now.

"I need to get dressed." I point to the door. Mostly, I kept the bite out of my voice. Mostly.

She doesn't budge. "Your mom wants to know if you want chocolate cake or an apricot tart."

Of course, Mom sent her. Heaven forbid I have half an hour of privacy. I stomp around my bed to the door. "Mina hates cake, so make both!" I yell down to my mom. I need that cake to drown my sorrows. I turn to Mina and point to the stairs. "Out."

Mina gasps and when she walks directly up to me, I subtly cover my junk with one hand...she'd never, but I might deserve a dick punch for talking to her like this.

"Do you know how many times I've eaten cake this week?" she demands. Her dark brown eyes are flashing at me, her cheeks pink, and damn she's gorgeous when she's pissed off. My heart is breaking all over again.

And seriously? She's mad because she felt pressured to eat something she doesn't like? When I'm mad at the whole world?

I lose my shit. I don't realize it until I've backed her to the wall and she stops me with a hand on my chest. I've caged her in, my hands on the wall, my body so close to hers I can feel the buzz of something between us.

She's breathing at least as hard as I am, and she taps her hand against my chest. It's a warning. Back off or else.

I don't care what she's going to do to me. It's almost cute she thinks she could do anything at this point. I bend my head until the tip of my nose brushes hers. "Mina." I want to sink so far into her that I never have to come out and face my life, and the fact that I can't makes me want to cry. "Unless I'm unresponsive, my room is off-limits to you."

Her face tilts up toward mine and for a stupid second, I think...maybe. Maybe she's going to kiss me and it's going to be hot and angry and loaded with years of wanting. But it's all in my head because she taps my chest again, harder. A final warning.

God, what the hell am I doing? She didn't want me before, she's never going to want me now. I step away from her, raising my hands.

I can't stand to see the pity in her eyes, so I stare at my *ficus*. When did I water it last?

"Timothy—"

"I want one room, Mina." I am raw. One giant, exposed nerve. I need some time by myself to figure out how to make it stop hurting like this. "One room where I don't have to—" My voice chokes off my words.

"Be near me?" Her voice is tense, a rubber band stretched too far.

It's not just her. It's everyone and everything. My whole life, coming undone.

I nod and the rubber band that is Mina snaps.

"You asshole." She pushes past me toward the door. "If you changed your mind about me staying here, you should've said something before I spent your parents' money."

I follow her to the doorway. Of course, she doesn't get it. I'm tired of trying to make this woman see me while she deliberately misunderstands me.

I grip the doorjamb. The desire to tear it down leaves me shaking, but who am I kidding? I don't have the strength to try. "That's not what I meant, and you know it." My fingers dig into the wood until they hurt. I want her here, I want her gone; I don't know what I want.

I want my best friend and I don't know how to ask for that from her anymore. "They want me to retire."

Mina spins around. Her mouth moves, a soft *what?* I can't hear escaping her lips.

"I'm sorry I was a dick to you," I say softly. "I just need—"

Space is what I'm about to say, but she's up the stairs in two leaps, her arms wrapping tight around my waist as she presses against my chest. I have to take a step back from the force, but my arms go around her like it's the only reason they exist.

I don't need space. Space is stupid. I need this. Her. It hurts in the worst way how good it feels to hold her, so I pull her tighter to me, and dammit. I'm crying into her hair.

"I'm pissed at myself." The dam inside me is close to breaking, I have to relieve some of the pressure or I'll drown. I babble into her hair while her hands stroke my back, warm against my cool skin. "It shouldn't have happened. I've taken hits to the head before and walked them off. I'm angry, and..." I don't know what

I'm saying. I'm barely coherent at all. I know I'll never be as good at anything as I've been at stunt work and loving her, and the idea of walking away from both sucks.

Mina lets me get it out as I repeat myself four or five times. When I'm empty and quiet, she pulls away, cupping my face with both hands. "You can always be a stunt butt," she deadpans.

My mouth drops, a little hiccup of a laugh escaping, then—for no reason other than the universe is evil—my towel falls off, leaving me naked.

Mina laughs and I manage to get a hand over her eyes before her gaze drops. She *always* looks. I've always let her because I liked it when she looked at me.

Not anymore.

"That was unintentional," I say. "Sorry. Close your eyes and turn around."

"I've seen your trouser snake before, Timothy."

Is that hurt in her voice? "Yeah...well, not anymore, all right?" I have no idea how to build a wall around my heart—I never have—but it's time I learned. This is a start.

Mina turns around and I quickly scoop up my towel, holding it over my junk as I back slowly toward my door. "I'll be down in a minute. Thank you. For the cuddle." Everything is terrible, but I can get through tonight now. "I needed that."

I close the door, but I still hear her say, "Me too."

They're sitting at the dinner table when I join them. Dad's reading, of course, and pretending to be discreet about it by holding his e-book in his lap. I bump his shoulder, pretending to read silently over it. "Mom, what's a *tumescent*...I can't make out the next word...is that *rod*?"

My mom sighs, picking up her wineglass. "It's a boner, Timothy." She turns to my dad and rolls her eyes. "Put it away, William."

"Yeah, no boners at my table, Dad." I drop into my seat and grin at Mina. She won't meet my eyes.

"I'm reading a literary criticism. It's in regard to language, not rods." He shuts off his e-reader, sets it on the table, and sniffs. "I'm saving my historical erotica for later."

"Did you bring earplugs?" I ask Mina. Her eyes go adorably wide. "Never mind, I have extra."

"One time," my dad mutters as Mom downs her wine.

"A lot of therapy," I point out, refilling her empty glass when she sets it down.

"Maybe we can talk about something else?" My mom gives me a look, telling me I'm *this* close, and this, right here, is what I need. Normalcy. When no one starts in on a new topic, my mom takes charge. "Have you given any thought to what you're going to do now that you've retired? You know you need to keep busy. If we have something in place, you can step in as soon as you're—"

"No." I push my plate away. Goodbye normalcy, hello trying to keep my shit together.

"You could come work for me," my dad suggests. I raise an eyebrow and he shrugs. "Or not."

He would murder me in under a week. Mom, funny enough, doesn't offer me the same deal. I'm banned from the set where she films her cooking show because she doesn't have a sense of humor.

"I can work as a stunt coordinator," I say reluctantly. It's my only hope and I know how the people I love the most are going to take it.

Mina freezes.

Mom puts her fork down a little too hard.

Dad stares.

"Or not," I add, picking up my fork, pulling my plate closer again, and chasing a cherry tomato around my salad. My appetite hasn't returned, but I need something to do with my hands.

I wouldn't have to do the stunts, but...I wouldn't be able to help myself. They know it. I know it. It would be under the guise of demonstration or just plain showing off. But now it's out there. Maybe they can ease into the idea of it because I'm not giving up yet.

"How many concussions have you had?" Mom demands.

I pop the cherry tomato into my mouth with my fingers while she glares. "Two little teeny tiny ones," I say casually.

"Broken bones?" She arches a brow.

"A dozen?" I have no doubt she knows the exact number. I could get there if I listed them all.

"Metal plates, screws, et cetera?" Mom's eyebrow is practically in her hairline and I open my mouth to warn her against her face getting stuck like that.

"I don't like cake," Mina declares out of the blue. "I never have. Even if it's moist, it still gets stuck in my throat."

We're all staring at her now, Mom's jaw hanging open.

Mina spears her cherry tomato effortlessly. "Buttercream is disgusting too. It's so sweet and it does nothing to help swallow down the cake itself."

"Sweetie." My mom still looks aghast. She got her start in fancy cakes and branched out into every other food imaginable, so this is immensely personal to her. "You haven't had *the right* cake." She whips back to me, stabbing her fork in my direction. "Stitches and sutures. How many?"

"Cheesecake is okay," Mina continues, unstoppable now. "But only because of the cheese."

I love this woman for rushing to my defense, but watching her throw cake in my mom's face isn't exactly how I want their relationship to start.

"Cheesecake is delicious," Mom concedes, "And you're allowed your opinions, honey, but you're wrong."

"Technically," I interject to save Mina from whatever self-destruction she pulls out next, lest it implicates me. "Most of my injuries were from before I started doing stunt work."

"You need new hobbies," Mom grumbles. "Bake the poor girl some cake."

"No, I like her." And my balls where they are. "Besides, Nic makes all the cake." Including the ones Mina forced herself to eat thinking my mom had baked them, I'd wager. "He's still staying here?"

My mom sighs, but she takes the bait and Nic saves the day without being present.

My backdoor into the stunt world is still there, a lifeline that, for the moment,

I need, even if a part of me suspects it isn't open at all.

Chapter Thirteen

Timothy

My bed is a fluffy cloud, but I can't fall asleep. The anger I felt earlier is gone, and in the quiet of the night, I feel lost.

Through my cracked bedroom door, I hear the rattle of ice hitting a glass. Nic, home after a long day of filming. I push myself up slowly. The world barely spins, but I take my time, pulling on some lightweight sweats and shuffle-stepping out of my room in case I get dizzy or miss a step in the dark.

Mina left her door open a crack.

Farther down the hall, my parents' door is closed, but I can still hear Dad snoring through it.

I'll have to apologize in the morning for my attitude at dinner. I know Mom's pecking comes from a place of love, but Christ on a stick. I'll find another job and safer hobbies when I'm good and ready.

Or never. Never's good too.

I pause at Mina's door and listen for the soft sounds of sleep, but instead, I hear a muffled sob.

"Mina?" I push the door open and step into her room. It's dimly lit and I make a mental note to order some blackout curtains. She stiffens before rolling over to sit up. The desire to scoop her into my arms is so strong fighting it leaves me shaking. But I'm working on boundaries. "What's wrong?"

She sniffles, wiping her eyes. "I didn't wake you, did I? I'm sorry."

"You didn't wake me." I step closer. I've seen Mina cry a few times, but only once because she was sad, on the night we met. Every other time it's been her awful periods. "Do you need a heating pad or some pain relief?"

"What? No." Her hands drop to the bed. "It—everything finally caught up with me, I guess. The accident, my job, my apartment, all of it. And I'm scared."

"Of what?" I ask, sitting on the edge of her bed.

She shakes her head, bites her lip, and finally spits it out. "I don't want you to go back as a stunt coordinator."

Shit. I'm the reason she's crying. I hate that. I want to make her laugh like I always do, but I can't think of a goddamn thing to say to accomplish that.

The masochist in me reaches out to tuck a strand of hair behind her ear. Her eyes are dark, shimmery pools in the dim light and she stares at me in that soul-drinking way.

Mina has never kept her dislike of my job a secret, so this isn't a surprise. She doesn't like to hear about the stunts themselves, so over the years, I've tailored my conversation with her to be about the people when I talk about the job, rather than whatever cool stunt I did. It sucks, but I get it. She lost her parents to a climbing accident—of course, she doesn't want to hear about the time my parachute tangled or the time I bounced off an airbag and broke three ribs.

"Okay," I hear myself say. Acknowledgment of what she wants, not acquiescence. I'm not going to fight her on this right now.

Her head falls forward until it rests against my shoulder and since her body is shaking again, I wrap my arms around her and pull her close to me. So much for my fucking walls.

"Life isn't risk-free," I say softly into her hair. "A piano could fall on my head while I'm walking down the street."

She ignores my attempt at levity. "You promised," she says, her lips brushing over my collarbone. I'm so caught up in the sensation, it takes me a moment to realize what she said. "You promised you'd retire, Timothy."

I did when I woke after surgery, and I even meant it in my drug-addled post-surgery brain. But now...I don't want to give up my career for a friend. Even a best friend. That's not fair.

I can't make any promises, so I say nothing, holding her close like she held me earlier. She must be exhausted because she falls asleep in minutes. I want to lie next to her, listening to her soft breathing until I doze off, but that's the opposite of building a wall, so I gently lay her down, pulling the blankets up to her shoulders.

Placing a soft kiss on her forehead—I am really not good at walls—I head downstairs.

In the dark of night, with the glow of the pool lights reflecting off all the glass windows, it's easy to admit the truth. I've built so much of who I am around what I do for fun and work. If I retire, I'll become a ghost. There is nothing left of me without my career.

I grab a tumbler from a cupboard, filling it with ice before pulling a bottle of sparkling water out of the fridge. I know my mom, and it takes me ten seconds to find her stash of edibles. I grab one and hide the rest in a cupboard where she'll never find them. Not without a ladder.

Nic's sitting hunched over his—*my*—whiskey, one hand cradling his head. Cute. Maybe he feels my pain.

I slide open the glass door and step outside. He turns at the sound. I give him a little wave. He's on his feet instantly, wrapping me in a hug. "Fuck, Timothy. I'm sorry."

There's nothing to do but nod, because I'm sorry too.

"I should've tried harder with the choreography," he says, holding me tighter, and I swear to god if he cries I'm going to push his ass into the pool. I can't do all the emotional heavy lifting for my friends when I'm struggling under my own. Mina was there for me earlier, sharing the weight, but Nic's been AWOL for four years.

"It's not your fault." I slap his back. "Just an accident." It's my fault as much as anyone's. "You could have visited me." Honestly, bigger things have been weighing on me. My recovery, my job situation, Mina. But Nic not being there—at all—stung.

Nic lets go of me and drops into his chair with a heavy sigh. "You had Mina."

"You didn't come," I say more forcefully. The pool lights cast an eerie light show over his face as he stares straight ahead. We've known each other since we were boys. Grew up together. How did we grow so far apart?

"I *tried*. Couldn't make it to the waiting room." He makes a disgusted sound. "I'm sorry. I've been a shitty friend."

It must be my turn to be the shitty friend—I forgot he hasn't stepped foot in a hospital since the deaths of his parents. I'd lose it too.

I've been in and out of hospitals so many times I should have a loyalty card.

"Get up," I say. "We're hugging this out."

He grumbles, but he knows he's not getting out of this and he gets up and hugs me back just as hard. "I still love you," I tell him.

"You too."

We settle back into our seats like old men.

The first night in this house, we sat right here by the pool, drinking whiskey and talking about bright futures. Nic was getting better roles in bigger films. I was working my ass off. We were going to take the world.

And here we sit, scarred and battle-weary, fallen so far from those hopeful, optimistic pricks. I hate who we were, and I'd give anything to go back to it right now.

I crack the sparkling water, filling my glass. Whiskey would be better, but this isn't my first rodeo. Alcohol does not mix well with head wounds. I pop the gummy dinosaur in my mouth and chew, staring out at the water of my pool.

I can't shake the image of Mina's eyes shining up at me in the dark.

You promised.

Going back into stunt work will hurt her. She might have turned me down, but she loves me. It was there in her eyes. So what if it's platonic? She still loves me, and she's not just some friend. The idea that maybe I won't walk away the next time a stunt goes wrong—or maybe even right—scares the shit out of me when I think of her. I don't want to leave her.

God fucking dammit.

"I'm retiring," I spit out. The words taste foul, but just like that, I cut myself free from the stunt world. It's official. I'm done. Lost in the fucking dark, no clue what to do now that I'm a shadow of my former glory. I never thought I'd be here. Maybe in my seventies or eighties, but not when I'm in my prime. But here I am. Retired.

"Me too," Nic says with a dark chuckle.

Irritation with the situation rises and if it weren't for lifting restrictions, I'd throw his ass into the pool. "I'm serious."

"Good." He holds his empty glass out and when I refuse to refill it, rattles the ice. I ignore him because it's my whiskey and I'm not his servant. With a sigh, he grabs the bottle and pours it.

Suddenly I don't want to talk about me. At all. Not even a tiny bit. "Why do you want to quit? Pissed you're only the Second Hottest man in America?"

He rolls his eyes. "Seriously? You think I've enjoyed anything about the last four years? The last ten?"

Nic followed me out to LA and tripped into a modeling career, then stumbled into acting. He has a rabid fan base thanks to the Warwick role. They might love him, but critics don't. No one casts him for his ability to act, and while I knew he didn't love acting, I hadn't thought about whether or not he was happy with his life.

"You're such a surly bastard, hard to tell sometimes," I say, leaning back and melting into my lounger. "What would you do if you quit?" *Give me ideas because I don't have a clue what to do with myself.*

"Fuck if I know," he grumbles.

Helpful.

My phone vibrates in my pocket and through some sort of sixth sense, I know it's my twin calling.

Nic catches a glimpse of her picture flashing on my screen, and since she's trying to video call me, he grabs his whiskey and stalks back into the house with a grumbled *good night.* If she catches a glimpse of him after I swipe to accept the call, she doesn't acknowledge it.

"Timothy, you shit-for-brains fucktoast!" she hisses. It's sunny in Italy and she's sitting outside. On a balcony, I think. A tear slips out before she hastily brushes it away. "How—how—dare you."

"Hi womb-mate," I chirp at her because it will piss her off. "Guess how many staples are in my scalp?"

Finding out about my accident via email from Mom's assistant five minutes ago has not left my twin in a good mood. She makes me tell her everything that happened, everything the doctors said. I don't want to, but I do because she's my twin. My little sister.

Mom and Dad are in so much trouble with her. Possibly Amanda, too, since my older sister was Nic's second call.

Nic's dead to Jessie already, so ironically, he's safe.

"I'm coming to LA," Jessie announces, though she looks queasy at the thought. "You need someone to look after you."

Like hell. The last thing I need is Jessie and Nic and their damn dramas while I'm trying to recover.

"I have a friend staying with me," I tell her.

She snorts. "I know what kind of loser friends you keep."

That's a dig at Nic, not any of my other friends, who Jessie would like. I haven't told her about Mina. Jessie gets a bit overprotective, and since Mina doesn't love me, it would be a waste of energy to tell my twin about her.

"Nic's living here, too," I add. Since it's not something the tabloids have picked up on, Jessie possibly doesn't know. Both she and Nic keep their personal lives out of the family group chat, preferring to contribute memes (Jessie) or lurk (Nic).

She sips her coffee and makes a face. "Oh."

"Coffee too bitter?" I ask, glancing over my shoulder, curious if I'll find Nic hanging out in the kitchen or near the stairs, listening in.

Nope. He's gone.

"You scared the hell out of me," Jessie says in a small voice.

"I'm fine, J." I don't want to be living this—talking about it is intolerable. "How's your vacation?"

"Hot."

"Nah, can't be that hot. I'm not there."

She finally smiles, though it's weak. "I see your ego has escaped unscathed."

My ego is in tatters. I look ghastly on the screen, pool lights reflecting off my skin. Pretending isn't working for me, but I don't know what else to do. "Come on, look at me. I'm perfect. Sorry, I got all the good genetics."

"Oh wow, you think you can still say that?" she says. "Did they even find a brain in that head of yours, or was it just three squirrels fighting over a Red Bull?"

I shrug. "Basically, but that's better than the unicorns with dildo horns prancing around in your head."

She laughs. "I love you, you gigantic…" she's struggling for a word that isn't prick or dick or asshole—I've given her shit about expanding her vocabulary—and I raise my eyebrows and wait.

"Meatball." The euphemism clicks two seconds after she says it. She swears and bangs her elbow on her chair. She swears again, rubbing her elbow.

I laugh. "Dork."

"Weenus! It's the skin on your elbow! You're a gigantic weenus!"

"What's that?" I say loudly. "The connection's shit. I have a big penis? That's why you were so small at birth because I took up all the room in the womb with my gigantic schlong?"

"For fuck's sake," she mutters, but she smiles. "I love you, too, dickhead. I'm glad you're okay. Call if you need anything?"

I salute her but I'm a bit teary because she didn't ask me to stop doing stunts or stop having fun. She's my twin and even though we haven't been close in twenty years, she gets me on a basic level.

Or, more likely, she figured it was pointless, which makes me sad. She ends the call, leaving me alone in the dark.

Shit's been weird with Jessie for a long time. We were besties until Nic came along. It's been hard navigating her hurt. His hurt, too, because Jessie can figuratively nut a man with one perfect eyebrow raise.

"Are you serious right now?" Mina's voice, annoyed and thick with sleep, nearly makes me drop my phone. "Why are you out here yelling about your penis? Do I need to take you back to the hospital?"

I get to my feet—slow again, because the edible kicked in and I feel like molasses—and smile at her. "Nah, typical Tuesday night at Casa Timothy."

"It's Sunday," she says. "Come on. Back to bed."

"It's Monday," I point out, just so she'll glare at me. She's so damn cute when she's annoyed.

"Timothy Alexander Foley, if you don't get your ass in the house, I will—"

I fold her into a hug and the fight drops out of her. She sighs.

The last week has been hell for her. For everyone. I love my family, and I love Nic, but Mina's been here for me in a way no one else has, since the day we met. I count on her in a way I don't count on them. Maybe all we'll ever have is friendship, but I'm grateful for that. Even though it hurts.

"Thank you," I say softly. "For being here. For putting up with me."

"Anytime," she says, taking my hand and pulling me back into the house.

Chapter Fourteen

Mina

Timothy's parents leave and over the next two days, he retreats to his room, spending most of his time where I'm not allowed.

He's recovering, but I thought we'd hang out. Lounge on the sofa and talk. When we'd watch movies at my apartment, he'd often lie on the sofa, his head in my lap. He can't look at a screen for long right now, but he could lie like that and nap while I watched something on my phone. We could play a short game of pool, or he could help me cut fabric—he's done that before. Instead, he's hiding from me.

I chose the bold colors for my autumn release, hoping I could draw strength from them, but it's not working. My nerves are fraying as my scissors cut through the fabric. What if he has another brain bleed and I don't notice because he's in his room? I check on him every few hours, which irritates him, but too bad.

Fabric cut, I move on to sewing gussets. Another day's work and I'll be back on schedule. I set up my portable table in the living room and lined the wall next to me with plastic tubs of cut fabric, organized by size and style. I purchased a new embroidery machine with some of the money from Timothy's parents and sold my old, finicky one. I'm not ready to embroider anything yet, but I test it out on a few scraps, just to try it.

The noise of my sewing machine is the only sound in the house and it's eerie.

I want the old Timothy back. I want him looking over my shoulder, asking questions about what I'm doing, pulling a pair of underwear over his head, and asking if he looks hot in them.

The front door opens and Nic walks in, locking it behind him and toeing off his shoes. I finish my gusset, then lean back in my chair, rubbing my neck. Done for the day.

"How's Timothy?" he asks in a quiet voice as he heads into the kitchen.

I glance at the clock. It's 9:30. Timothy went to bed an hour ago. I follow Nic into the kitchen. "He's too quiet." The last two nights when Nic asked, I told him Timothy was fine, and physically, I believe he is. Mentally, I'm not sure.

Nic stops rummaging in the fridge and closes the door with a sigh. "Yeah."

"What do you mean, *yeah*?" I ask, irritated when he doesn't say more. Not that Nic's been around to see how quiet Timothy is. He's busy on set.

"The doctor said he'd sleep a lot, right?" He reaches for the chocolate cake on the counter and slices off a tiny wedge. "Don't tell my trainer," he says, leaning over the sink to eat it. Like I give a shit if he breaks the ridiculous diet the studio has him on. He's all muscle and bones anyway.

"It's not the sleep. When he's up, he's different. Quiet and...not himself."

Nic shrugs. "He's still coming to terms with his retirement, and if his head hurts, he probably doesn't feel all that chatty."

I saw the misery in Timothy's eyes when he made his retirement official before his parents left, and of course, his headaches will make him quiet. This seems like something more. "You aren't worried?"

He polishes off the cake in three bites as he considers. My throat goes dry and I fight the urge to gag because cake is disgusting.

Nic brushes the crumbs off his fingers and grabs a glass, filling it with water. "Not yet," he finally says after a long drink. "I think he just needs time."

Maybe Nic's right. He's known Timothy since they were kids, he should know him better than I do.

Still, it doesn't feel right to me.

Nic says good night a few minutes later, heading downstairs while I clean up my sewing space.

I turn off all the lights on my way upstairs, and that's when I hear it. A soft moan from Timothy's room.

My heart seizes and then pumps adrenaline through my body. He was fine when he went to his room, but he could've slipped in the shower. His brain could've started bleeding again while he slept. I don't know, but a million worst-case scenarios race through my mind as I tear up the stairs and whip open his door and—

Timothy's sitting against his headboard, his head tipped back, eyes closed. One arm is bent over his head, gripping the headboard behind him. His lips are pressed together tight, the faintest sheen of sweat on his brow, and I take one step into his room, convinced he's dying, before I notice his other arm. It's moving fast, muscles bunching and pulling.

Oh. *Oh.*

My eyes drop down his bicep, down his forearm to where his dick juts out of his fist as he pumps it hard and fast.

Desire floods my system, hot and thick. I need to turn around and leave before he sees me, but I can't move. I want to see him get off.

Like he senses my presence, his eyes fly open, locking on mine. I feel his gaze, hot and dark, on my skin and for the span of a breath, I might as well be next to him. On top of him. Under him. My hand wrapped around him, his hand slipping between my legs. The moment between us lasts only a second but it's so thick I feel everything.

Time might stop, but his hand doesn't. He gasps in surprise, jerks, and—

He shoots himself in the face.

A second startled gasp escapes his lips and he flails, like he's not sure what to do because he's still coming, his eyes flying between me and his cock and the mess he's making. Finally he snags a pillow, covering himself.

I can't help it. I giggle.

Timothy blinks like he doesn't understand what happened. "Fuck," he finally says, wiping his chin.

"Oh my god, Timothy!" I double over in laughter, squealing as I slam the door shut. "Put a sock on the door. I thought you were dying."

"I am now," he says sheepishly. "Can we pretend this didn't happen?"

"No way."

His voice takes on a gently chiding tone. "You know this isn't my most embarrassing masturbation story. Not even top five, Mina, so settle down."

"You shot yourself in the face." Tears are streaming down *my* face, but at least it's not jizz.

"You can admit you found the whole thing intensely erotic," he calls out. I can hear the smile in his voice, and relief drenches me. My Timothy is still in there and he's going to be okay.

"Good night, Timothy." I giggle back down the steps to my bedroom, but after I put on my pajamas and climb into bed, that's not the image that stays with me.

I huff a sigh and roll onto my side, but I can't shake it. I'm going to be picturing the way he gripped that big dick of his, the slide of his hand from the base to the tip, the way his thumb flicked over the wide head every other stroke...

Flopping onto my back and staring at the ceiling, I try to think about Wild Things instead. Making enough panties for a pop-up shop. Including a candle or something in the subscription box.

Twenty seconds later, I'm back to Timothy fucking his fist. Was he thinking about me? He was, I decide, because I want to imagine the details. If he was thinking about my hand or my mouth, or my pussy...how would it feel to have his hands on me? Or my hands on him? A little shiver of excitement runs through me.

I need to sleep and there's only one way that's happening. I dig my suitcase out from under the bed and pull out my vibrator. For a moment, I think about getting up to lock the door. I don't, in the interest of fairness.

Also, because I can't wait that long.

I slip my pajama shorts and underwear down, flicking on the vibrator. It's quiet, at least. I don't think Timothy can hear it. Not sure I care right now. The wild part of me I usually keep locked down wants him to hear me getting off.

Usually, I conjure up some man with indistinct features for my fantasies. This time, the mystery man's face keeps turning into Timothy's until I give up in frustration and let myself indulge in imaginary sex with my best friend. Timothy on top of me, moving slowly, kissing my neck. Me, riding him while he pinches my nipples. Timothy, bending me over the arm of the couch, taking me from behind.

There are too many ways I want him and I don't get through many before the pressure builds and breaks and keeps breaking. I bite my lip to silence my cry as I ride it as long as I can. After, I flick off the vibrator, blowing out a long breath.

Holy shit.

It's my best self-induced orgasm possibly ever and I'm mad about it because I know next time, I'll be thinking about Timothy again.

I'm up early, *definitely not* thinking about Timothy as I shuffle about the kitchen wearing a robe and bunny slippers. I'm deep conditioning my hair because it's been a while, so it's wrapped in a towel twisted on top of my head, but I need a coffee while I wait to rinse it. Celia taught me how to use Timothy's fancy espresso machine, and today, I want a latte with hazelnut syrup.

I'm not saying the great orgasm last night has inspired me to spend the morning treating myself, but I'm not denying it either.

I'm pouring steamed milk when I hear Timothy walking down the stairs.

My cheeks warm. I'm going to have to face him, despite what I saw last night, and what I did after. I don't know how.

"Want a coffee?" I ask without looking.

"Wow," Timothy drawls out. "This must be embarrassing for you."

My face goes center-of-the-sun hot and my spine snaps straight. The normal thing would be to glare at him, so I turn to do that, only—

He's standing in the kitchen wearing a robe with neon pink zebra stripes and T. rex slippers, with a plain white towel wrapped around his head. He motions at his robe and slippers with an imperious flick of his wrist before making the same gesture at me.

I laugh, all awkwardness gone. "Yeah," I agree dryly, "I'm the embarrassed one here." This is the most Timothy he's been, and the relief at having my best friend back leaves me giddy.

Maybe Nic was right. He just needed some time.

Timothy grins. "Turning up in my kitchen wearing the same thing as me." He shakes his head and tsks.

"You wear it better," I say, grabbing another mug from the cupboard.

"I can make my own coffee," he says, stepping closer and taking the mug from my hand.

There's the smallest hint of an edge to his voice, so I flick his arm. "I know that. Maybe I want to make you a coffee."

"Maybe I want to make you breakfast," he counters. "As an apology for last night."

It takes everything I have to keep my cool as my face heats. I tap my finger against my chin and look at the ceiling, pretending to concentrate. "Last night, last night...what happened last night?"

He grins again. "I'm not forgettable."

I smile and sip my coffee, giving him a little shrug for an answer before I turn to lean against the island.

Timothy passes close behind me and I feel his breath on my neck as he bends close, saying, "Can't be sure, but I thought I heard some buzzing coming from your room."

"You didn't," I say with a breeziness I'm not feeling. When he peeks around at my face, I blush.

"Huh" is his reply as he goes back to making his coffee. "Sit, I'll make you breakfast."

"You nervous about today?" I ask, taking my coffee to the table. He's getting his staples out this afternoon.

"No," he says, going quiet as he pulls some green onions and peppers out of the fridge.

I drink my coffee and watch him as he starts chopping. I like watching this domestic version of him. He looks so comfortable, so calm, even as he bobs to a song in his head while cracking eggs. I'm sure he knows I'm watching him, but he gives me the space to do it. He cuts the omelet in half with a spatula before sliding it onto two plates.

He sets the plates on the table, along with forks and knives, and takes the towel off his head before he sits next to me. My eyes drop to the deep V of his robe. He's shirtless—no surprise—but now I'm wondering if he's wearing anything under those zebra stripes.

"A little nervous," he concedes to the question I asked him ten minutes ago.

I reach my hand across the table and take his, squeezing his fingers. "I'll be with you."

"That helps," he says.

After breakfast, I force Timothy to rest on the couch while I go upstairs to rinse the deep conditioner from my hair. I come back down dressed for the day in shorts and a T-shirt.

Timothy's not on the couch. The dishes are done and I told him to leave them for me, so he's officially in trouble, but when I notice the gift basket sitting on the table, my irritation dissolves.

I know exactly what's inside it, because every twenty-eight days, Timothy sends me one. It's full of tampons and pads, fancy chocolates and nice lotions, face masks, and nail polish. Sometimes a candle or a book.

Not long after we met, he came to visit me at work, finding me curled under a rack of clothes. My period had come early, and I was unprepared for the pain. Instead of freaking out and calling an ambulance, or slowly backing away, he sweet-talked my boss into giving me a couple of days off, then took me home. He ran a bath for me, and when I came out, he had chicken noodle soup ready to go. My fridge was fully stocked, my prescriptions were filled, and he had two bags full of tampons and pads, not knowing which ones I preferred. There were fancy chocolates and nice herbal teas. A new, expensive heating pad sat outside my bedroom door, and he'd told me whatever I wanted was mine. I just had to ask.

It was...a lot, considering we hadn't known each other for long. I'd appreciated everything he'd done, but I was tired and in pain, so I'd thanked him, offered to pay him back, and hinted I'd like to be alone to try to sleep through it.

He took the hint with a smile and a *call me if you need anything*. And exactly twenty-eight days later, a gift basket turned up at my apartment, full of everything anyone bleeding through a maximum absorbency pad every hour would need.

I tried to get him to stop, but he's saved me a fortune on personal hygiene, and the chocolates are the expensive ones I love but can't justify buying. Besides, Timothy's not very good at listening to anything he doesn't want to hear.

I dig through the basket and pull out the chocolates. Six months ago, I had a hysterectomy. I've been meaning to tell him, but I kept putting it off. I can't live in his house and lie to him about this. Not that my periods or lack of them are his business. They aren't. But I want to tell him.

Chocolates in hand, I climb the stairs and knock on his bedroom door. He opens it after a short wait, drying his freshly shaven face with a towel. He's dressed now—mostly. In dark blue shorts. Nothing else.

I can't help it. My eyes skim over him. Barbell through the right nipple. Kraken tattoo wrapped over his shoulder and upper arm. A light dusting of sandy hair over his chest. Normally he waxes it, but he hasn't yet, and I want to touch it before it's gone.

Timothy closes the door in my face.

"Just a moment," he calls from the other side. When he opens it again, he's wearing a white T-shirt.

Right. He's discovered modesty in my presence.

I hate how much it irritates me, but that's not what I'm here for. I hold up the chocolates. "Can I come in? We need to talk."

He frowns. "Do I need to adjust the delivery date again?"

"No, it's—" I take a step as he steps out of the room and we shuffle around each other before he manages to close the door behind him. Seriously? He's still keeping his room off-limits?

He motions for me to sit on the steps, then takes a seat.

I sit next to him, but maybe I should've sat on a different step or remained standing. He's re-writing the rules of our friendship and I don't know what I'm allowed to do anymore. I don't like any of this.

"I had a hysterectomy," I blurt out.

Timothy stares at me.

I clasp my hands together and shove them between my knees. "That means they took my uterus out. I don't get periods anymore." Birth control didn't do anything except guarantee my periods came with some measure of regularity. I couldn't have an IUD, thanks to the shape of my uterus. I couldn't go on missing work every month, spending days in bed crying and vomiting when the pain got too bad. Sooner or later, like most of the other jobs I've had, they'd fire me.

It took me a decade to find a doctor willing to perform the procedure, and I spent every last penny of my savings to pay for it.

It was worth it. But I never told Timothy about that struggle. It was too personal.

"When?" he asks, sounding confused and hurt.

"Six months ago."

I can see him doing the math, thinking back to where he was and what he was doing. Wondering how he didn't notice. He didn't notice because he was off skiing with Nic and I had a fast recovery.

"Why didn't you tell me?" he asks. The distress in his voice catches me off guard. "I know it's none of my business, but please tell me you weren't alone."

I can't, so I don't.

He doesn't say anything, just pulls me into a hug. I wind my arms around his hard waist and bury my face in his T-shirt and bite back the whimper dredged up from god knows where.

"I'm sorry," he says into my hair, his voice sounding choked. "That must have sucked."

I'm not going to cry. I spent years crying from the pain and that's over now. The whole thing is over. My life is better. It's mine every week of every month.

"I would've been there for you." He squeezes me tighter.

"I know."

"I'm so—"

"I'm happy." I don't want to hear *sorry* again.

Timothy leans back and looks at me. His eyes are shiny, but maybe that's because mine are brimming. "I'm happy too," he says. "But I'm sorry I made you my emergency contact without asking you first. I forced you to be there for me."

When I wouldn't let him be there for me. It hangs unspoken between us.

"It's okay, and it's different. I chose to have a procedure done, and I was happy going alone. You didn't choose what happened to you. Whether or not I was your emergency contact, I'd have been there."

He's quiet for a moment, his light brown eyes searching my face before he nods. "I'm still sending chocolate every month."

"You don't have to." I'm not going to fight him over the chocolate that I desperately want. Not when he has a trust fund.

He gives me a stern look. "Come on. You still get moody."

I gasp in mock outrage and gently push him away. "Rude."

Timothy laughs, but it lacks his usual joy. "Just accept the chocolate as inevitable."

"Okay, fine." I need to do something for him, and suddenly I know exactly what. "But you need to accept my underwear once a month."

His jaw drops.

"I will sew you underwear," I grit out, annoyed at myself for my choice of words. "Boxers, briefs, or boxer briefs?"

He smiles and this time he looks happy. "I'll take whatever you make me."

"I think I have some dinosaur print. Definitely need to get my hands on something that says bam and pow and wap like in an old comic book. Maybe some animal print or rocket—"

That last word dies on my tongue as Timothy grabs my chin, tilts my face up, and kisses me. It's firm and quick, platonic rather than romantic, but I lean in any way. Except he gets to his feet, oblivious, and carries on downstairs like nothing happened, leaving me lurching after him.

I touch my lips lightly.

They're tingling.

Chapter Fifteen

Timothy

I'M AN ASSHOLE. I forced Mina to be there for me when she wasn't willing to let me be there for her. She's not mad, and she's going to sew something for me and—oh shit.

I kissed her. It stops me in my tracks.

"Sorry, got carried away," I call back up. I mean to glance at her for half a second, but I do a double take. She's still sitting on the step, two graceful fingers lightly touching her lips. She looks dazed.

Have I been too busy trying to wall off my heart, too busy sulking about my life to notice? Is there the slightest possibility she's changing her mind about us? There was that moment in the kitchen where I'd implied—with no evidence whatsoever—I'd heard her vibrator, and she'd blushed.

It might be something. It might be nothing, but I'm an optimist.

"I can't wait to wear your underwear," I add, winking at her. I don't wait for her to respond, carrying on down the stairs.

Mina rolls with it, giving me an exaggerated, exhausted sigh. Thank god. I'm pretty good at destroying awkward moments—usually ones I caused in the first place—but I'm not sure I can top my efforts from this morning. Dressing like Mina, with the robe and slippers and towel on my head, hopefully erased my masturbation misfire from her memory.

Not from mine, unfortunately. I groan as I walk into the kitchen for a glass of water. The first bit of self-love since the accident, and I can't believe I hit myself in the face when she walked in on me. I was too stunned, too deep in the fantasy for my hand to catch up with the situation, and now I'm going to be hearing her laugh every time I get my dick out.

Not exactly the reaction I want. Laughter belongs in sex, but not the first sexual encounter. Not that last night counts as a sexual encounter. Maybe a sexual encounter of the first kind? Isn't that look but don't touch? The third kind is anal probes? Or abduction? Maybe there isn't a one-to-one between alien encounters and sexual encounters. Pretty sure one of the many audiobooks Dad downloaded for me—since screens give me a headache—addresses this...

It's making my head hurt, so I let it go. I have to go see the doctor in a couple of hours and I need to look recovered.

I don't feel it. The headaches aren't as bad, but I'm exhausted. Fake it till I make it isn't working yet, and I'm afraid it might never work. I might never be okay. Having the doctor confirm these fears are grounded in reality is the last thing I want.

Mina's on the couch when I finish my water. She has a towel under her foot and she's painting her toenails a bright, cheery blue. I sit a full cushion away from her, propping my feet on one of her plastic tubs of underwear.

I fall asleep and wake up with blue toenails. Leaning my head back against the couch, I wiggle my toes and laugh. Seriously, building walls is not working out for me. Why did I ever think I could build them in the first place? I couldn't build shit with Lego as a kid, so it's no wonder my walls are wobbly and hole-ridden.

I love this woman more today than I did when I asked her to marry me. Walls aren't going to change that.

Mina comes downstairs and warmth spreads over my skin when she smiles at me. I love being the center of her attention. I'd do anything to stay in it.

"Ready in five?" she asks.

Shit. Doctor time.

The staples come out, and the doctor doesn't have some magical power to see inside me. Well, she does with CT scans and MRIs, but she determines I'm progressing fine and since things looked good inside my head when I was discharged, we can forgo the peek inside today.

I don't ask her if I'm ever going to be myself again because I don't want to put my hope into cardiac arrest.

Mina, though…

She slaps a notebook on the doctor's desk and holy shit. I grab it before the doctor can, but Mina must have it memorized. She lists off all her concerns while I read through the daily log of what I've been doing.

According to her, I'm sleeping a lot—although she doesn't know that several of those hours have been dedicated to intense sulking because I've done it in the privacy of my room. What she does know is detailed. What I've eaten, how my mood appears to her, guesses at the intensity of my headaches plus my assessment of them, if I gave one.

I skip ahead to last night and thank god she omitted me jerking off. No *he hit himself in the chin with an above-average load.*

The doctor is looking at me when I set the notebook back on the desk. "Rest is important," she's saying to Mina, "But I agree with you. Isolation won't help. Have some people over for dinner or a quiet activity."

"What about sex?" I ask abruptly.

The doctor flips through Mina's notebook. "There's nothing to indicate you can't slowly and gradually ease into more physical activity. Maybe start with short walks around the neighborhood, stopping if it makes your head hurt before you jump into group sex."

I laugh.

Mina squirms. "He didn't mean—"

"No, no," I interrupt. "I was wondering if dinner parties could lead to orgies, and now I know."

Mina gives me a dirty look—and not the fun kind—but I catch the twitch in her lips. She's trying not to laugh.

After the appointment, as we're walking to Mina's car, she nudges my arm.

"Why don't we invite Danny over for dinner this weekend?"

My stomach dives. I like Danny, but I don't want to see him. I don't want to see anyone except Mina and Nic. "Why don't I take you out somewhere nice instead?" I ask, trying to sound casual. "I'll buy you another Mioe dress." This time, I nudge her with my elbow. "You can pick it out."

Mina doesn't take the bait. "Why don't you want to see Danny?"

"He's a bit loud. Noise sets off my headaches. Not your sewing machines," I add quickly when she rounds on me. "They don't bother me."

Her lips press together. "Someone else then?" she asks.

"Nic?" I offer up as we reach her car. "Bonus, he can cook us dinner and we don't have to go out."

Mina frowns as we climb into her ancient hatchback. "You don't want to go out."

God, can she see right through me? "We have to start slow," I say, grasping at whatever comes to me. "Hand stuff before orgies."

Her sigh is long-suffering and very hot.

"Give me time," I say when she chews her lower lip. "I'm still recovering."

For a solid minute, as she negotiates the parking lot, I'm convinced she's going to argue with me. She doesn't.

We get home and I immediately head for my shower to shampoo my disgusting hair. It feels amazing, except when my fingers graze where they drilled into my skull. That feels weird, and not in a good way.

I've been spending too much time in my room, and if I want Mina to stop worrying, I need to show her I'm okay. Maybe she won't see through the lie. I head downstairs for a late afternoon of watching her sew.

It must work. She doesn't bring up Danny or anyone else all weekend, though she does drag me out of the house for short walks around my neighborhood. Now that the staples are out of my head, I start swimming too. Mina keeps an eye on me from a lounge chair, declining to join me.

By Monday, I can't sit on the couch and watch her sew anymore, so I pepper her with questions about her machines, about what she's doing, and finally, if I can try.

She humors me, motioning for me to take her seat, which I do. Mina digs through a tub and comes back with two squares of fabric with colorful dinosaurs. She places them together, so the print is on the inside, leaning over me to put it on the machine. Her body brushes against my arm. I inhale the dark floral scent of her perfume and immediately drift off on a daydream of hot, sweaty, intoxicating nights buried deep inside her.

When she's ready, she crouches behind me, her left hand on top of mine. Her face hovers close and her breasts graze my shoulders.

I can't concentrate like this.

"I'm going to sew my hand to this fabric," I tell her softly, turning to look at her, "with you this close."

She turns toward me a little, too, bringing her lips within a couple of inches of mine. Her dark eyes are hooded, focused on my mouth. I don't breathe. I don't move because I need her to be the one to take this kiss. I'm pretty sure she can hear my heart pounding as the moment stretches between us. I tilt my head to bring my lips closer in invitation, but she straightens abruptly, muttering an apology as her hand leaves mine.

My body is cold without her, and a disappointed sigh finds a way out of my lips before I can grab it and yank it back.

Her hand covers mine again, but she's not kissing-distance close anymore. "There's a pedal under the table," she says, trying to hide how flustered she is with an overconfident voice and failing. "Think of it as a touchy accelerator, and a traffic cop is watching you. Go slow."

I don't know why everyone assumes I'm some crazy-fast driver. Okay, I know why, but they're wrong.

Slowly, I press my foot to the pedal, and the machine springs to life. Mina shows me how to guide the fabric before removing her hand and coming back to turn the fabric ninety degrees. The second turn I do myself.

"There," she says as she snips some loose threads and turns the fabric right side out. "You made a pocket." She hands it to me and I inspect it.

Huh. I made a pocket. Cool.

Mina's phone dings and her face brightens. "Hey, Danny wants to swing by tonight to say hi."

Not Danny again. "Not tonight," I say, taking my pocket back to the couch.

"Why not?" she asks. "We don't have plans."

"I have plans." I pop my earbuds in. "This audiobook. I'm finally getting to the good stuff." I drop my voice to a stage whisper, "Pegging."

She gives me a look that is eerily similar to one my mother might give me.

A good number of the audiobooks my dad downloaded for me fall into the erotica category, but there are some spy novels and stuff. Which I'll get to after the sexy books. Never know when I might learn a new trick. Plus, I'm a sucker for a happily ever after.

Mina steps in front of me, nudging my leg with hers. "What about tomorrow?" she asks when I remove the earbud.

She's not going to let this go. I stand to leave because I don't want company and I don't want to explain why. "I'm going to my room to jerk off. Ignore all sounds for the next fifteen minutes—I'm not dying."

Yes, I have been announcing my personal time to her, even when I have no intention of masturbating. It gives me thirty minutes of guaranteed privacy, but it also puts a pretty blush across her cheeks. I'd bet anything she spends the entire time thinking about me getting off. This means I'm thinking about her thinking about me, and then I need to get off, whether that was my original intent or not. It's a vicious cycle.

"Wait a sec," she says, bending to dig in one of the boxes at her feet. "I got you something."

I'm halfway to the stairs, but I'm intrigued, so I come back. It might be nudes. Laminated for easy cleanup. Or better yet, it could be her.

She hands me an old-school hockey mask.

I laugh and put it on. Not as good as laminated nudes, but I'll take it. "It was your fault I shot myself in the face."

"Sure it was," she says, giving me a knowing look as she walks into the kitchen, stretching her arms over her head. For a moment I'm dazzled by the muscle in her arms and the grace in the way they roll as she moves. I want to learn every inch of her body with my hands, my tongue...

I push the mask up into my hair and shake myself. Time to go before she catches me staring at her like a creep.

"Have fun," she calls out. "Make sure you stretch first."

I start up the stairs. "I don't know what you think I'm doing that requires stretching."

"Exactly why I'll be Googling pegging."

I miss a step, landing on my knee.

Pain blooms, but I hardly notice as Mina dashes from the kitchen toward me.

I hold up a hand and she skids to a stop. "Don't," I snap, getting back to my feet. "I'm fine." Christ, I missed a step at the idea she might want to peg me, I'm not in danger of passing out or breaking a hip.

She presses a hand to her chest and takes a deep breath. "You scared me." Not an accusation, not exactly, but—

Oh.

OH.

A piece of the puzzle that is Mina slides into place. "I scare you," I say softly.

This time, she doesn't deliberately misunderstand me. Her eyes are saucers and when her mouth fails to produce any words, she nods.

She has feelings for me that go beyond friendship, but she's holding back, too scared to open her heart to me.

She's scared of a lot of things, but I didn't think I'd be one of them. I've done everything I can every step of the way to prove to her she's safe with me and whether deliberate or not, she hasn't seen it.

How can I fix this? I'll need to think about it. Good thing I've got thirty minutes of me-time to noodle on this problem. Well...twenty-five after I jerk off because let's be honest. She's going to google pegging.

"You're not paying attention," I tell her, turning and walking up the stairs.

Chapter Sixteen

Mina

Timothy accused me of not paying attention and three days later I'm still irritated. The moment he walks into a room he yanks all attention to himself—he knows I'm not immune to that, so what the hell?

Even now, when all he's doing is sitting at the table, quietly eating his Cinnamon Toast Crunch, I'm paying more attention to him than I am to the coffee I'm making. When I spill a little on the counter, I blame it on his thighs sticking out from his shorts. They're thickly muscled and one is a canvas for a trio of watercolor stallions.

His other leg won't stop bouncing. I want to straddle him to make it stop.

So yeah, I'm paying attention.

I sit across from him and immediately wish I'd stayed in the kitchen.

He's wearing a sleeveless T-shirt today and the Kraken tattoo on his shoulder comes to life every time he reaches for his orange juice. Maybe my fixation with his arms has to do with his restorative hugs and how familiar I am with the feel of them wrapped around me. Or maybe I'm deluding myself like my life depends on it, because it does. Or my heart does, anyway.

Timothy glances up and catches me looking. He doesn't scowl or look upset, something that's happened a few times since he came home from the hospital. He looks contemplative.

He finishes his cereal and gets up to bring his bowl into the kitchen. It takes a monumental effort not to watch him. The way he moves through any space is fascinating. I don't typically do menswear, but for him, I'd take up suit-making.

"You know," he says, flicking the sink on to rinse his bowl, "I've had two serious, exclusive relationships as an adult."

Now I have an excuse to turn and look at him—surprise. "You have?" How did I not know? Wait—"You mean you dated someone for a few weeks?"

He doesn't turn to look at me, doesn't react to my words. Just puts his bowl in the dishwasher and tidies up the kitchen. "I was with Jake for two years until his touring schedule got to be too much—he's a drummer—and we amicably split. After that, I was with Elle for three years. We lived together, she'd met my parents. Then she moved out East to take over her aunt's sex toy company and neither of us wanted to do long distance. My twin sister works with her. We're still friends."

My jaw might be on the ground. Timothy has five years of solid relationships under his belt? "When was this?"

He turns and easily hops onto the counter. "I was twenty when I started seeing Jake. About six months after we broke up, I met Elle."

Timothy had serious relationships before we met. I must be still staring at him in open-mouthed shock because he laughs abruptly.

"You should know about Nic," he says, his nose wrinkling like he really doesn't want to tell this story. "He moved into the house across the street when we were fourteen. We were best friends from day one and because I was a dumb teenager, I had a huge crush on him." He laughs again, and this time it's a bit self-conscious. "This is the only thing in my life I'm embarrassed about. When we were fifteen, I needed to...I don't know...*know*. About him, about me. I told him I thought I was into guys as well as girls, and maybe we could kiss, so I'd know for sure. Nic wasn't into the idea, but we were friends, so he agreed."

Timothy pauses, his sense of timing perfect. I'm hanging on his every word, even though, knowing Nic as little as I do, I can guess where this is going.

"Worst kiss of my life." He's grinning, but I can feel the cringe in his voice. "His too. My crush on him popped like a balloon. He wasn't a dick about it, but I think he'd rather forget it ever happened."

"I won't tell anyone," I say, biting back a giggle. "I can't believe you asked him for a kiss."

Timothy shrugs. "I was a dumb kid with a huge crush and I've always been optimistic. I slipped him my tongue. He was not happy."

Oh my god. I can't hold in the laugh anymore. "Timothy."

"My point is, my friendship with him survived my feelings. It survived the distance after he married."

The way he's looking at me...shit. This isn't about his dating past, or his ability to maintain a friendship after complications. Or, rather, it is, but it's about us. He's knocking down my excuses.

I'm not afraid of our friendship dying. Timothy would never let it. It would change, though, and I like it the way it is. But maybe we're already too far down that road. I'm not sure I could be this close to him if he started dating someone seriously.

"I thought we'd go to the zoo today," I say, changing the subject like the coward I am. I've been trying to get him out of the house every day. He can't keep starving himself from people—he's an extrovert. He needs the energy of a crowd, even if he's not ready to step back into the spotlight.

Timothy looks at me for a long moment, like he knows I've caught on to him, but he's letting me off the hook this time. He hops down from the counter. "Sounds good. Might go for a quick swim first."

I'm already nodding when he pulls his shirt over his head and drops his shorts and underwear to the ground. He strides to the sliding glass door stark naked.

We're back to nudity? After doors closed in my face and his hand over my eyes?

I've seen Timothy naked dozens of times. The man does not need an excuse to streak at a party. He's not lewd about it and he knows I'm not bothered by nudity, but the sudden shock of seeing his dick lying thick and heavy between his legs reminds me of the sight of his fist wrapped around it, stroking.

My whole body goes hot, desire swooping low because it could be my hand wrapped around him. All I'd have to do is tell him I want him.

I clench my jaw and drop my gaze to my coffee. I'm not doing that. I have reasons, even if I can't remember them right now.

Timothy stops by the door. "Want to join me?"

"I'm good," I manage, my voice tight as I stand. No way am I getting into the pool with him, but I do have to keep an eye on him. Make sure he doesn't have a medical event and drown.

I'm just doing my job.

If I repeat it often enough, maybe I'll go back to believing it.

The zoo was a bad idea.

We've spent the afternoon wandering around, talking about animals, while inside, I'm twisting myself up, wondering how sex with Timothy would be. Is he a tiger in bed? A bear? A wolf? A honey badger?

I blame his dick. If I hadn't seen it again, I might be able to concentrate. Instead, my body is pointing out to my brain my heart is safe because he's had a couple of relationships, while my brain is screaming at my body to stop being horny and my heart is racing around in a panic.

I leave him by the monkey enclosure while I get us a couple of ice cream cones. It's about a million degrees out and my gutter brain isn't helping. Temporarily putting some physical distance between us isn't helping either because I can still see him, hands in the pockets of his shorts, watching the monkeys. The three buttons on his short-sleeved blue-gray shirt—none of them done up—give a peek at his golden chest.

He's so still. I've never seen him like this. He's always moving or fidgeting. I hurry back, ice cream cones in hand. He looks at me from behind his mirrored shades when I nudge him. "You okay?" I ask, handing him an already melting ice cream cone.

He licks around the base of the ice cream and I watch, fascinated, wanting to taste the vanilla on his tongue. I know he knows what I'm thinking—his dimple pops as he grins. Then he breaks the spell by chomping half the soft serve. Five seconds later, he winces and I laugh.

"Dumbass," I lick a drip of my chocolate ice cream before it can reach the cone.

The brain freeze passes, and he grins. "Nope. I have a plan. Eat all mine…" He takes another bite, smaller this time. "Then I can eat yours."

I hip-check him gently and we watch the long-armed swing of the gibbon moving about the ropes and poles as we eat our ice cream cones.

"How badly do you want in there?" I ask, realizing too late he's been watching me, not the monkey.

I can feel the heat in his eyes, behind his mirrored sunglasses. "So fucking bad," he murmurs, head dipping as he looks down my body.

"In *there*." I point at the animal enclosure while I go hot all over.

He shrugs and turns back to the exhibit. "I've planned seven different routes through it. One I could only do if I were a monkey."

The tone in his voice is a little sad, so I slip my free arm around his waist and give him a half hug. His arm comes around my shoulders and he squeezes me to his side. "I'm okay," he says in a quiet but firm voice as he lets me go.

Immediately I want back under his arm, despite the heat of the day and the heat of his body. I want to smell the faint sweat under his cologne and feel his lips, cold from the ice cream, against my temple. Against other places.

No. I'm not going there. "Want to check out the tropical reef exhibit?" The brand-new exhibit is inside, where the temperature will be cooler. Hopefully.

He holds out his hand, and I take it because friends can hold hands. Even if he keeps tracing his thumb over the back of mine. It feels natural. He feels like a boyfriend.

He's been a boyfriend. Two years, three years. The idea I don't know him as well as I thought keeps tugging at me. He keeps plants alive and his house isn't a giant shrine to adrenaline.

You aren't paying attention, he'd said. Could he be right? How much of this man have I set aside as Not For Me, refusing to see the rest of him?

"You never stop surprising me," I say as we amble along behind a stream of young parents pushing strollers.

Timothy tugs us out of the way so he can toss the paper from his now-gone cone in the trash. "How so?"

I hand him the rest of my cone. "You've been a boyfriend."

He nods, eats the last few bites of my cone, and tosses the garbage away. "I definitely mean to brag—I am the best boyfriend. Ever."

I roll my eyes, but he's an amazing friend. He'd be an amazing boyfriend.

We step back into the stream, and soon we're in the cool building housing the reef exhibit. I stop to watch a turtle glide alongside the floor-to-ceiling glass. Timothy drops my hand to stand close behind me, leaning to whisper in my ear. "At the hospital, you accused me of seeing hundreds of people."

Shit. I'd forgotten. How could I forget? This is so clearly my Get Out Of A Potential Heart-Destroying Relationship with Timothy Free card. I need to play it right now. Put a stop to this. Then I can quash this physical attraction that has my body bending toward him every time he's near. We can stay friends, my heart can stay safe.

"You said"—Timothy's hand slides up and down my arm and I shiver—"I couldn't love you and be with all those other people."

My excitement over playing this card goes up in flames because it still hurts.

"I tried to fuck you out of my system for a few months after we met. It didn't work, and I felt awful. It wasn't fair to my partners that I was never thinking about them. So I stopped. Every 'date' I've been on since the day I bought you that ring has been strictly platonic."

"Platonic?" I'm staring at the glass, but I'm watching his reflection. I can't see more than the shadow of it, the way the light bounces around.

"No romance, no sex." His breath ghosts my ear and a shiver zips down my spine, my skin breaking out in goose bumps.

"The woman from the bowling alley?"

He makes an unhappy noise. "A part of me gave up, seeing you with Dex, but I couldn't even kiss her."

The last of the hurt I've held on to from that night dissipates. "I didn't want Dex," I blurt.

His hand settles over mine and he laces our fingers. "You didn't?"

What am I doing? I can't stop the words, though. Can't let Timothy feel the way I felt that night for another minute. "I was never going to go for that drink. I wasn't interested in him, he isn't..." Isn't *what*? I don't know, so I leave it hanging.

"He's not me," Timothy says softly.

I turn my head and he smiles at me like he's joking, but his lips don't turn all the way up. He's not joking. He's right.

"No. He's not you." The whisper slips out of me before I can catch it.

"I want you, Mina," he says softly. "I want to kiss your sweet lips and take you home and worship every inch of your body with every inch of mine. I want to cook for you and rub your neck when you spend too many hours at your sewing machine. I want to give you everything you want and spoil you and fight with you and make up with you. Maybe you weren't paying attention, but maybe I've held back. I want you to know all of me, even the things I don't want to talk about." He lifts our linked hands, pressing a soft kiss on the inside of my wrist. "I'm not asking anything from you. I only want you to know. I'm yours."

I don't know what to do, so I turn my gaze back to the tank in front of me. It's too much, all at once. He hasn't been seeing anyone this whole time. He's been in serious relationships before. He loves me and he's retired and he's perfect. It's a different woman who raises her hand and weakly says, "Look, a shark."

Timothy's lips brush the edge of my ear and I can feel his smile. It seeps into my skin, warming me gently. "It's been a long time since I've had sex. I need to go stand somewhere else for a few minutes, or everyone will know I'm packing a Moray eel in these shorts."

I snort, but maybe some physical space will do me some good. I need to digest this and recalibrate. The cool air where his warmth was makes me shiver again and I miss having him close the moment he slips away.

All those gorgeous men and women who would've happily jumped into bed with him, and he went out on friendship dates? Who does that? It's so weird, but it sounds exactly like something Timothy would do. He lived alone. Nic was on Addison's short leash. I was always working. Timothy needs people and attention and fun, or he wilts.

All my cards are gone. All my excuses. If I want Timothy, all I have to do is tell him. My heart is still bashing around my chest. I don't like this out-of-control freefall.

I turn around and find him immediately in the crowd. He's over by the touch tank, pointing something out to a couple of seven or eight-year-olds standing near him. He looks up immediately and smiles, and I remember. My last card.

I can't have kids. Timothy wants them and he deserves to be a dad. He'll make a great dad.

Dammit, I didn't expect it to hurt this much.

I turn to the tank in front of me and watch the lazy progression of a silver fish floating through the water as I try to get my emotions under control. I am not crying at the zoo. And I don't regret my decision.

When I look back at Timothy, his entire arm is submerged in the touch tank and he's noisily pretending the stingrays are devouring him to the delight of the kids nearby. Even the moms are entertained—why wouldn't they be, when his tanned, muscled arm emerges dripping from the tank?

Warmth radiates through me and I smile because he's everything to me. His eyes lock on mine and he smiles back, and I know.

I love him. In every way it's possible to love another person, but most definitely as more than a friend.

It can't be—*we* can't be. I need to smother this, fast, before it consumes me.

I walk over to put an end to his fun before he gets banned from the zoo for causing emotional distress to a tank full of stingrays, but he pulls me close, sliding his wet hand over mine and pulling it down to the water. A stingray swims up, breaking the surface. Timothy guides my fingers to it, and it's like touching the baby of a mushroom and a sponge. Soft, in a way. Cool and wet.

The stingray swims on, water drips from our joined hands, and Timothy nuzzles against my neck. "You okay?"

"Perfect," I say, watching as he glides our hands through the water. It's calming. "I can't have kids."

When Timothy gives me a confused look, I sigh. "You want kids," I remind him. "No uterus, remember?"

Timothy cuddles me tight, his hand protective over my stomach. "Bisexual, remember? Not having the possibility of biological kids isn't a deal-breaker for me when it comes to relationships and I'm happy you aren't suffering every month."

My face heats. I am an absolute dumbass for thinking he'd expect more from me than he would a boyfriend. And without all my excuses, I recognize what he probably figured out a while ago.

I'm scared to love again.

He kisses my cheek gently. "If you want kids, we'll figure it out—adoption, surrogacy, whatever. If you don't, that's fine too. Anything else holding us back?"

"I don't know." The fact that I'm terrified isn't enough for him.

"When you're ready, you know where to find me." I can feel his smile against my neck. "I'm right here."

Chapter Seventeen

Mina

Jax is here to take Timothy out, but Timothy has disappeared into his room. He's still not willing to see Danny or any of his old crew, but he readily accepted an invitation from Nic's trainer. I don't know Jax, but Timothy assures me he's a joyless, quiet grump of a man with a fondness for torturing his famous clientele with grueling workouts.

Everything about the man screams strict discipline, so I think Timothy will be safe with him.

Hopefully, Timothy hasn't changed his mind. I'm half afraid if I turn Jax away, he'll make me get down and give him twenty-five push-ups.

I stop outside Timothy's bedroom, my mouth suddenly dry.

It's been a week and I'm treading water, waiting for some excuse to pop into my head. Any reason why a relationship with Timothy would be a bad idea. Nothing is coming to me. There is no reason we shouldn't be together, beyond the fact that I'm still scared.

Timothy's not hiding from me anymore. Nope, he's right there, where he said he'd be. He's not pressing me for more, but he's playing dirty. More naked swimming. Presenting me with cherry stems he tied with his tongue after our ice cream sundaes last night. Little touches and hungry looks that turn my stomach into butterflies.

I'm not sure how he escalates this situation next, and that's thrilling, which is disturbing because I don't like thrills.

I'm probably safe since Jax is here. I knock.

The door opens and Timothy grins at me. "Now you knock? You only barge in if you hear me jerking off?"

I go hot at the memory of Timothy stroking himself, and it takes all my self-control not to look down at his shorts. My eyes dip anyway, but I laugh. His shorts are a hideous plaid, but at least they match his icy blue polo shirt. He's dressed for mini-golf with Jax.

"I thought you were dying," I say with exasperation.

"Sure you did, champ." He beams at me. "When I hear that jackhammer vibrator of yours, should I knock down your door to make sure you aren't remodeling my bathroom?"

"You can't hear me." Not unless his ear is pressed against the door.

He winks. "I don't need to. I know when you're thinking about me."

I don't bother to deny it, though I'm tempted. "Jax is here," I say, turning to go back down.

Timothy bundles me into a hug, kisses my forehead, and promises he'll be home by eight.

And I'm alone.

Almost immediately, I begin conjuring up disasters. Someone who sucks at mini-golf will shank a ball and it will smack Timothy right in the forehead. He'll slip on a rogue banana peel and bash his head into a windmill. Out of the blue, his brain will start to bleed again and no one will notice.

Maybe I should've gone with them.

I sit at my sewing machine and shove these thoughts out of my head.

If anything happens to him...

Grabbing the nearest pile of unfinished underwear, I throw myself into work, letting the whir of my machine even out my heart rate.

I love him.

Finished underwear pile up and I keep working, forcing myself to con-centrate. One after another. There's a rhythm to it and repetitive nature that soothes me, but it's not working today. My thoughts are running wild.

Whatever I'm afraid of already has the power to hurt me, so why not put my heart in his hands? Timothy's the most trustworthy person I know.

And maybe I don't want to be alone anymore. We have the foundation of our friendship to build upon. We could be amazing together.

A little buzz of excitement builds in me, and with a blink, I realize I've stopped sewing, possibly a while ago, and am staring at my reflection in the sliding glass doors.

I haven't had sex in five years.

That jolts me and I stumble to my feet. I can't imagine sex with Timothy being bad—he's too considerate to be a selfish lover—but what if we're awkward together, elbows in the wrong places, teeth knocking together? If it doesn't feel right?

What if I'm a disappointment?

I punch that thought in the throat. I'm not a disappointment, whatever my stupid cheating ex said. He was trying to find excuses for his actions. The way Timothy looks at me—I don't think I could ever disappoint him in bed.

No, if it's awkward and weird, we'll do it until it's not.

I'm too keyed up to sew, so I put my stuff away and head downstairs to switch my laundry. Timothy's load in the dryer is done, so I fold it and stick it back in a basket.

Am I really doing this?

Yes. I am. Tonight, I'm seducing my best friend.

There's a soft, worn white button-up on the top of Timothy's basket and I throw it on over my tank top. I'm swimming in it, my little gym shorts barely visible, but I want him to come home to me in his shirt. When my laundry's tumbling away in the dryer, I take Timothy's basket upstairs and wander into the kitchen to find a snack.

High on a shelf, I find three pretty glass jars of what looks like homemade candy. I bet his mom made big batches of these candies for Christmas and gave them to everyone. Timothy hasn't touched them. Behind a jar filled with hard red candies, I spot a Tupperware filled with dinosaur gummies. That's what I want. Fruity, sugary goodness.

Timothy has always stayed away from edibles while working and he was always working. Nic would keep them downstairs if they were his.

They must just be gummies.

They taste fine, and when I feel fine an hour after eating a few, I eat the rest. And dance around the house a little because I have the energy to burn.

It takes another hour, but it hits me when I can't stop touching the turquoise throw pillow. The dinosaur gummies were definitely edibles.

I giggle, and still clutching the pillow, I reach for my phone.

> Hypothetically speaking, if I were to eat some gummy dinosaurs from your pantry, do I need to order a pizza or call a doctor?

ME

My phone rings.

"How many did you eat?" he asks. I can hear the concern under the calm in his voice and it freaks me out.

"This isn't my first rodeo, Timothy," I say, trying to sound unruffled. I micro-dosed during my periods, back when I had them. It helped a little, sometimes.

"They're Mom's. I'll give her a call and find out how strong they are."

Celia Foley, America's chef, making edibles. "I'm all right."

"I know. I'll call you back."

Time ticks by as I melt into the white leather sofa. I love this sofa. It's so smooth. The leather is cool under my hands and I don't even mind if the sofa absorbs me and I become sofa-people.

Timothy calls back. "They're low-ish dose. How many did you eat?"

"Eight-ish. Maybe ten. Like two hours ago? Anyway, I'm good. I'm in love with your sofa. It was definitely all of them, by the way, and the dinosaurs were adorable. Did your mom make them?"

There's a moment of silence. "I'm on my way, so...stay on the sofa."

"OOOH! Bring tacos. No...ribs. Oh! Onion rings. On second thought, I want guac and chips. I wish your mom was here, I bet she makes the best snacks. But maybe she'd be pissed I ate all her edibles. Can you bring some tacos?"

He laughs. "Sure, baby. See you soon."

He ends the call before I figure out how to make my thumb do it. I toss my phone onto the cushion next to me and lean back.

Huh. The picture on the wall is a TV but for a long minute, I think I'm hallucinating it. I hadn't noticed it before. There's a bigger screen downstairs but we haven't been watching movies because he gets headaches. And he's still sad about his retirement.

My phone chimes.

> Sorry about my unlabeled edibles! How are you feeling?

CELIA

> Good!!!!

ME

Is that too many exclamation marks? Too late, I've already sent it.

> Want me to call you? Timothy said you're alone.

CELIA

> I'm okay. I'm going to watch some TV.

ME

> Have fun. Call if you need me.

CELIA

I find the remote and flick it on. Apps fill the screen, and oh my god, is that Maude? They're an expensive porn streaming service, but the production company is run by women and they're progressive as hell. Top shelf stuff from the little clips I've seen floating around the internet.

I sit up on the couch, glancing around. Nic's not here, but I'm not sure when he's coming back. Timothy's on his way but stopping for food.

Screw it. I want to see what this is about since it's out of my price range. I click on the icon and it starts mid-doggy style. It hits me I am very likely picking this up where Timothy stopped it after he came. It sends an excited little flutter to my core.

This is good quality, though. The lighting, the acting. There's so much tenderness between the actors. The handsome man pulls out and they shift on the white leather sofa until she's sitting, legs spread wide apart, while he kneels to—

Wait a minute.

I glance down at the sofa. Glance back at the TV.

That's the sofa I'm sitting on.

I can see the railing of the stairwell behind it. The lamp is the same.

The edibles cannot be low dose. This is porn-ception.

It's weirding me out, so I go back and pick another porno at random. A couple is making out in a pool. I relax again because this is good and my body might be turning to rubber anyway. Or a polymer. Either way, my sofa isn't on TV, which means I'm not on TV.

The man lifts the woman onto the ledge of the pool to eat her out. A doorbell rings. I look over at my front door for a second. Did I order a pizza? I pause and go to the door. No pizza. Damn. I want pizza.

I start the porno up again and the couple turn their heads because the doorbell was in the porno and yeah, I almost fell for it a second time. The camera changes, looking into the house where a hot man is walking through the doors, and—

THAT'S MY SOFA!

Is this an out-of-body experience? Celia needs to label her fucking Tupper-ware.

I back it up a few frames and hit pause.

The dining table is the same. The art on the wall is the same.

This is so weird. It's like...this screen is playing out my fantasies in my head. Am I dreaming? I stare at my hand for a minute, then at the screen. No, that can't be right, because my fantasies are all Timothy and neither man on screen is Timothy. And my hand looks like my hand...but also not like my hand.

What if there were two Timothies?

I can't move while I think about it, but eventually, I decide the world could not handle two Timothies, I could not handle two Timothies and thank god there is only one.

I pick another porno. Then another. Every one of them is shot in this house. I barely look at my phone as I type out and send a quick text.

> YOU LIVE IN A PORNO SET? HOT BUT HOW?

ME

I die when I see who replies to my text.

> Wrong number sweetie, and yes, Timothy does live in a house where a dozen pornos were shot. Don't worry, it was professionally cleaned before he moved in.

CELIA

I hide my phone from myself under the couch, convinced Celia Foley knows every dirty thing I want to do to her son and would be mad because none of it involves cake.

Then I spend an unknown quantity of time playing a stoned Spot the Dif-ference. My eyes only zero in on the lamp. It's the same, but I double-check it at least twenty times. Just in case.

When Nic comes home, I'm boneless as a jellyfish, my feet up over the back of the couch, my head hanging over the edge, watching a couple have sex in the kitchen. Upside down.

I'm upside down. Not the couple. That would be impressive, though.

Nic edges into my line of sight. "Um…Mina?"

I lift my head to look at him, and it's more than a jellyfish can do. My head drops again. "Hey, Nic."

"Are you okay?"

"I'm a jellyfish. Yes. Did you know this house is a porno house?"

"Yeah…where's Timothy?" Nic takes a step not closer but into my field of vision, his fingers flying across his phone screen.

"Not in this porno," I answer. "Did you know jellyfish don't have bones? I wouldn't want to touch one. Timothy made me touch a stingray. It was hot. Not the stingray, that was cold."

"O-kay," Nic says like he's afraid I'll sting him with my jellyfish tentacles. He doesn't know I can't move them. I am washed up on this beach and I have to watch all these pornos before the tide brings me back out to sea.

Nic's phone chimes. "Timothy will be here in five minutes."

"Do you think it's a bad idea for me and Timothy to date?"

There's a brief pause and the silence between us is filled with a loud "fuck yeah, baby" from the porno.

"If you love him, you're serious about him, and you're willing to support him as he deals with his retirement, then no, it's not a bad idea. But I don't want to see my friend hurt, so if you're not certain, please don't."

"Okay." I wave my tentacle at him. It's my foot tentacle, and it takes a lot of effort to unstick it from the sandy shore.

"I think you might have been right last week," Nic says after a moment. "About Timothy hiding."

"He's out with Jax," I say slowly. Everything is slowing way down. My tongue too.

"He's not returning Danny's messages. Or Curtis. Or any of the other people he worked with."

I try to nod, but I'm a jellyfish. I don't have a neck. Do I? I touch my neck, poking and prodding.

Nic frowns at me, then shakes his head. Because he has a neck. "I've invited them over for a poker game tomorrow night."

I give up on my neck and rest my hands on my stomach. "Do they know this house is a porno house?"

Nic sighs, asks if I'm good alone, then disappears down the stairs.

I watch my porn, stuck to the couch.

It feels like I've been watching this for hours. I flick back to my favorite one, where a man who looks a tiny bit like Timothy is getting sucked off by a woman who has dark hair like me. Her boobs are bigger than mine and that's not fair...I cup mine and bounce them. Nah, I love not needing to wear a bra. My tits are the tits.

On TV, the Timothy character is fingering the Me character like a champ while her head bobs on his lap. In a few minutes, he'll be stretched out on the white leather couch I'm sitting on, licking her pussy with a competent enthusiasm that I hope earned him employee of the month.

I know Timothy will be just as good. Maybe better. He's so attentive and intuitive. He always wants the best for the people he loves. For everyone.

Horny feelings have come back, now that I'm thinking about Timothy. I want him to do all these things to me on this couch. And I want to do things to him.

I want him to come home. I must wish for it hard enough, because he bursts through the door on a taco-scented breeze, takes one look at me, one look at the cunnilingus on TV, and cracks up laughing.

"Nic told me to get my ass home," he says, dropping on the sofa next to me and reaching for the remote. "He sounded pretty freaked out."

"He's afraid of me. Don't turn it off," I roll toward Timothy and somehow end up sprawled across his lap.

"Like this one, do you?" He laughs, scooping me off him and depositing me next to him, his eyes twinkling. "Love you in my shirt, by the way." He leans forward to unpack our dinner.

I glance down. Huh. I am wearing his shirt. "I'm keeping it. I'm sorry I ruined your playdate with Jax."

"Oh, no, I'm not missing taco and porn night for anything. We should do this once a week." Timothy sits back with a wolfish grin.

The tacos smell good, but Timothy looks better.

"Why do you live in the porno house and why didn't you tell me? How much semen is on this sofa?" I run my hand along the smooth leather back of it until I bump into Timothy. I touch him next. His neck. His arm. I melt again when he opens the guac, loads some onto a chip, and stuffs it in my mouth.

"Everything was professionally cleaned, I never told you because I forgot, and I got the house cheap because one of the producers had to liquidate some assets before her divorce. We had a mutual friend who knew I was looking for a place."

"Have you been in a porno?"

"Almost, when Nic and I first came to LA. He talked me out of it because the contract was shit. Plus, I'd rather jump onto moving trains."

I'm not even a little surprised. We eat tacos and critique orgasms and honestly, this is the best. Timothy is the best, and I can't stop looking at him. He's so golden, despite the fading dark hair dye. He's already my whole world and all I have to do is reach out and he's mine.

He smiles at me, amused and curious. There's warmth and love in his eyes and when he looks back at the TV, the world feels colder. I want his eyes on me. His everything on me.

The edge of his tattoo peeking out from his shirt sleeve catches my attention. I push his sleeve up and get close enough that my nose bumps his bicep. I've looked at this tattoo so many damn times. It's a Kraken on a background of stylized waves, tentacles curling around his arm.

Timothy's a Kraken, I'm a jellyfish. There's some meaning to be found in this somewhere, but I'm not high enough anymore to be distracted by it. Not when I want to feel every inch of his amazing body up against mine.

"We should have sex," I blurt out.

Timothy chokes on a chip.

I straddle him once the coughing subsides, my hands skirting the collar of his shirt, toying with the cotton.

"Mina."

It's a warning, the way he's saying my name, so I kiss him to stop it. His lips taste salty from the chips. He takes one kiss before turning his head away. "Not tonight. You're stoned."

"I'm not." I curl into him and kiss his neck. His groan makes my lips buzz.

"You were making some insane claims about Krakens and jellyfish a minute ago," he says. He's not touching me, so I grab his hands and place them on my waist. They stay when I let go, but his touch is light.

"Is he eating her pussy on TV right now?" I whisper into his ear.

He audibly swallows. "Yup."

"I want you to do that to me. Right here on the couch. Just like that."

There's a moment of silence where I can feel him weigh what he's about to say.

"Not just like that," Timothy concedes, his voice growly. "I'd do it for a hell of a lot longer than eight minutes. I'd eat you until you begged me to stop."

I clench, aching. "Yes, let's do it." I tip off his lap, sprawling on the sofa.

"Not tonight," Timothy says with a tight laugh, grabbing my shorts with one hand and holding them in place when I start to tug them over my hips. The tips of his fingers brush the top of my curls and I know it's an accident, but I shiver anyway.

"I'm not that stoned," I protest, shimmying a bit to see if his hand will move closer to where I need it. It doesn't. "Make me feel amazing, Timothy."

His eyes are so dark right now. "When you're sober, I'll make you feel on top of the world."

Chapter Eighteen

Timothy

I WAKE WITH A smile on my face and an erection that could poke out a giant's eye. Mina is half on top of me, half sandwiched between me and the back of the couch. Her head fits perfectly in the crook of my shoulder like I knew it would. Nic must have put a light blanket over us when he left. Late morning light fills my silent house, closer to lunch than breakfast.

I'm not 100 percent sure, because she was stoned off her ass last night, but I think Mina might be ready for us. She doesn't like casual sex, so her suggesting we fuck has to mean she wants a relationship. I hope.

Or she was stoned, nothing's changed, and I'm going to live out the rest of my miserable life in the friend zone.

As bad as I feel about Mina getting into my mother's edibles, stoned Mina was undeniably cute. The way she went from intensely focused on my tattoo to throwing herself onto the couch, asking me to eat—

My dick pulses, and considering her inner thigh is directly on top of the not-at-all little guy, I need to think about something else or I'll cream my shorts from the friction when she eventually slides her leg off me.

I'm not sure I'd be able to maintain my reputation anyway. Being inside Mina the first time would likely end me early. Two, maybe three thrusts in her tight—

Don't go there.

Even if nothing more happens between us, last night was fun in the most unexpected ways, and I am going to cherish that. We watched Sponge Bob. Mina grumbled a bit, but I figured with her jellyfish fascination, she'd get over not watching more porn. I was right, as usual. She settled down next to me, giggling these little infectious giggles, and forgot all about trying to seduce me. Not sure when we fell asleep, but I'm glad to wake up with her.

I hold her and breathe in her intoxicating scent—jasmine, sandalwood, and honey. I want her in my lungs, on my skin. There's no guarantee I'll get another morning like this, so I'm going to savor every minute of it.

Mina yawns and stretches, but nestles back into me with a cute little noise. She doesn't go back to sleep. Instead, her fingers trace lazy patterns over my shirt, her touch light. She might know I'm awake, but if I don't say anything, maybe we can stay like this a little longer.

Her touch creeps downward slowly until she reaches my navel, circling it through my shirt. My still-hard dick throbs under her leg and maybe she feels that because her breath catches, her fingers pausing. I hold my breath until she starts moving again.

A heavy awareness settles between us now, in the knowledge we're both awake, and this is intentional. Her fingertips trace my flesh right above the band of my boxer briefs, to my hip and back, her touch so light I break out in goose bumps. I'm hard enough to cut glass now. Maybe metal.

"I'm sorry about last night," she says softly.

I mumble something, but Mina's slowly dragging her leg off my dick and the ache she leaves in her wake is all-consuming. "How are you feeling?" I manage to ask when I can function again.

"Sober." There's a mischievous, teasing tone in her voice. I suck in a breath at the ticklish drag of her fingertips over my skin as they dip below my waistband. Every muscle in my body tightens in anticipation the lower she goes.

"Do you remember last night?" I ask.

She stops. Her fingers are so close, it takes all my self-control not to shift so I can nudge her hand with my dick.

Touch me.

Mina doesn't hear my silent prayer. She slips her hand out of my shorts, but then she climbs on top of me and maybe she heard my prayer after all. Her knees bracket my hips, her hands are on either side of my neck, she lowers herself until her breasts press against my chest, and all I can think is *yes, yes, yes*.

She smiles at me, a slight blush coloring her cheeks. "I remember asking you to go down on me. You said no."

"Technically, I said *not tonight*, because you were stoned and I care about consent."

"And I appreciate that." Her brown eyes are dark and full of heat as she looks at me. "It's morning now. I'm sober."

It's happening. Oh. My. God. It's happening. Mina and me. Holy shit. I am not prepared. What do I do?

Confirm I'm not imagining this. Plus, after five years of pining for this woman, I need certainty too. "Are you all in?"

She bites her lip, but a smile escapes as she nods. "I'm jumping and you'd better catch me because I'm terrified."

"I'll always catch you." I tuck a strand of hair behind her ear. "And you'll be careful with me? Turns out I'm not indestructible."

"Must be hard, living like the rest of us mere mortals." She looks at me for a long moment and what I see in her eyes as they sweep over my face realigns my entire world. Warmth and a deep understanding, like I'm inside her as much as she's inside me.

Mina leans down and finally, *finally*, kisses me.

Her lips are gentle and warm and she kisses me like I'm something cherished, something precious. It's soft. Careful. The pent-up longing makes each press of our lips even sweeter and we kiss like we have all the time in the world to learn each other.

Her lips part, mine follow, and the hunger builds slowly. A nip here, a suck on a lower lip there, still slow but deeper. Needier.

I could kiss her forever and I don't want to stop, but there are so many places I have yet to taste. I yank the blanket off and Mina cries out in alarm when I tumble her, rolling us. The couch is big, but it's not the easiest place to maneuver. Still, I manage to get her underneath me, to press her into the cushions where I can slow everything back down with thorough kisses from her jaw to her neck. She moans and wraps her arms and legs around me, and this is where I belong. Well, as close as I can get with our clothes on. Speaking of, I get to work on the buttons of the shirt she's wearing. My shirt. Hers now.

"I love you," I whisper against her soft skin. The words tumble from my lips, no longer something I can contain. Maybe it's too much, too fast. I hold my breath as I wait for her to respond, to push me away because she's scared.

"I love you, too," she says, a tremble in her voice.

Her words give me a rush, zipping through my blood like adrenaline and lighting me on fire. I catch her lips and kiss her breathless. She loves me, and it feels like flying.

I kiss my way to her collarbone, tugging her open shirt out of the way. She's not wearing a bra—she doesn't wear them much around the house, which has been torture—so I slip my hand under her tank top, sliding up her flat stomach and over the smooth, small mound of her breast. Her nipple hardens against my palm.

I have to remind myself to take my time. It's taken us five years to get here—it's not going to be over in five minutes.

Mina gently but firmly pushes me off her, and I don't have time to be crushed because she whips her shirt off, her tank top, too, and tosses both aside. They land somewhere. I don't know or care because that little glimpse I got at the bowling alley was nothing compared to the glory of Mina topless.

"Fuck," I murmur, cupping her, slipping my thumbs over her dusky pink nipples, back and forth as they tighten. She reaches for me and I come to her, meeting her lips before kissing down to her breasts. The sound she makes when I suck one of those tight buds into my mouth is otherworldly.

"I need you," she whimpers, and who am I to argue? I need her too.

"You can have me," I say, grabbing the waistband of her shorts and the panties underneath, sliding them over her hips, down her legs, and tossing them clear across the room.

The curls between her legs are dark and neatly trimmed. I push her legs wider, opening her to me. She's so pretty, the same shade of dusky pink, glistening with arousal. "But I made some promises last night I want to keep first."

Her laugh is breathy and we shift until her head is resting on the arm of the couch, a pillow behind her, knees up, and legs open. I lie on my stomach, propped on my elbows.

"Any last words before I destroy you?" I don't know how I manage to tear my eyes off her pussy, right in front of my face, but I'm glad I do because Mina tipping her head back and laughing in the golden sunlight flooding my house is something I want to capture forever. She brushes her fingers over my cheek and I turn to kiss her palm. "I've got you. Always."

Mina nods and finally—*finally*—I bend my head, nuzzling that soft patch of hair before I spread her with my thumbs and give her a light, teasing lick.

"Oh," she whispers on an exhale.

I groan and sink into her because holy shit. She tastes divine, better than I imagined, and I've spent *a lot* of time thinking about this. It's an effort to go slow when I want to make her come so damn bad, but promises are promises.

"Yes, that," she tells me when I do something she likes. Her moans, the way she tilts her hips to give me better access—I want to learn every single little thing that will drive her crazy.

She's so wet my finger slips easily inside her tight pussy and the feel of her clenching around my finger has me humping the couch with how badly my dick needs attention.

Slow down. My brain is screaming at me to make this last, to ruin Mina for anyone else, but my body isn't listening.

Her legs press open wider, her hips rocking, and when I look up, Mina has her hands over her head, gripping the arm of the couch, eyes closed. She's so sexy, with those perky tits and all her smooth, creamy skin flushed pink. God, the taste of her, the feel of her on my tongue...I need to be inside her so bad I could cry.

I need to slow the fuck down—I don't think it's been a full minute yet and Mina's getting close. I'll stop touching her while I bring out the dirty talk. That ought to ease her down so I can build her back up. But when her eyes open and look at me with such warmth and adoration, the words die on my tongue, buried under the weight of my feelings.

"Timothy," she whispers, and it's in her voice. She feels it too.

I kiss her inner thigh, letting her cool off before I bring her back to the brink with slow licks, soft sucks, and the gentle but steady thrust of my fingers.

"I'm close," she says with a moan, "please, Timothy."

I could go longer, but my dick is also begging for release, so I crook my fingers inside her and flick my tongue fast over her sweet little clit. Mina comes with a gasp, clenching my fingers, flooding my mouth with the sweetness of her release. It's my name on her lips that I love most, though. The way she says it, full of wonder and ecstasy and love.

I keep going, drawing it out as long as I can, until Mina's breathless *stop*.

She's glowing and smiling, unbelievably beautiful as I kiss a line up her stomach, between her breasts, up the smooth column of her throat, and murmur, "How was that?"

"Timothy, you—"

She doesn't finish. Just pulls me onto her and kisses me.

Chapter Nineteen

Mina

I'm still shaking when I gently push Timothy back. My entire body feels electrified, every single nerve alive and buzzing, but it's the warm, expansive feeling in my chest that has me tingling.

"Sit." My voice is thick and hard to find, but Timothy immediately sits on his butt, swinging his feet to the floor. "Off." I tug on his shirt and he obeys, pulling it over his head before he turns a wide smile to me.

I think my smile is just as big.

"And these." I pluck at his hideous shorts and he obeys, taking his boxer briefs with them.

He leans back against the sofa, clasping his hands behind his head, his dick jutting up and swaying when he shifts to get comfortable. He's beautiful, each muscle perfectly cut, his skin golden. I run my fingers through the dusting of light brown hair on his chest. He's still smiling, but that smile shifts into something wicked and his eyes go half-lidded when I toy with the small barbell piercing his right nipple. When I bend to lick and suck, using my tongue and teeth to tug and soothe, he moans.

He's strung so tight he's practically vibrating by the time I run my hands over his abs. It's hard to ignore his dick and the bead of precum gathered at the tip, but I want to torture him. When I trace my fingers over his Adonis belt, he loses it, shaking with laughter and grabbing my hands, but not before I manage to tickle him a little more.

"Gentle," he says with a grin, guiding my hands down. He lets go when I wrap my hand around his shaft. One slow, light stroke, and suddenly he's serious again.

"Come here," he says with a stuttering breath, pulling me onto his lap.

After I caught my asshole ex cheating, Timothy went with me to get tested. He got tested too—something he did regularly. We both celebrated our clear results with some drinks, and I can't get pregnant. We probably don't need protection, but I don't know what he's comfortable with. "Do you want me to grab a condom?" I ask.

Timothy's thumbs stroke my waist as he looks at me. "I've never had sex without one, but it's your choice. I'm willing and I'm still clear."

"I want you. Nothing between us."

"Nothing between us," he echoes with a nod, pulling me close for a kiss. I can still taste myself on his lips and I kiss him back while I reach between us.

He whispers my name when I slide the fat head of his dick through my slickness. His hands tighten on my hips. "I need you," he says against my lips.

I need him, too, so I notch him into place and slowly, slowly lower myself.

"Fuck," Timothy gasps, his hips lifting, pushing deeper.

The stretch is incredible. Five years is a long time, and he has girth as well as length. Every inch I take leaves me unbelievably full.

His hands rise to my breasts and he twists and tugs at my nipples, bending forward to suck one into his mouth while I work him deeper. When he's fully seated in me, I pause just to feel him.

Timothy leans back on the sofa to take me in from my head to where we're joined. "You're a goddess," he says, reverentially, his eyes tracking back up, his hands returning to my tits, thumbs brushing over my nipples until they ache.

I run my fingers through his hair and rest my hands on his shoulders, leaning forward to kiss him. "You'll tell me if your head starts to hurt?"

He grins. "Only if you promise not to stop bouncing on my dick."

I don't know if I should laugh or strangle him. "Timothy."

He crushes me against him, capturing my mouth and kissing me deeply. "I'll tell you, but I'd rather you were thinking about how good I feel inside you than worrying about my head."

"You feel so good," I tell him with a roll of my hips. We both moan.

"Gentle," he reminds me as I start moving. "Nice and slow, or I won't last."

I want his nice and slow, his fast and hard. But I won't last long either. Not with him filling me and touching me like he is.

We find a rhythm, achingly slow and deep. The entire time I ride him, the pad of his thumb circles my clit and his other arm holds me close and we kiss, lips and tongues and teeth matching the gentle but intense way we're fucking.

I've had good sex before, but this is something else. Because this is Timothy, because he's my best friend. Because I love him. I'm getting close. I break off the kiss and bury my face in his neck. His skin has a sheen of sweat and he's salty on my tongue when I kiss him.

The circles his thumb traces grow erratic—he's closer than I am.

I lean back, bracing one hand behind me on his thigh, and replace his thumb with my fingers. He grabs my hips, his eyes hot and greedy as he watches me move on top of him.

This new angle does something, his dick hitting exactly where I need it. I come apart, gasping his name. Timothy's right there with me, jerking up and pulling my hips down and crying out a *fuuuuuuuck* that makes me laugh, even as my orgasm still flows over me.

By the time our bodies stop moving, we're both laughing and smiling, looking at each other a little shyly. I don't know when I've ever felt happier.

"I love you so much," Timothy says, grabbing my face and kissing me long and hard. I all but collapse into his kiss. I'm worn out—maybe more emotionally than physically, but my body feels limp and sated and my head feels light.

"I love you, too," I say softly when he finally lets the kiss end.

"As soon as the doctors say I can, I'm going to fuck the hell out of you," he all but growls. "If you want. Of course."

"I want. I want to fuck you too. If you're open to it."

His eyes go wide and hungry. "Yes." He pulls me into another kiss, mumbling against my lips. "You'd be hot as hell with a strap-on."

I think he's getting hard again inside me, but I don't get to find out.

The front door swings open.

"I got the house!" Nic shouts as he walks in.

Timothy moves fast—I'm underneath him before I can register what happened, his big body covering mine.

"What the fuck Nic, knock!" He doesn't look angry, just annoyed as he reaches for the blanket and pulls it over us.

The door closes and Nic's footsteps move toward the stairs. "Sorry. I didn't know you two were...I'll be downstairs." His steps fade and disappear.

Timothy sighs and smiles down at me, a rueful look on his face. "I'm sorry."

Nic wouldn't have seen anything except my startled face, and he lives here. We should've gone to Timothy's room. "Do you want to go talk to him?"

He grins. "No. Pretty sure I don't need to explain to him that sometimes adults like to cuddle naked."

I laugh. "I meant about his divorce."

"Later," he says, pulling out of me before pulling me to my feet and wrapping the blanket around me. "Right now, I want you in my shower."

Can't argue with that.

Chapter Twenty

Timothy

"You got the house?" I ask, thundering down the stairs an hour or two later.

Nic's standing at the wet bar, drinking a glass of water and looking mildly annoyed. "You and Mina, huh?"

"Yup." I don't give a shit what he thinks—he's jaded by his divorce and we both know it. Still would be nice if he could be happy for me. I'm happy for me. I'm so fucking happy.

"Be careful," he says after a moment. "I'm not sure she's all in like you are."

I wave him off. "She's all in."

"Last night she wasn't. She asked if I thought you two would be a good idea."

Huh. Mina doesn't ask for second opinions on stuff like this. If she's unsure, she keeps it to herself until she is sure. Remarkably perceptive of Nic, but he's missing the bigger picture. "Last night, she thought she was a jellyfish. She was stoned. Doesn't count."

Nic yanks the tap on, refilling his glass and slamming it off. "I don't want you to end up where I am. Just...be careful."

"I'm always careful. What?" I demand when he gives me a doubtful look. "You know I'm careful." Except for the twenty seconds leading up to my career-ending injury, but we're not going to talk about that.

"Fine," he concedes in a tone that feels a lot like he's humoring me. "Contrary to all appearances, you are surprisingly careful."

Damn straight, I am. The outside world doesn't see the work that goes into building the muscle memory I fall back on. They don't see me assess a situation. They don't have the understanding I do of my abilities. To them, I look impulsive. Reckless.

Non-stunt example: Timothy bought a porno house, sight unseen, from someone he barely knew, a day after being told it was going on the market.

I'd seen this house in many pornos and a few hours of hyper-focused research told me the price was good, the place wasn't a lemon, and I had the money.

I'm careful. I'm sure about this. Mina is my person. And nothing about waiting half a decade for her is impulsive. I get why Nic's worried, especially coming off his divorce, but Mina and I have years of close friendship to fall back on—loving her is a muscle memory. We know the dark corners of each other's souls. We've carried each other through difficult times.

Except she went it alone with her hysterectomy.

Maybe I don't know all her dark corners, but I want to. I think she'll let me.

I shrug off all of Nic's concerns. "Mina has my whole heart. If she wants to rip it out, throw it on the ground, and jump on it for a while, it's hers."

He looks unimpressed. "Maybe...take things slow."

"We are taking things slow." Mostly because Mina will take things at her pace.

He snorts. "She's taking things slow. You've probably bought a ring."

He has me there. Asking her to marry me was a bit premature, but I regret nothing.

Nic's face drops. "You bought a ring? Christ, how do you not scare people off in the first five minutes of a relationship?"

I want to point out I never bought a ring for Jake or Elle or anyone else, but something in his words irritates me, so I go with a joke. "I have a great ass. Sparkling personality. I give great hugs and amazing oral." Not a joke, since all of it's true.

He shakes his head and I laugh, but he's right. I am a lot to deal with. I've been dumped a lot, often after a few weeks. Right around the time people decide I'm more annoying than fun.

My whole life I've heard *settle down, can you stop,* and *sit still* and *oh my god shut up*—the last one mostly from my twin. I'm the reason my mom couldn't have nice things.

Maybe I'm careful, but I'm still a lot.

Mina knows me. She knows what she's getting and I will do everything I can to make being with me worth her while.

"So you got the ugly-ass house," I say, changing the subject. "How'd that happen? I thought Addison would get it."

He pulls out his phone and a moment later slides it across the bar to me.

TMZ has a huge photo of Addison—dated a year ago—and while it's blurry, it's obvious she's naked and the man she's riding is not Nic. The exclusive is a tell-all from an inside source about up-and-coming Addison Kincaid cheating for years, and when the marriage started to go south, how she fed rumors to the tabloids to make it look like Nic was the unfaithful one.

I whistle. "This whole time? That's shitty."

Nic drops his elbows to the counter, his hands in his hair. "Yeah." He takes a shuddering breath and lets it out slow and controlled. "I should've known, right? How did I not notice my wife was sleeping around?"

"Insane schedules," I say softly. "She was pretty good at hiding it too. What she did—it wasn't your fault."

He huffs out a sad little laugh and says nothing. I'm not going to get more out of him, not without alcohol, and I'm not going to encourage Nic to start day drinking.

"When did all this come out?" I ask. I don't read tabloids or clickbait. It's a bit of a sore spot, considering they nearly ripped my family apart when I was a kid.

"A couple of days ago. The timing is too perfect, with our court date..."

"Maybe Addison has an enemy." I wouldn't be surprised if my mom's behind this. Addison came for her favorite. "So, does this mean you're moving out?"

"Do you want me to?"

"I don't know." On one hand, I want to be free to explore this new thing with Mina without Nic in the way. But I'm supposed to be keeping an eye on him and that's easier if he's living here. "Stay."

Nic side-eyes me. "Mina okay with that?"

"I can ask her, but this is still my house." Mina will be fine with it. I'm sure. Mostly sure. Nic's still filming, anyway. It's not like he's around all that often. "But if you're going to be a dick to her because you hate happiness, you can leave."

"I'm not going to be a dick. I'm happy for you."

He's not happy, he's worried I'll get hurt. I'll be too much for Mina. He has a point—I can be a lot—but Mina can take me. I'm pretty sure.

Doubts creep in like they always do, and maybe I need to cover my bases. Give her a million reasons to stay.

Mina takes the next twenty-four hours and obliterates those doubts. She wasn't exaggerating when she said she was jumping—she's all in, holding nothing back, showing me in every kiss, touch, and look how much she loves me. She might be scared, but she's trusting me to catch her. I love her even more for it. Plus, it's hot as hell.

We spend most of the day in my bed, exploring each other and all the gentle ways we can come together. Mostly, we cuddle. Mina's still worried about my head, but it's been nearly a month since the accident. The headaches are gone and I'm itching for some semblance of normal. Especially when the man I see in the mirror looks fine. Apart from the patches of hair they shaved off, anyway.

Mina forces me to slow down and the unhurried, deep sex we're having is brain-meltingly good. I'm already imagining how good it will be when I'm "allowed" more strenuous activity. It's annoying I need a doctor's note to fuck her against a wall.

Mina and I are cleaning up dinner when the front door swings open and Nic walks in, turning to say something over his shoulder to...

Danny. Curtis. The entire damn stunt crew pours into my house behind him, everyone talking at once.

"Hey, Timbo!" Danny roars, holding a six-pack of beer and a bag packed to the brim with snacks up in the air as people jostle to slip shoes off at the door.

Dex is the last one in.

Our eyes meet and he looks down at his feet, but not before sneaking a glance at Mina that turns my stomach.

"Ready to lose some money?" Danny asks, drawing my attention away, a wide grin splitting his face.

"Poker night," Nic says, and the way his gray eyes are watching me is unsettling. Like he's judging my response.

I can count on one hand the number of times Nic invited people over to my house, or his.

This is an intervention.

Mouths are moving and eyes are crinkling in smiles directed at me and I assume people are saying something—it's been a while, they were worried, I'm looking good, that sort of tripe. I can't hear any of it. Just the flatline alarm of my previous life.

Mina touches my arm, and I realize I've frozen.

Nope. I'm out.

I can't get upstairs without getting close to the crowd and I don't want their hugs and their back slaps or the pity underneath it all, so I walk into the living room, step onto the couch, then the back of the couch. Grabbing the railing of the stairwell, I swing myself over onto the first landing, ignoring Mina's alarmed shout.

"I need to call someone." I meet Nic's eyes. He has the nerve to look disappointed. "Jessie," I add, because it's the only way to get back at him. His jaw tics, so I'm claiming victory. "I need to call my sister. You guys have fun. Catch you later." I take the remaining stairs two at a time.

"Timothy—"

Mina's voice halts me but after a second I keep going. She knew about this, didn't she? Did I disappoint her too? When I'm safely in my room, I close the door, stuff my shaking hands in my pockets, and hide in the closet.

Too late, should've picked the bathroom.

My snowboard is still sitting in the corner. I can smell the snow, feel the bracing cold on my face, the thrill of going weightless when I fly through the air.

It's not fair and the fact that physically, I could still do any of this stuff and be fine kills me.

The door to my room opens and closes, the footfalls to the closet soft.

"I told you no company," I say to Mina. I'm sitting, my back against some built-in drawers. I don't remember sliding to the floor.

Mina comes closer until her toes touch mine. "You need to stop hiding," she says in a firm voice that immediately turns me into a petulant four-year-old.

"I'm not hiding."

"You are."

"Fine. I am." I say, my fingers twisting the hem of my shorts. Untwisting. Twisting again. "I'm not ready to have my former colleagues rubbed in my face."

"They're your friends," she says, sitting next to me and resting her head on my shoulder.

They were. They were all my friends and I'm no longer one of them. Tears burn behind my eyes.

"Tell me," she says in a soft voice.

I rest my head against the top of hers and the softness of her hair is comforting. She won't understand—she's never understood my job or why I loved it—but she's still my best friend and right now I need that. I need her. "I don't belong down there."

She takes one of my hands and clasps it between both of hers. "They're your friends and they love you."

"They love who I was before."

"Timothy, you haven't changed. Only your career."

"I am my career!"

I tip my head back against the drawers, eyes closed, as I try to get myself under control. It's not her fault, and I didn't mean to shout at her. "I'm sorry," I whisper.

Mina doesn't speak. She rubs my hand between hers, and I find myself watching her do it. Her thumbs press into my flesh, but I barely feel it. The disconnect, coupled with the silence, undoes me. Words rush in to fill the space.

"They know the Timothy Foley who will do anything on a dare," I say in a breathless rush. "The one who makes them laugh and shows them a good time. The reckless, indestructible, adventurous guy. That's not who I am anymore. It's like I'm in a Timothy suit and it's the wrong size. This isn't me. I'm...*fuck*." My voice cracks. "I'm nothing. I don't know who I am."

"I know you." Her voice is a whisper and I close my eyes because as great as the past two days have been, I'm still not sure she does. Or ever will.

"You were right when you told me I wasn't paying attention," she says after a moment. "I didn't look far beneath the surface because it was easier to accept our friendship as it was, but I know you." She shifts to face me. "You've always been yourself with me, and I've been lucky enough to see a side of you the rest of the world hasn't. I've seen you at rest. When you take off the protective gear and just sit. You haven't had to be this other Timothy Foley for me to love you."

One of her hands lifts from mine to rest lightly over my heart.

I let it sink in. I don't know. Maybe she's right. She's always been this calm place for me. Even now, I can feel myself settle, that twitchy, skin-too-tight feeling easing.

"I love you," she continues when I meet her eyes again, "not because you make me laugh or because I have wild stories to tell about the shit you get up to when we're together. I love you because you opened yourself up to me and let me come in. You made me feel safe when my world turned upside down and every day after. Your friends are the same because you do the same for them. You've never had to be some wild, adrenaline-seeking person. For any of us."

This is the part she'll never get. "I do for me."

She's unfazed. "You'll find other outlets. You don't have to figure this out today or tomorrow. You loved your job. It's okay to grieve it, but don't let that grief consume you. I won't let it. You're too important to me."

I pull her into a tight hug, then pull her onto my lap and for a long time we hold each other until my eyes cool and dry and my heart slows to match hers. "I don't want their pity."

Mina shrugs. "Fine. Don't accept any pity. But don't let friendships you value die because it's hard."

That hits me. I don't want to lose them, but it's going to hurt to keep them. To hear the stories about their days at work. To know I won't be a part of them. That's the hardest part, and I'm going to have to learn to deal with it because I value these guys more than what they are.

"You're sexy when you kick my ass with logic," I say, nuzzling in for a kiss.

Mina kisses me back before pulling away. "I'm sorry we didn't tell you. I sort of forgot." Her cheeks go a little pink. I can guess why she forgot, so I forgive her.

I kiss her, more deeply this time, and when I stop, we're both smiling. "We could stay in here, play with some of my toys—"

Mina laughs and climbs off me. "Go play poker with your friends. You're a starving extrovert. It'll feel good."

I am an extrovert. She might be right. "Come play with us."

She shakes her head and holds out her hands. I let her pull me to my feet.

"Okay," I say, "if you don't want to hustle these guys out of their paychecks, let me find something to occupy you while I take all their money."

Mina's nose wrinkles. "Cute that you think I'm bored when you're not around."

I laugh, but walk to the other side of my walk-in and grab a box off a shelf, handing it to her. "For when you miss me."

"It's a poker game, not summer camp," she says, looking at the box. She holds it up. "Why do you have so many sex toys? Do you give them out at Halloween?"

I can hear the real question under her quip—does my ex with the sex toy company send me products? Or a.k.a. is that door really closed?

"My sister sends them. I got her the job with my ex and if great-aunt Glenda gets toys, I do too."

Something catches her eye, and she fumbles the box. "This one is four hundred dollars!"

"It's a limited edition, and that particular model is the Ferrari of clitoral stimulators." I motion to the boxes on the shelf. "Anything in a sealed box is brand new and all yours. Anything in this drawer is mine. If you're curious. You can snoop."

Her cheeks go pink.

I let out a low whistle. "Mina Andrei. You've already snooped. While I was in the hospital."

She doesn't confirm or deny, but the pink deepens on her face. "The orgasms from these things are supposed to suck your soul out of your body," she says, redirecting the conversation. I don't care that she snooped—I only want to know if she liked what she discovered.

I pull her into my arms. "No baby, only I can do that." I kiss down her jaw to her neck. "Want me to give you a hand with this Ferrari of a sex toy? I'm a professional driver, and this is a closed course."

She moans a little and her body melts into mine. For a moment, I think I'm going to get away with it. But Mina's control is too damn good. She breaks away from me. "Go play with your friends, and if you don't disgrace yourself, after, you can play with me."

I scoff because I'm not going to disgrace myself. I'm pretty good at poker. "I'll take enough of Nic's money alone tonight to buy you another Mioe dress, so think about what you want."

This isn't true, we keep it low stakes and the most I've ever won in a night is one hundred dollars, but I can't help it. Mina smiles at me because she knows I'm full of shit and I kiss her until she makes me stop.

I'd still rather spend the evening with her, but at least I know she'll be in my room, giving herself knockout orgasms with that toy. Grabbing my wallet, I head down to the basement.

The room goes silent when I walk in. I can feel Nic's eyes burning into me and I have to pretend Dex doesn't exist, but I survive.

"Can I join you?" I ask.

"How's your sister?" Danny asks, and I can't tell from his voice if he knows that was an excuse or if he thinks I was talking to her, but I do catch the dirty look Nic gives him.

I grin. "She's good. Still in Italy, sampling the locals."

Nic's eyes turn to me and he is unamused. I grin back. "Take a seat," he says, the tone in his voice telling me he doesn't want to hear about Jessie.

I grab a chair and push in between Nic and Curtis so I can talk all night about my sister. Not that I need to play dirty—Nic can't act, which means he has more tells than anyone, as long as he doesn't settle into his resting dick face. Those tells are more subtle. Not for me, but for everyone else at the table.

It hurts when they talk about work and I'm reminded of everything I'm missing, but there's more to the conversation than the job. Danny's stories about his five-year-old daughter Freya get laughs, and Curtis talks at great length about his teenage brother's antics.

Dex is still mostly quiet, but Mina loves me and he was nothing more than a brief bit of fun for her, so I can deal with it. I'm not ready to apologize for my part in the accident—the loss of my job is still too raw—but I can put him at ease by treating him like everyone else.

As the hands go by, I start to feel more at home. More myself. My friends still accept me, and it might be hard, but it's going to be okay.

Chapter Twenty-One

Mina

I come downstairs after my shower one morning to find Timothy doing yoga in the living room, P!nk blaring over the house's sound system. He's wearing navy blue boxer briefs and nothing else, his firm ass pointing to the sky as he does Downward Dog. A light sheen of sweat coats him, and he smiles up at me when I stop at the edge of his yoga mat.

"You better not be doing this too hard," I say over the music.

Timothy's smile widens. "Just hard enough."

"I'm talking about your head, not your cock," I say, heading for the coffee.

"My head is fine," he calls out.

Thank god. I'm not sure where yoga falls on the spectrum of harmless to deadly. Probably depends on the pose.

"So is my cock," he adds. I don't need to turn around to know he has a wolfish look on his face.

In the last week, we've had a lot of sex. Too much free time and the newness of an intimate relationship is an intoxicating combination. We're lucky we make it out of the bedroom some days. I'm not complaining, but...

I hope I can keep up when he's back to full speed. The irrational fear he's going to get bored with me and that all this will end creeps in when I think of what our relationship will look like once he's fully recovered. I trust him, and I trust he knows what he's getting himself into with me, that five years of friendship means this relationship will last. Doesn't stop the fear, though.

I grab a coffee and hop onto the counter where I have a better view of Timothy's lithe body. For a muscular guy, he's insanely flexible. I could watch him all day. Hell, I have.

"We should talk about what we're going to do with all the surfboards and wingsuits and parachutes," I say. His mom emailed me this morning, asking me to broach the subject with him. But even if she hadn't, it's been on my mind. He can't use them, it might be best to remove temptation.

"Too soon," Timothy grumbles, just loud enough for me to hear, and I decide to let it go today.

It's been a good week. Timothy's gone out a couple of times with Jax and Danny. We've gone to his gym to work out together, though he's still limited in what he's allowed to do. Nothing high intensity. Nothing that would require him to strain. He wiggled his eyebrows at me as he did arm curls with two-pound weights.

His recovery—beyond the physical healing—is finally moving forward. I don't want to push him backward by arguing over gear gathering dust on closet shelves.

I'm proud of him for finding the strength to make the best of his shitty situation. For finding happiness where not all that long ago, he struggled. My heart is as full of him as my head, and watching him from my perch on the counter makes me ridiculously happy.

He comes out of some pose I can't name and walks up to me, pushing my legs apart to stand between my knees.

"Did I tell you good morning yet?" he asks, skimming light kisses along my jaw.

"You did. Did you forget?" I hate that I can't tell if he's flirting or bleeding out in his damn brain thanks to Downward Dog and gravity.

"Of course, I didn't forget." He points to a couple of pink lines streaking his chest. "You gave me these." He taps the hickey he left on my neck. "I gave you that. Then I gave you my dick until you screamed my name—"

"I didn't scream."

Timothy's hands slip around my waist and he nuzzles against my neck. "You screamed. Want me to call Nic? Bet he heard. Or maybe I'll just"—he jerks me to the edge of the counter, dropping down until his breath coasts along my inner thigh—"push these little shorts aside and"—he licks my over-sensitized center and I nearly fall off the counter—"make you do it again."

"Timothy!"

He pops back to his feet at the tone in my voice, concern in his golden eyes. "What?"

"We had sex an hour ago."

He grins. "I'm the fucking energizer bunny. Of fucking. One of the perks of dating me." There's a wobble in his grin and an uncharacteristic flash of insecurity in his eyes. Every alarm in my head goes off.

"Perks?" I raise an eyebrow because what is this nonsense?

His grin falters. "Yeah."

"What do you mean, *perks*?"

He's caught, and he knows it. The panicked look in his eyes shifts to resignation and he sighs. "I have orgasms on tap for you, any time you want one. Anything you want, outside of those too. Just let me know."

"Are you trying to keep me in a dick coma so I don't see some supposed failing?"

He doesn't say anything, but it's in the shift of his expression. He is.

"Timothy." My heart breaks a little. I brush my fingers over his cheeks, pulling him close for a kiss. "Being with you isn't some hardship."

He's silent for a moment, studying my eyes. "I can be a lot sometimes. Even if I'm not as much as I used to be."

My mouth goes dry. Haven't I been worried about the same thing? That I won't be able to handle him when he's fully recovered? Is it possible he's noticed my worries, and he's trying to make up for them? I hope not. I'm going to do better locking out those little voices from now on.

"I love you. When you're a lot, when you're quiet—all of you." It's true, and it's what I tell myself when I doubt. But even if he's detected my concerns, this feels like it's bigger than me. It feels like baggage. "I'm sorry anyone has ever made you feel you have to compensate for having a big personality.”

A grin flicks across his face. “I also have a big—”

“Timothy.”

“Well, I do,” he says sheepishly.

“You do,” I admit because he does, “but…you don’t need to give me multiple daily orgasms, or anything else, to keep me happy.”

He rubs his thumb over my thigh, a smile sliding over his lips. “Getting you off is also for me.”

I pull him close, kissing him long and deep. His arms wrap around me and he holds me tight. Finally, I rest my forehead against his. “The night we met, you spent hours listening to me cry over a guy who didn’t deserve it. You sent me monthly gift baskets because my periods sucked. When I got fired, you wanted to find me a job. You’re always giving. Sometimes, I want to give.”

His fingers work their way up my hips and under my shirt. “What do you want to give me?”

“I’m not talking about sex. Well, maybe a little,” I concede when he kisses the spot on my neck that turns my blood to warm honey. “Just be with me, Timothy. Relax. You don’t have to fix everything or look after me all the time or give me more than I need. Let me ask. Let me give. Tell me what you need.”

“Look down,” he whispers.

I do, and he’s hard, tenting his jockey shorts.

His lips brush my cheeks. “I need you.”

“Then let me take care of you,” I say, slipping off the counter and pushing him back until he bumps into the island. This isn’t what he was hinting at, but it’s what I want. “And let’s spend the rest of the day hanging out.”

Timothy looks unsteady, but he nods, shuddering when I brush my fingers over his erection.

“It’s hard for me to not be extra,” he says, his eyes fluttering shut as I free his dick and stroke him the way he likes.

“So be extra. I love your extra.”

He sighs, but it’s a much happier sigh. “I don’t know how I can love you more every day, but I do.”

I take him into my mouth and take away his ability to talk. Or at least to say anything beyond dirty talk, because let's face it, Timothy is still Timothy.

"Fuck," he stutters as I suck him deep and stroke what doesn't fit in my mouth with my hand. He gathers my hair, holding me loosely. "I love watching you suck me."

My mouth is busy, so I try to smile through my eyes. I love making him feel good, but I also love the way he feels in my mouth, the salty, musky taste of his precum, and how gentle he is with me. He knows I hate gagging, so he doesn't move, not even the tiniest thrust. I'm in control and he's more than good with that. It's a turn-on and if I didn't need a break, I'd have slipped my hand into my shorts by now.

He brushes some loose strands of hair out of my face. "You're so pretty with my dick in your mouth," he murmurs. "Mmm. Just like that, god you feel amazing."

I lightly drag my nails down his thighs and he falls back against the counter with a moan. The kitchen fills with the sloppy sounds of me blowing him and the satisfied, incoherent rumblings that soon replace his words. I focus on my task, varying my touch, running my tongue over his length, along the ridge. Stroking and sucking, fast and slow, deep and shallow until he's shaking under the hand I've braced on his thigh.

"Look at me, baby," he whispers, and I do. His face holds so much open vulnerability, so much love. I don't stop or slow, but I keep my eyes on him and what passes between us is deeper than a blow job in the kitchen. It's a promise I'll take care of him too. That he can let me without needing to reciprocate. That he understands how much I love him. All of him.

"I'm going to come," he says roughly, giving me the choice of letting him come in my mouth. We don't break eye contact, though his close when his face pinches with pleasure. I keep going, taking him as deep as I can and swallowing before the texture makes me gag. He moans through the end of his orgasm and when he slumps against the counter, I release him gently and pull his boxer briefs back up.

When he moves—probably to grab me a glass of water—I still him with a touch.

"Let me," I say, kissing him on the cheek. "Remember?"

"I don't remember my name," he says with a sheepish, dreamy grin. "Move in with me. For good."

What?

It takes Timothy four days to convince me to move in with him, and another four days for me to convince him I should pay rent and split the bills. He doesn't give in graciously. He pouts, sulks, and tries every trick in the book, but in the end, I win. As soon as my job keeping him out of trouble ends in three weeks, I'll start paying. He's undercharging me, but I let him, so he thinks he wins too.

In truth, I've been too wrapped up in Timothy and busy sewing underwear to look for a new apartment and find a new roommate. I haven't started looking for a new job, which I'll need if I'm going to pay my share.

A little voice in my head warns me I'll regret it. I lived with my cheating ex and the apartment was in his name, so when I left I had to rely on the generosity of Danny and his now ex-wife, sleeping on their couch until I could find my own place. As kind as Danny and Linnea were, I hated it. I lost my home and the man I thought I loved.

Timothy would never do that to me. I know it, and yet, the little voice is still there, telling me I'm being reckless. Telling me I won't be enough for him, this thing we have will fizzle out, and then what?

It creeps in again while Timothy's out playing mini-golf with Jax and I'm trying to finalize my embroidery for the autumn release. I can't get my pumpkin spice latte right—not the new machine's fault. This is all on me and my lack of actual artistic ability. Daisies are easy. Last year's fall leaf was easy. A takeaway cup with a pumpkin on it? Impossible.

If I'm after a beige cylinder with an orange spot, I've nailed it.

My phone rings—Charlotte video calling me—so I quickly swipe to accept the call. Maybe she can draw a cup that actually looks like a cup when my machine is done with it.

"Guess what?" she bursts onto the screen with a smile, then shakes herself. "Oh, wait. How's Timothy? You two still—all the time? Am I interrupting?"

Lexi crowds next to Charlotte. "For this, she can multitask. Tell her."

"Timothy's out," I say with a laugh.

Charlotte makes an impatient noise. "You remember the shop on Grand and Aspen?"

I draw a sharp breath. "Yeah." I know the shop immediately. I lived in a small apartment with Lexi and Charlotte before Nan died, and we used to pass the family-owned bridal shop on the way to our favorite café. The window displays were always soft, romantic, and beautiful.

It reminded me of home.

After the accident that claimed my parents, my grandmother moved us from California to Connecticut to be closer to her family. Her sisters ran a boutique bridal shop a lot like the one on the corner of Grand and Aspen, but they had to close the business the summer before I graduated from high school.

For two generations before that, the Andrei name walked brides along the East Coast down the aisle. My childhood was the sound of gossip and quiet concentration as my Nan and her sisters hand-sewed tiny seed pearls onto bodices or created gorgeous lace by hand for a select few customers with deep pockets. I learned to sew and helped out in the shop until I was old enough to work on the dresses. When I had a bad day at school, they made me hot chocolate and settled me in a cozy corner with old catalogs. When I was lonely, they told me stories as they worked.

That shop was home. The shop on Grand and Aspen had the same feel.

"My dad bought the building some ten years ago," Charlotte says. "The Chandlers are retiring and none of the kids want the business. The lease is available from January, and he's willing to keep it off the market for a few weeks to give you time to decide whether you'd want to take it on, so would you want to? Dad will drop the rent ten percent for you and we'll get my cousins to do some free reno so it's a great deal. You can give Wild Things a home." She's out of breath now, beaming at me on the screen.

"*You* could come home," Lexi says softly.

"It's perfect," Charlotte adds.

It is perfect. I can see myself in it, expanding to include T-shirts and dresses. A workroom in the back where the sound of shears and sewing machines mingle with the music my employees and I take turns choosing. Shelves of fabrics I saved from landfills in an array of colors and textures. A wall covered with inspiration. The shop out front, where customers browse, happy to warm up on a cold winter's day.

I miss winter. LA's been sucking me dry. My once-interesting wardrobe job on a period drama—before I lost it—had become a slog and I'm not looking forward to finding a new one. It's not what I want to do. I want Wild Things so bad I can taste it.

Except it isn't about what I want. It's about what I can safely afford. I need to keep my feet on the ground, where I don't have so far to fall.

Charlotte gives me a rundown of costs and for a moment, I dream of it. I have until January to save. Timothy's undercharging me. With my experience, it'll be easy to get another wardrobe job, and if I pick up some bartending shifts on the weekends…it's so close to doable but it's not a sure thing. I'm not willing to risk it.

"Even with cheaper rent," I finally say, "I don't have enough money to comfortably expand yet. And I don't have any connections out there." The idea of starting over and finding places out East to source fabric is not appealing. It's nauseating.

If I leased the shop and overextended myself, promised things to customers I couldn't deliver, or if I couldn't afford employees and couldn't fill a shop…A full shudder runs through me. It would all be for nothing. Everything I've built over the last five years would go up in flames.

No, I'm not ready to expand. One day. Maybe in a couple of years.

"So make some connections," Charlotte says, like it's easy to go begging for someone else's trash.

"It would be nice to have you back," Lexi says.

"I would love to be closer to you two," I say, "but I can't do it now."

"Remember Matthew McJackass of cheating ex-boyfriend fame?" Charlotte's eyes harden as she says his name. "He said you'd never get this off the ground, and look at how well you've done! You have a waitlist, Wild Things has attracted heaps of followers online. Opening your shop would be like standing on his nuts."

I want to stand on those nuts. Jump on them. Feel them pop beneath my heel. "I'll work on building my brand a bit more, wait until I'm ready. Then I'll jump on those nuts."

"Except you *are* ready."

I wish I had her confidence. "But what if it doesn't work? What if I put all this money into it, and it flops?"

"Then you go back to wardrobe. Or try something else."

"I'm too old for all this," I grumble. When I was twenty, when I should've been open to risks, I didn't have the resources. Now that I'm in my midthirties, I'm too afraid of losing everything I've worked for. It's wildly unfair.

"I'll email you everything," Charlotte says, sensing weakness. "You have a couple of weeks to think it over."

"I'll think about it," I promise, "but I don't think it's the right time."

"Is this because of Timothy?" Lexi asks. "He's from somewhere out here, right? Maybe he'd be willing to move home? He might consider investing too. It wouldn't hurt to have a partner."

No way. If he left, I'd lose my home, half my business, and my heart all at once. I won't risk it. Except...he might be willing to move. Before his accident, I don't think anything would've taken him away from LA, but now...maybe.

We're taking things slow, so I'm not going to talk to him about it until I figure out what I want to do. I'm 99 percent certain I'll pass on the lease anyway. But right now, it doesn't hurt to indulge in the daydream.

Chapter Twenty-Two

Timothy

Life is great.

I haven't had a headache in a while, the sun is shining, Mina's already up, and I get to spend the day with her, which makes this the best day. I love it when every day is the best day. After our talk in the kitchen last week, I'm feeling a lot more relaxed about not scaring her off.

But I know about the shop.

She lets me use her laptop anytime I need to—as long as I don't close any of her ten million tabs or use it to look up anything that might land her on a watch list—and one morning it's on the table while my phone is still upstairs and I want to order her some of the chocolates she likes.

And there it is. A building for lease in Connecticut.

I don't tell Mina everything, and she doesn't tell me everything. That's not how our friendship has worked and it hasn't mattered because we know each other on this deeper level. She'll tell me when she's ready, and the fact she hasn't yet might mean she's not seriously considering this opportunity. Or she's too scared to ask me to go with her. Which I will happily do.

It doesn't help I have all this pent-up energy. Fucking like bunnies was a good outlet, but we've slowed down, and now that excess energy fuels my doubts, turning it into some frantic Whac-A-Mole game in my head.

We're fine. I know we're fine. Better than fine. I'm not going to let it get to me. There's nothing cagey in Mina's actions or words. She's figuring things out on her own and I'm not going to pressure her.

I wish she'd tell me, though.

A slight breeze wafts into my room, carrying with it the scent of some flowering shrubs in my garden and the soft splash of someone in my pool.

Mina.

I get up, ignoring my glorious morning wood, and pull on a pair of lightweight gray sweatpants in case it's Nic. He doesn't share my belief pants should be optional in one's home and I'm feeling generous this morning.

I stride out onto my balcony, and there she is.

My pool isn't huge—about twenty feet by ten. It's not ideal for laps but it's been great for physical therapy and recovery. Same with the small hot tub at the end of it.

Somewhere I have some pool floaties, and only one is an alligator because I'm an adult. Maybe I should dig them out and we can spend the day in the pool. Or maybe I'll lean against the glass balustrade and watch her swim for a while.

Either her swimsuit is the same color as her skin, or...

I don't pause to think. Mina might be naked. I needed to be down there five minutes ago. I swing one leg over the glass, then the other, my back to her as I use the gap between the panels to lower myself, letting my legs hang as I move to grip the concrete edge of the balcony. I'm disappointed to discover I've lost some strength, but it's to be expected given how little I've been able to do while I recover. Still have plenty in reserve, though.

Mina screams.

I ignore it and drop, landing softly on the cool concrete. When I turn, she's hauling herself out of the pool, water sluicing off her body. Dammit, she is wearing a swimsuit. Not much of one, though. It's a bandeau bikini two shades darker than her skin and it's nearly as hot as being naked.

She stomps up to me, but it's all in slow motion and I'm gaping at her because she's gorgeous. She has my whole heart, and she's so fierce and—

She snaps me out of it with a flick to my left nipple.

I yowl and leap back, covering myself with my hands.

"What the fuck, Timothy?" She's pissed. Hands on hips, eyes spitting fire pissed. Nipple-flicking pissed. "You could've fallen and hit your head!"

"I wasn't going to fall." Thank god she wasn't here when I flipped into the pool after Nic's Nerf gun ambush. She'd never let me touch her again if she'd seen that.

"You dropped from your balcony! That's like ten feet!"

"It's only a couple of feet since I was hanging by my fingers and I'm six three with an arm span of…"

Mina, it turns out, doesn't care. "Your foot could have caught on the balustrade and you could've landed face-first on the concrete."

I laugh, because no, that was never going to happen. My body awareness and balance are better than that, plus I've done this so many times. And I'm recovered now—can't she see it? Or feel it? I'm practically vibrating.

"I could've tripped running down the stairs," I point out, and that's not what she wants to hear.

"I'm supposed to stop you from doing this shit." She rubs her eyes and I take the chance to admire her body. More lithe than curvy, but the curves she has are perfect and they're pulling me in. When her hand drops, I'm inches away and she startles.

She might punch me in the dick—poor guy is already confused and can't decide if it would be best to stand tall or retreat—but I move slowly, wrapping my arms around her and drawing her against my body. Her skin is wet and cool, and she rests her forehead on my sternum before her arms wrap around my waist.

"Please don't do that again," she says softly, her breath fanning across my skin.

"I was careful," I say, tipping her chin up. "But I won't do it again if it's important to you. I promise."

Her lips part, beads of water still clinging to them, and I kiss her before she can say anything. The kiss she returns is angry and hard. Fuck, this is hot. I can barely keep pace and I want more.

I cup her ass, my fingers slipping under the cheeks of her bikini bottoms as I lift her, turning to press her into the column holding up my balcony, wrapping her legs around my waist. Her moan when I grind into her is music. She's slick against my chest and if I don't have her, I might actually die.

"Can I take you right here?" I murmur, moving to her neck. I can taste her beneath the salt of my saltwater pool and she's divine.

My question snaps her out of it. "Put me down, you shouldn't be lifting me!"

"I'm not lifting you, the column is taking most of your weight." No way would any doctor disapprove of this, and those lifting restrictions will expire soon. What's a couple of weeks?

"Timothy."

She sounds more worried than angry, so I do as she says, lowering her to her feet. My dick throbs at the loss of her warm pressure against it.

"What about the lounge chair?" I ask, palming myself through my wet sweats.

She pushes past me for the outdoor shower, shaking her head.

I follow her, leaning against the privacy screen separating the shower from the patio.

She yanks on the water and steps under. "What was so important you couldn't take the stairs?"

Her hands are in her hair, rinsing out the salt, so I reach over and hook a finger into her bandeau top, giving the fabric a little tug toward me. I don't let go. "I thought you might be skinny dipping."

"This," she says, motioning up and down her body, "is not worth falling off a balcony."

I wasn't going to fall. "My dick and I beg to differ," I say instead, again tugging on her bikini top.

"You and your dick can't enjoy this dead or in a full-body cast," she snaps.

I move slowly so she can stop me if she wants, pulling the wet fabric down, down, down until it slips off her wet breasts and settles low on her waist. My throat goes dry and I lick my lips because Mina has the most perfect dusky pink nipples. Small and hard, getting harder by the second. I need them in my mouth.

Mina slips everything over her slick hips, kicking it aside. She's standing under my outdoor shower naked.

I fall against the privacy screen and bite my fist. Every time I see her naked is like the first time. I think I whimper at the sight of neatly trimmed dark brown curls that I want to tickle my nose.

"You going to invite me in?" I ask when she continues to ignore me. Watching her hands rub soap over her skin has me so fucking hard.

She looks me over, her tongue wetting her lips. "If you promise to behave."

"What do I get if I do behave?"

"I'll peg you," she says softly. "Tonight. If you think you're ready."

I bite my fist again and nod enthusiastically. We may have slowed down, but we've been working up to this, adding a bit of anal play into the bedroom. It's hardly a surprise, but it still feels like Christmas.

Mina grabs the waistband of my sweatpants and pulls me into the shower. I pull her into a kiss that doesn't end until we're both gasping and I work my dick inside her and fuck her hard enough that after she asks how my head is.

My head is excellent.

For five years, I thought I loved Mina as fully as possible, but I was wrong because every day I love her more. There's no limit on what I feel for her and it's thrilling.

I'm ready for tonight. I don't bother to dress after my second shower of the day. Just wrap the towel around my waist and head into my walk-in. I already know what I want. This is something I've been dreaming of for years, and I'm glad Mina's into the idea of it.

The harness I picked for Mina is brand new, with thinner straps around the waist and hips, and a thicker strap in the crotch. She'll get a good deal of friction right over her clit while she's thrusting.

My ego might be big, but I don't have delusions of grandeur over what I can take up the butt, especially after a five-year sabbatical. The dildo I grab is small and skinny, a lighter shade of purple, with a slightly bulbous head. Got to start somewhere. In general, I'm more of a giver than a taker, but if Mina enjoys this, we can work up to something bigger.

I lay them out on the bed, then go back for a big-ass thing of lube. Some more towels, too, because this is going to get messy and I want to take care of all the messy stuff so she doesn't have to. I want tonight to be comfortable and stress-free for her. I want her to love this as much as I'm going to.

When she walks in, she doesn't take one look at the harness and dildo and walk back out, or laugh at how small it is. She looks at everything laid out on my bed and walks up to me. Sliding her hands over my chest, over my shoulders, and around my neck, she pulls me to her for a kiss that takes my breath away and sets my world on fire.

"Are you going to yell at me if I throw you onto the bed?" I ask when she finally pulls back.

Her eyes turn stern. "Don't." She kisses me again to take the sting out of the fact that she doesn't think I should.

"Then get on the bed." I smile against her lips. I could throw her around all night, but I'm not going to argue.

She grabs me by the towel, taking me with her, her kisses pulling me harder than her grip. She sinks onto the mattress, scooting back. I follow on an invisible string.

One tug from Mina and my towel is undone. I toss it to the floor, pulling her leg up my hip as I press her into the bed and kiss her breathless.

I snatch the harness as I trail kisses down her body, lifting her hips and holding her pussy to my mouth while I go to town on her. Wearing Mina's thighs like earmuffs is my favorite—feeling the strong muscles in her legs tighten and tremble drives me wild. When she's impossibly wet and gasping and my dick has turned to fucking stone, I slip the harness on her, kissing her skin under every strap and taking my sweet time tightening the buckles, tasting her.

"Size does matter," I say, and Mina laughs, watching as I slip the ring over the dildo, attaching it to the harness. The purple shaft disappears into my hand and I use it like a handle as I dive back between her legs to finish what I started, pushing straps out of the way. Her fingers wind through my hair, carefully avoiding the incisions, even though she has no chance of accidentally fingering my skull. It's an unwelcome reminder that my life might be great, but there's a hole in my heart that, unlike the ones in my head, might never close.

I put the job I miss out of my head and concentrate on the woman I love.

Mina comes with a soft whimper and I keep going until she taps me because I can't get enough of her. I kiss my way up her body to her lips and for five minutes, or ten, or more, we make out. When I finally pull away, she's smiling at me.

It's like standing on the edge, ready to drop from a plane, knowing I'm in for a fucking awesome ride. My heart rate picks up in anticipation and I grin. I love her so much and I wish I could give her a quarter of the thrill I'm feeling. Actually...maybe I already do.

Chapter Twenty-Three

Mina

"How are you feeling about this?" Timothy asks, tugging at the dildo. I suck in a breath as the strap rubs against my clit.

Just because I don't have casual sex doesn't mean I'm a prude or my tastes run vanilla. I've done some stuff. Just not *this*. But I'm curious and I like that I'm getting to experience this for the first time with Timothy. I like that he's really into it.

"Excited," I answer honestly, "but a little worried I'll hurt you."

He grins. "Lots of lube, start slow, and you'll be great."

I bite my lip and glance down at the dildo. Thank god it's small. "What if I suck at it?"

He shakes his head. "I've seen you move. You can fuck."

I laugh. "You'll guide me?"

"Every step of the way." He rolls onto his side next to me, taking my hand and lacing our fingers together. "If you change your mind, or you're uncomfortable, at any time, tell me and we'll stop."

I squeeze his hand. "Likewise."

He grabs a pillow and throws a thick towel over it, lying down, hips propped, legs apart. "It would probably be easier for you to fuck me from behind, but I want to watch you. I want you to see how much I'm going to like this."

I kneel between his knees, nodding. I don't know what to do, so I touch him, running my hands up and down his legs, over his stomach, up his chest. Do I just...lube up and stick it in?

"Come here," Timothy whispers, pulling me down for a kiss. "You're incredible," he murmurs into my mouth. "You've got this. You've got me."

He doesn't let me go, and for a long moment, we only kiss, but it's enough. The tension leaves my body, I can feel my arousal returning, and when I reach down and stroke Timothy, there's already a drop of precum at the tip of his dick. He groans.

God, I want this. When I pull away, I'm ready.

"You look sexy as hell in a harness," Timothy says with a smile, tugging at a strap on my hip. "I should buy you more things with straps."

I reach for the lube, pouring some into my hand before setting it on the towel next to me. I rub it between my hands, warming it up, then realize everything I touch is going to get lubed.

"Get messy," he whispers.

I laugh, then slap my hand on his thigh. "Like this?"

"Mmm." He grabs my free hand, bringing it to his dick. "And this." When I stroke him, he tips his head back and sighs. I slide my other hand up his thigh to his balls, giving them a very gentle squeeze, and playing lightly with them before moving to his perineum. "Yeah," he murmurs as I massage him. His dick is so hot and hard in my hand.

I press my slick finger to his back entrance, circling while I continue lazily stroking his dick. Timothy shifts his hips a bit, and I slowly press in, gently stretching him until I can work a second finger in.

"Fuck," he murmurs.

I stop immediately. "Is that okay?"

"Trying not to come," he says tightly. "Don't judge. Also, don't move. Or look at me. Maybe hold your breath."

I laugh and wait until he nods. This time I don't stroke his dick—I just hold him while I finger him.

He wraps his hand around mine, tightening my grip and sliding my hand up and down his length for a few beats before stopping us with a happy sigh. "I'm ready," he says, pulling my hand away and placing the bottle of lube in it. I'm generous with it, coating the dildo and Timothy, pouring some into his hand before I drop it on the towel and scoot closer.

"Nice and slow," he says, grinning.

I position the tip of the toy at his back entrance, then slowly, slowly press forward. Timothy makes a satisfied sound when I withdraw a tiny bit and press in again. It only takes a couple more slow thrusts and I'm there.

He lowers his legs around my hips and grips his dick. "That feels fantastic. Fuck me, baby."

I slide my hands over his thighs to his hips and test out a tiny thrust. The friction of the strap between my legs is amazing and a little *oh* escapes my lips. The look on Timothy's face is pure pleasure, so I do it again, a little harder. His eyes drift over my body as I pick up the pace a little, making me hot as the strap rubs me just right.

"You're doing great," he says, stroking his dick. "So fucking good."

I love watching him touch himself, and watching him do it while I fuck him? Even better.

Sweat slicks my body, and I pause a moment for more lube. Timothy guides me. Shallow thrusts, then deeper, slower, then faster until we settle into a rhythm that leaves both of us gasping.

Timothy reaches up with his free hand, palming my breast, squeezing and pinching my nipple as he fucks his other fist. "Come on, come for me. I can't hold on much longer."

The strap between my legs is slick and I'm nearly out of my mind with how badly I need to come when Timothy twists my nipple. I shatter and the struggle to keep thrusting into him drags my orgasm on and on. I reach for his dick, gripping him just above his hand, tightening my thumb and forefinger over his crown, moving with him.

Timothy comes with a shout, each stroke painting his clenched abs, dripping down my hand.

When he's finished, I collapse beside him, kissing his cheek, his jaw, and his neck, while he catches his breath. While I catch my breath. Muscles I didn't know I had ache, but it's a sweet ache.

Timothy's smile is lopsided and dopey. "You were fantastic, baby."

He cups the back of my head, pulling me in for a kiss, and I grab him back. We both freeze the moment we realize our hands are still very lubed.

"Sorry," he whispers, pulling his hand away. Strands of my hair are stuck to his palm and I laugh.

"Stay here a minute," I say, even though I don't think he can move right now.

"Your ass looks amazing in that harness," he calls as I slip into the bathroom. I laugh again, giddy and happy and so tired as I start up the bathtub and slip the harness off.

I bring a wet towel out to Timothy and clean him up. He smiles as I tell him how much I love him, how much I enjoyed that.

He gets to his feet and while he walks slowly to the bathroom, I gather up all the towels and drop them in the hamper.

"How's your head?" I ask, lighting a few candles and dimming the bathroom lights.

He sighs as he lowers himself into the tub. "Perfect. Sunshine and fucking rainbows."

I wait for him to get comfortable before I climb in, settling between his legs, my back against his chest. Sunshine and fucking rainbows are exactly how I feel too.

Chapter Twenty-Four

Mina

Timothy walks by the sliding glass doors, mouthing *help me*, even though his mom, on the video call, can clearly see him.

I shake my head and go back to my embroidery machine, laughing softly as his mom chews him out. He's been avoiding this call for a while now, so serves him right. She's pissed off he isn't taking job hunting seriously. Honestly, if I had his money, I wouldn't either. But I get it. This is more about giving him something to focus all his energy on that doesn't involve jumping off roofs.

The embroidery machine finishes, delivering me a perfect pumpkin spice latte. My tweaks to the design finally worked. I'm giddy and when my phone rings with an incoming video call from Charlotte, I point my phone directly at the cute little cup.

"Nice!" Charlotte says, followed by a short pause. "Not sure about the dinosaur print pumpkin spice combo, but...it's quirky."

I laugh, waving the little square of fabric at Timothy. He glances at me and walks to the glass for a closer look. The smile that breaks across his face fills me with such a high I can't stop myself from dancing.

Timothy's grin widens, then he rolls his eyes as his mom demands his attention.

Leaving the fabric on my workstation, I head upstairs for privacy. Not that Timothy can hear us over his mother, but...still.

I haven't told him about the shop. He was unwilling to move out East for the girlfriend he dated for three years, I doubt he'd do it for the girlfriend he's dated for mere weeks. Ugh, I don't know, maybe he would, but every time I think about taking this leap, I feel like I'm going to throw up.

"So, the building on Aspen and Grand…" Charlotte wiggles her eyebrows.

"I still have a few weeks to decide, right?" I ask. I have to admit, daydreaming about Wild Things in that building is addicting. I don't want to turn her down and put an end to it, even though that's exactly what I'm going to do.

"You do." Charlotte grins. "But I got Dad to drop the rent. Fifteen percent instead of ten. And of course, we don't need a deposit from you because we know you aren't going to wreck the place."

A true perk of being a careful person. It makes me smile. "Thanks, Charlotte, but—"

"No 'but.' Just think about it. Talk to Timothy, see what he thinks."

"Fine," I say, though I have no intention of bringing it up yet. Deep down, I think I'm scared he'll encourage me to do it, whatever that might mean for us. Yet another reason I immediately break into a cold sweat. Things are so good right now. Why change them?

Charlotte has to go—she has a date tonight—so she says goodbye and I go back downstairs.

Timothy managed to get rid of his mother. He and Nic are sitting by the pool, drinking beer and talking.

I put my earbuds on and test out another embroidered pumpkin spice latte. It turns out perfectly. Spending some of the money from Timothy's parents on this machine was a good investment.

It's nice to daydream about the lease, but I won't take it. My to-do pile shrinks as the finished pile grows, and maybe I'm not ready yet, but I'm moving in the right direction, one step at a time, the way it should be. I'll leap one day when it isn't so far.

Timothy comes up behind me, bending to kiss me on the cheek. He pulls out my earbud. "We're going to have a few people over. That okay?"

"Of course." I stretch my arms up and around his neck and he nuzzles into the crook of mine for a bit before Nic calls him away. I could use a break anyway. Since I know Timothy and the kind of friends he has, I put my embroidery machine in the garage so it doesn't get broken during an impromptu game of in-house football.

It's not just the machine, though. My stuff is everywhere. Boxes of finished and unfinished products are stacked in corners, cluttering the coffee table. My foldable sewing table. Bolts of fabric and plastic containers filled with notions. It's all got to go.

Timothy and Nic help me move the bigger things but when people start arriving, Timothy leaves to play host and Nic gets to work making drinks, leaving me with a handful of smaller boxes.

Timothy and I have very different definitions of *a few people*. These aren't just stunt people, either, although they're here too. There's a social media influencer, a couple of models, a washed-up pop star, a few actors, and a couple of young athletes. A lot more people I don't recognize.

Almost everyone is dressed in something fashionable and I'm hauling boxes in yoga pants and an old T-shirt.

I drop the last box in the garage and run upstairs to change clothes. When I come back down...

Three women—the influencer and a couple of models—are wearing my thongs, and nothing else. The box they found is open, panties all over the floor, while they pose for selfies.

I can't sell these thongs and who knows how many from the box they've tried on. I'm going to have to start over, sew another fifty.

My chest tightens and I don't know what to do. Most people would kill to get their clothes on these women, but if my brand is recognized in their photos...

Most people don't hyperventilate at the thought of an already long waitlist of customers exploding.

I can't afford to go big before I'm ready. What do I do?

Timothy is nowhere in sight, and I don't know if that makes this better or worse.

Nic hands me a drink. "I told them not to."

Panic hasn't made me stupid. I raise an eyebrow at him. "You tried to stop a trio of attractive women from getting naked?"

He looks at me like *really?* "No. Of course not."

I want to punch him in his too-handsome face, but I settle for holding a grudge. "Do you have any idea how much money these women cost me?" I can't demand they pay for the thongs. People like them get this shit for free and I should be grateful they liked them enough to notice.

"They're thongs." Nic sounds exasperated. "How much can they cost?"

"You were married to a lingerie model, what do you mean *how much can they cost?*"

"Fine. I'll pay you. Remind me later." He starts to walk away but stops, pointing at the influencer. "She could make you a million with these pictures."

I want to throw something at him. "Not if my brand blows up, I can't produce, and I get a ton of backlash."

He shrugs, spots Timothy wrestling a massive alligator floaty toward the pool, and heads that way.

I follow. I make it two steps before Danny crushes me into a hug. "Mina!"

Ugh. I want to scream. I want to grab my thongs, run to my room, and spend the night hiding.

"So, it finally happened, huh?" Danny says, holding my arms and studying me. "Always knew it would. You two have been circling each other for years. I'm happy for you. Take care of him, yeah?"

Then Danny's gone, following my new thong-clad friends out to the pool. They jump right in the water and start splashing each other—at least until Danny strips to his boxers and cannonballs right in the middle of them.

Serves them right.

I drain my drink, then grab the box and the thongs that have spilled all over the floor and stuff them into the garage, away from my other stacks. I can't bring myself to put all that hard work into the trash right now.

Timothy finds me in the kitchen. He's down to his shorts and is dripping wet. He wraps his arms around me from behind and cold water seeps into my clothes. "Come ride me in the pool."

I glance outside. A blond woman in a black T-shirt is perched on Danny's shoulders and a topless redhead is on Nic's. "Absolutely not. And you shouldn't be doing that either."

"Why not?"

"Because you'll take an elbow to the head and die."

Timothy turns me in his arms, pressing his forehead to mine. "I won't. Come on, baby."

My body is vibrating with irritation now. "No. I'm not going tits out on your shoulders."

"I'm not sharing your tits with these losers, keep your shirt on. Just get on my shoulders and help me take down Stella and Danny."

Nic and the redhead are down already. Stella has her hands in the air, cheering.

"This isn't my kind of thing, Timothy."

His face scrunches. "The woman who caused my shopping cart to crash while racing down Broadway—cheap shot, by the way, and I think Mrs. Kiki Foxx would agree—doesn't do a little pool wrestling?"

He has a point and I hate it. Racing shopping carts with drag queens on board was a very memorable friendiversary night, but it was before his accident. Things are different now. "Timothy, please. Don't risk it."

"You don't want me to, huh?" Hurt fills his brown puppy eyes, whipping guilt up inside me.

I don't want it to be like this with us. I don't want to hold him back until he resents me. Until he moves on to someone who won't tell him no.

"You might be back at full strength, but your mom is still paying me to keep you out of trouble. Please, Timothy."

His expression shifts into a smile and he kisses me. "Okay."

Danny calls him in a big, booming voice. Timothy smiles at me apologetically, kisses me quickly, and struts outside, hollering back at Danny that he's out. I wish I didn't hear the chorus of boos, but I do.

His friends will grow to resent me too. The girlfriend who doesn't let her boyfriend have any fun.

All I want is to keep him safe.

Timothy is good on his word. He finds a beach ball somewhere and jumps into the pool. This is marginally better than the wrestling, as far as stray elbows are concerned, but I'm not about to drag him from the pool like he's a child in front of all his friends.

One call to Celia and I could end this party right now. Not sure Timothy and Nic would forgive me, though. This shit is exactly what I feared when his mom asked me to do this.

I sit on a lounge chair by the pool and resign myself to watching Timothy like a hawk, wishing I could smother him in Bubble Wrap and hating how raw my nerves are.

The influencer eventually comes and talks to me about the thongs. We exchange contact info and talk a bit before she's pulled away by one of the models. She seems nice and Nic had a point—she could make my brand huge, and that's worth a box of thongs I can't sell. Or it would be if I were ready. The pictures are already online, but she agrees not to tag me. I'm lucky that she's interested in helping me launch a marketing campaign when I'm ready to expand.

I don't feel lucky.

Timothy's in his element. Laughing, shouting, and being rowdier than he should be, but not doing anything I can directly yell at him for. We were so tightly wrapped in our little bubble, I forgot about this part of him, and now that we're here, the fear he'll get bored with me is back and loud.

The feeling in my gut tells me a clock has started ticking, and it isn't the one marking when I'm done keeping an eye on him. It's our relationship. I'll smother him, and he'll fray me until all that's left of both of us is hurt and resentment.

Pushing these thoughts away is hard. I try to ignore them, but they cling to my shadow.

I'm pulled into dozens of conversations—I know too many people—and in the chaos of the party, I lose track of Timothy. I trust him, but some ugly thing deep inside me calls me stupid for it, reminding me of him disappearing with that woman at the bowling alley.

The sun goes down. I'm tired of haunting this party. I tell Nic I'm clocking out on Timothy duty and it's his turn. But I fix myself a drink and plant my ass on the second flight of stairs, high enough that I can still keep an eye on things. Guess I'm not really off the clock. I pull out my phone and look at my mood board for my shop, hoping it will help soothe my nerves.

I'm not tied to a job or an apartment. Maybe if I'm going to move cross-country, this is the time. The situation with the influencer changes the equation a bit...if I can rely on her to keep her word once I'm ready, and who knows when that will be?

I jump when someone sits next to me. Relief eases the tightness in my stomach until I turn and see it's not Timothy.

It's Dex.

"Hey," he says quietly.

"Hey."

There's no reason for this to feel awkward—we met once, exchanged numbers, set a date that never happened, and didn't talk to each other again. But it does feel awkward. His jaw is set and there's a stiffness in his posture now.

"Sorry we never made that date," he says when our attempt at small talk dies.

I reach for something to say but can't think of anything. "I'm..."

"With Timothy, I heard." He taps his phone on his leg a few times. "I didn't realize there was something between you two, or I never would've asked. I'm sorry."

"You don't have to apologize. There wasn't anything between me and Timothy then."

Dex side-eyes me. "There was on his side, and I didn't realize he was serious."

"Oh." I didn't either.

Whatever is weighing on Dex drags his shoulders down. He sounds tired. "Shit got out of hand, for both of us. I want you to know I'm sorry. I can't get the sound of him hitting that pole out of my head. If I hadn't—"

The kid is two seconds away from crying, and I'm five seconds away from kicking Timothy's ass. Maybe Dex's too.

"What—" I want to ask what happened, but I need to hear it from Timothy, not from Dex. I shake my head and pat Dex on the shoulder. "It was an accident."

He nods. "At least you two are together now," he muses.

"Yeah." For now.

"Why are you sitting here, all alone?" he asks suddenly, turning toward me.

I shrug and stare at the black screen of my phone. "I don't know where Timothy is."

"I was kicking Danny's ass at pool," Timothy's cool voice startles me and Dex goes rigid. Probably pale, but the lights are in some dim party mode and I can't be sure. "You would know that," Timothy continues, "If you looked for me."

Dex gets up. Timothy doesn't even glance at him when he walks past.

I stand. I want to fight with him, scream at him, cling to him while he fucks me and I'm not enjoying this mix of emotions. "I'm going to bed."

Timothy holds a hand out to me. "Ask me to come with you."

I stare at his hand. "How did the accident happen?" I ask quietly.

His hand drops as he exhales. "I was a dick, baiting Dex, and I got carried away. The rig tilted. I think I moved into his kick instead of away."

My heart lurches. *Baiting Dex?* Why? Over what?

Over me. Over that stupid fucking date I was never going to go on. Tears fill my eyes. "It was my fault?"

"No," he says immediately, his voice firm. "No," he repeats, louder. "Never your fault. It was mine. I was in a bad mood."

"You don't have bad moods."

"Everyone has bad moods, Mina. I'm just better at hiding them. Most of the time. Not that day."

I clamp my hand over my mouth. My throat is burning with the effort it takes to keep the tears in my eyes from falling. He was in a bad mood, just like I was, after that disaster of a friendiversary night. Fuck, if I'd just talked to him...

Timothy moves to the step below me. "I'm grieving my career, but I need you to understand I wouldn't change any of this. Okay?" He brushes a runaway tear from my cheek. "None of it is your fault. None."

I can't speak, so I nod.

"Right now," he says, "I need to know you want me." His voice might be calm and firm, but his eyes are not. They're full of worry.

I swallow the lump in my throat. "I always want you."

He wraps his arms around me. "I love you. More than anything. I'm sorry I've neglected you tonight. I never stopped thinking about you, even when you weren't by my side."

I wrap my arms around him. With him on the step below me, we're nearly the same height and I don't need to go on my tiptoes to kiss him lightly. A sad emptiness and a vague sense that we're failing settles over me. "Come to bed with me."

Timothy nods, then pulls back and whistles loudly. The house goes not exactly silent, but a lot quieter. "Hey, Danny, shut it down for me?"

Danny salutes and bellows out, "Party's over, folks! Grab your shit and go home!"

Timothy moves past me, pulling on my hand. "Come on."

Chapter Twenty-Five

Timothy

"Still ugly," I say as I follow Nic through the door of his Beverly Hills mansion. After our little (big) party yesterday, the paps have figured out where Nic was staying, which means the fans have as well, and now I'm helping him move back into his place, with his fancy security system on the large, walled, secluded property, because as much as I like having Nic around, I don't want anyone harassing Mina.

"I didn't pick the house," he grumbles as his suitcase wheel goes the wrong way.

"Where's the bellhop when you need him? Concierge!" My voice echoes through the cavernous white room. Nic's house resembles a bland but extremely expensive hotel—white on white with orchids and simple but boring statement pieces—or purgatory. I bounce between the two as I see fit.

"At least no pornos were filmed here," Nic says pointedly.

"That you know about."

The small rental truck arrives with the stuff he kept out of Addison's hands by putting into storage, and it doesn't take long to unload everything. I don't think he's happy to be home, but at least he can enjoy his hideous, 12,800-square-foot victory. Hopefully, he keeps his dick in his pants while celebrating.

"I'll order us a pizza," I say from the doorway of an unfurnished bedroom.

Nic nods, stepping quickly in front of a canvas wrapped in plastic and covered in a blanket.

I know exactly what that is and why he's kept it all these years, but I'll let him pretend his crush on my twin is a secret.

What does he even do with that painting, though? Stare at it with lovesick eyes? It's a portrait of him, so I hope it's not masturbatory fodder. I walk away to give him a moment alone with it before he safely tucks it into the back of the closet, behind all his other scar tissue.

His kitchen is cold, massive, industrial, and soulless. I grab the bottle of whiskey I bought as a re-housewarming gift, or a happy divorce gift, and head outside. It's a warm evening. I pour a glass for myself and check my phone for messages from Mina.

Nothing.

I have a temperamental twin sister who excels at not telling me she's mad when she's livid, so I know Mina's still pissed about the party yesterday, even though she says she isn't.

She asked me to be careful, and I was careful. I was surprised I still had fun, but I was more surprised she wasn't by my side. Sure, she watched me from a lounge chair while we played a lazy game of pool volleyball, but after that...she disappeared. Then reappeared with Dex, which was unfortunate. I trust her, but seeing them together still made me feel like shit.

Maybe I'm overreacting. Or maybe she's realizing I'm not worth the trouble and the stress. I need to show her I am.

Nic drops down across from me, ruining my view of all the trees surrounding his wildfire-bait mansion. When he realizes I didn't bring a glass for him, he gets a shitty look on his face and swigs the expensive whiskey straight from the bottle like an animal. "What's up with you?" he asks, studying me.

I shrug. "Nothing."

Nic's already shaking his head. "No, lately you've had this smug, freshly-fucked look on your face. It's annoying as hell, but it's gone. What happened?"

"We shouldn't have had so many people over yesterday."

"She's pissed about that?"

"No, she's pissed about having her underwear stolen." It's more complicated, but I'm not going to try to explain it to Nic. I'm not sure I understand either. That influencer could've launched her brand big time, and Mina didn't want it.

"I paid for those thongs this morning," Nic lifts the bottle to his lips again but stops to change the subject. "Your mom wants me to ask how the job search is going."

"I'm not chaining myself to some desk." I'll become a chaos gremlin and get fired within a week, if not on the first day. "And it would be nice if you stopped doing her dirty work for her—you're already her favorite and she's been on my back since I woke up from surgery."

Nic shrugs. "Doesn't have to be a desk job."

I take a bigger drink of whiskey. So far, I've been sipping it. Taking alcohol slowly, like yesterday, to see how it affects me. Head injuries and alcohol do not mix, and while I'm recovered, I'm not willing to get unexpectedly hammered. "Mina's looking at a lease in Connecticut."

"She is?"

"She wants to expand her business—she's talked about it for years."

Nic frowns. "Thongs?"

"Yeah, among other styles." I turn my glass and it makes an obnoxious noise on the glass tabletop. "I'm not interested in looking for a job out here because if she goes, I'm going with her."

The whiskey bottle slams onto the table, hard enough to make my jaw clench.

"You fucking asshole," Nic spits.

Yeah, he's not going to take this well. "Thank you?"

Nic doesn't explode often, but when he does...whoa, boy. And right now, he's about to blow. All I can do is hold on to my ass and wait for him to be reasonable.

He shakes his head. "I didn't want to come out here, but I did because you wanted to become the greatest stuntman in the history of ever. And now what? You're leaving because you couldn't do it?"

Ouch, I'm going to be the bigger person and let that slide.

Nope. Can't do it. "Listen, you prick. I love her. If Mina wants to live in Antarctica, I will take her there and learn everything I can about penguins or whatever. This is about following her, not running away. And no one asked you to come out here with me. You made choices too, and now you're the face of a huge franchise. You're the Second Hottest man in America. You're doing great. You don't need me to hold your hand."

He snatches the bottle again, dark eyes sweeping away from me. "I hate it here."

"That's the divorce talking."

Nic glares at me as he downs another gulp.

"Maybe go easy on the whiskey," I suggest. "I'm not holding your hair back while you puke."

He runs a hand through his short hair, and his glare intensifies. After a minute, he asks, "You don't really want to go home, do you?" It's more of a plea than a question. "We came to LA to get away and have adventures. Let's do that again. We're not too old yet."

"Again, the divorce talking."

"This is your head injury talking," he snaps back. "I get you're hurt and upset about it, but this is a big decision to make, especially right now. You have a life here."

"Not without Mina."

A look crosses his face. Hurt and anger. Fear.

I take a sip and quietly say, "She hasn't decided to move yet, it might be nothing."

Nic grumbles something, but the pizza arrives. I go to get it, and when I come back, he's staring out at his pool. At the hot tub with the gas fire pit in the center of it. At the lounge chairs and closely cut brilliantly green grass. All of it Addison's choice.

"Know why I married Addison?" he asks in a flat voice.

He's drunk if he's the one bringing this up. I glance at the bottle and yeah. He must have pounded it while I went to get the pizza. "Because you were scared?" I venture.

"Because I was scared." He pauses, eyes narrowed at his own words as a scowl takes over his face. "No. Because I've got nothing."

"A lot of people would look at this ugly-ass mansion and disagree."

"I've got no one to make me want to be anything, or to do better, or to do anything at all. Allison—"

"Addison," I correct, smothering my laugh under my hand.

Nic doesn't notice he got her name wrong. "Addison had drive. So much drive…"

Is he talking about sex drives? I snatch the bottle and refill my glass to get the taste of that out of my mouth.

Nic sighs after a minute. "She wanted to be on the top."

"Is this about sex? Because—"

"It's not about sex," he snaps. "I'm talking about careers. She made me want to be better at my job. When we first came to LA, your drive to get to your dreams made me want to make something of myself. I wanted more than waiting tables and shooting Target ads. I wanted to make it too."

I wave my glass at his property. "You made it."

"And I don't care. I don't give a shit about any of this. I don't want it, and now, I'm all alone…why bother with any of it?"

"So don't sign onto any more movies. Do whatever ones you can't get out of, then do something else for a while." This isn't about that. He doesn't want to be alone. He never has.

"I've never wanted to do anything else."

"Pretty sure your bank account means you don't have to." Unlike me, he doesn't need a job to keep him out of trouble. Nic could happily do nothing for the rest of his life.

He shrugs.

"You'll figure it out." I tap my fingers on my glass.

He sighs and we fall into silence for a minute, maybe two, before he pushes the whiskey bottle away. "You lost the job you love. I lost the woman I didn't. Kind of funny how our lives are imploding."

"Yeah—" I draw out, squinting into the dark. "I'm not laughing, are you?"

He glances at me, the corner of his mouth ticking up before the laugh escapes. Suddenly we're both laughing and I'm not sure why, but it feels good, so I roll with it.

When we settle down, we eat pizza and talk about lighter things.

I still feel heavy when I head home.

If Mina moves across the country, I'm going with her, but I don't want to leave Nic alone in LA. He's not in a great place and without me, bad people can get to him. Namely, my cousin Ashley. She won't be off filming shitty reality TV forever and she's one step above a stalker and obsessed with Nic.

So I need to keep Mina here, for a little while at least. Maybe, it occurs to me as my rideshare pulls up to my house, I can do that and make sure she knows how much I love her with one move.

Chapter Twenty-Six

Mina

Nic Fontana is a dead man.

After a morning of sewing, I log onto my neglected Wild Things social media accounts, only to discover thousands of notifications and comments lamenting my website crashing.

In a cold sweat, I pull up my site.

One thousand new subscribers.

One. THOUSAND.

Thank god it crashed when it did, but the stupid technical glitch that allowed one thousand people to sign up for my autumn release means I now need to sew, embroider, package, and ship three thousand new pairs of underwear in four weeks. On top of the ones I still need to finish.

That goddamn horndog—he could have stopped them. Nic is officially on notice.

It takes me about five minutes to find out what happened. Yesterday a customer recognized the fabric of one of the thongs on the pictures from last week's party, connecting it to a teaser post about my autumn release on my social media, and left a comment. The influencer confirmed the commenter's suspicions, calling it a sneak peek.

I should've asked her to take the photos down the moment I knew they were up—what was I thinking? I knew the damn risks.

Even if I chain myself to my sewing machine and work all day every day, I won't be able to meet half this demand. I don't know what happens next, but unhappy customers tend to be loud about it. This is going to ruin me.

Goodbye expansion. Goodbye dreams. Might as well crawl back to Cruella de Vil and beg for my old job back.

My frustrated, strangled cry echoes through Timothy's silent house and I stomp into the kitchen because I can't look at my computer, and tech support has had me on hold for an hour.

Maybe it's good if my website stays down. No one else can join my subscription service.

Timothy's out, and for once, I don't know where he is or who he's with. He's been secretive this week. I know he's up to something and I should probably care more about what it is, but right now, I can't focus on anything beyond my disaster.

I should sew my ass off while I'm on hold, but I need to hit something. I'm going to the boxing gym instead.

I feel marginally better when I return, but it's not until Timothy comes downstairs and wraps me in a hug that I feel like everything will be okay.

"I needed this," I whisper into his neck.

Timothy's hands slip up my shirt, warm and rough against my shoulders. "You okay?"

"Yeah, I think so. How do you give the best hugs?"

He pulls me tight. "Because I don't hold back."

A little shiver zips down my spine, and I wish I could be more like him. "Don't hold back," I whisper in his ear. Maybe some of him will rub off on me.

Timothy growls and my shirt is gone, flying through the air. Even though Nic is no longer living here, we race up the stairs to the first bedroom—my room—shedding clothes, kissing and groping as we go.

"On the bed, on your hands and knees."

I want this so bad I complain when his hard dick brushes against me and he ignores it in favor of running his hands over me. Timothy laughs, but his hands slide over my ass to my thighs as he kneels on the floor behind me.

He licks from my clit to my entrance and I shudder at how good his tongue feels.

"That better?" he asks, doing it again. I answer with a moan. It's so much better, and it doesn't take him long to get me there. He lets me come, guiding me through it, pushing his dick inside me before it's ebbed and now I feel better.

The tight way he grips my hip, every demanding thrust...I am so thoroughly his and he's mine. He lets go of my hips, wrapping my hair around his fist and letting me thrust back onto him for a while. When he's had enough, he tugs me upright, I reach over my head to lock my hands around his neck while he kisses mine and plays with my tits. And when I barrel toward my next orgasm, he's right there with me, telling me how good I feel, how much he loves me, and how he'll always be there for me.

I'm sorry, but at this time, my label isn't for sale.

My website is up and running again, my subscription list locked down. I'm tempted to send a mass email to the one thousand new subscribers, explaining the situation and apologizing for not being able to take them at this time. The only thing stopping me is the fear that at least a few of them will mount a campaign against me and I'll lose both my credibility and ability to expand in the future. Everything I've worked for.

I'm tempted to sell Wild Things to one of the half dozen companies sniffing around me, so it's not my problem anymore. But I've been building this brand for five years. I'm not going to hand it over without a fight.

I need to figure out what to do. I want to tell Timothy and ask him for advice. He fixes so many problems in my life, though, and if I'm going to stand on my own and run this business, I need to figure it out. On my own.

I send the email declining the offer and toss my phone onto Timothy's bed, turning to the mirror on his dresser. Tonight is the Warwick wrap party, and while I don't want to go, I am happy to put on this brand-new Mioe dress. Pear green with an asymmetrical neckline, the silky fabric pours over my curves in the most magical way. It's not as short as the other dress, thank god, hitting just below my knee. It's the dress of a woman not on the brink of all her hard work collapsing, which right now, I aspire to be.

"You have an eye for this stuff," I say to Timothy's reflection as he steps out of the walk-in. As beautiful as this dress is, my eyes are immediately drawn to the way Timothy wears his Tom Ford dress shirt. His sleeves are rolled, and he has one more button undone than most men would wear that shirt, but it works for him.

"I have an eye for you," he says.

I turn as he stalks up to me, ready to warn him not to mess up my hair and makeup, but he makes it to my lips first, grabbing me and kissing the hell out of me.

"I have a surprise for you," he whispers when he pulls back, eyes twinkling.

I smile. "I have something for you too."

"Yeah, you do," he growls, hand sliding over my ass and hauling me tight against him.

I let out a sigh full of feigned exasperation. "On the bed."

"Yes, ma'am." He sweeps me into his arms, carrying me to the bed while I scream at him about his head. He just laughs.

"I'm fine now. Good as new," he says, gently setting me on the edge of the mattress. "I'd be even better if you let me have a little taste."

His present is lying on the bed, so I snatch it and hand it to him before he can get under my skirt. His eyes widen in surprise and he turns the plain brown paper package over in his hands a few times before he tears into it.

They're just cotton jockey shorts, but I designed the fabric and printed them for him. Little Superman logos with a capital T inside, instead of an S.

He tackles me onto the bed and I scream about his head and my dress, but we're both laughing and kissing and after, he helps me back into the dress. He's on his best behavior as I reapply my makeup and fix the mess he made of my hair.

I forget about the surprise he has for me until the driver pulls up in the back of a building on Robertson Boulevard. We're running late for the wrap party already, but Timothy isn't remotely concerned and grins as he helps me out of the car.

"What's this?" I ask as he leads me to the heavy backdoor, pulling keys out of his pocket.

"You'll see," he says, letting us in.

The click of my heels echoes in the empty room as Timothy leads me through the back to the front of the shop.

It's beautiful, with clean lines and shiny surfaces.

He hands me the key. "This place is yours."

My jaw drops. "What?"

"We'll get some decorators in," he says, looking at the exposed rafters and lighting fixtures. "Make it more your style."

"I don't understand."

We both turn at the sound of footsteps and my jaw drops as Soraya Williams, the designer behind Mioe, steps into the room alongside Eric Kouame, who only makes the most elegant handbags and clutches, and oh my god. I must be high. I got into the edibles again. These two are already big names and they're only getting bigger—how the hell does Timothy know them?

"Perfect fit," Soraya says, looking at the dress I'm wearing. Her dress, which Timothy rumpled to hell. There is no way she can't see how badly we've treated it.

Timothy winks at me. "Couldn't agree more."

I open my mouth, but my words stick.

Timothy introduces us—he knows Eric from his gym and Soraya through a mutual friend and I'm pissed off he never told me. Or I would be if I could emote. Instead, I'm so starstruck he has to guide me through small talk. I can barely follow but it sounds like they're talking about this place as a small boutique that would sell Soraya's dresses, Eric's accessories, and my lingerie.

That can't be right. My subscription service is a little exclusive, but that's because I'm only one person with so many hours. Both their brands are environmentally conscious, but that's the only thing we have in common.

I'm not anywhere near this caliber. I can't put my thongs or period panties in the same room as a Mioe dress or an Eric Kouame clutch.

"I'm sorry," I finally manage to get out, smiling because I'm afraid my face is twitching. "I didn't...Timothy, what did you do?"

He grins and tugs me close, wrapping me in a one-armed hug. "You know how I needed a job?"

Oh no.

"I bought this building. I was told a lingerie shop wouldn't be enough to make the bills, even with nice stuff like yours, so I called up Soraya and Eric, and they agreed they wouldn't mind having a place in West Hollywood to sell some of their product."

I close my eyes and take a deep breath. When I open them, nothing's changed. "You...bought a building. Like that." I snap my fingers.

"Well...with a silent partner. I'm not buy-a-building-on-a-whim rich."

"Nic."

Timothy puts a finger to his lips as he looks at Soraya and Eric. "He's very silent, though."

I don't think I can breathe. The emptiness of the shop crowds in on me and all at once this perfect dress is too tight and my skin is crawling. I can hear Timothy making excuses to Soraya and Eric but I can't focus on the words. They talk, they leave, I still can't breathe and I'm gripping the counter for dear life.

"Baby." Timothy's warm hand touches me between the shoulder blades, and I shrug him off. "What's wrong?"

"You bought me a fucking building!" My voice rises until the last word rings out, echoing in the empty room.

He frowns. "You don't like it?"

"You didn't ask me!"

"I wanted to surprise you." He holds an arm out to me and I stare at it, knowing at once I need one of his hugs to bring my heart rate down, but if I accept one, I'll forgive him and I'm not ready to forgive him.

"My business, the one I have slowly, painstakingly built for years, is on the cusp of either booming or collapsing, I have major fashion companies approaching me, wanting to buy my label, I'm drowning in orders and people pissed off they missed out, and you thought now was a great time to drop this on me?"

His expression turns to one of alarm. "What are you talking about?"

"That influencer from your party—I've blown up and I'm over capacity. I can't do this. I can't." My voice breaks. "I don't want to do this anymore."

"You should've told me," he says, his hand faltering as he holds it out.

I need to hold on to my anger—it's the only thing keeping me from breaking—so I turn and stomp over to the window, away from him.

"You've always wanted to do this," he says calmly.

"You've known me for five years, how the hell would you know what I've always wanted?" Cars drive by outside. A couple walks down on the other side of the street. I'm standing in an empty shop in a gorgeous evening dress and my world is collapsing around me.

"Because I know you." He joins me at the window, his knuckles brushing the back of my arms. "You're scared you're going to make this leap and fail."

It hurts so much because it's true, and I know it's true and I can't make it okay. "Of course I'm scared. If I fail, I don't have a trust fund to fall back on. This is a fatal fall."

His arms slip around my waist and the warmth of his chest presses against the exposed skin of my back. "You aren't going to fall. But if you do, I'm here. I'm your safety net."

I wiggle out of his arms and walk back to the middle of the shop. It's not the shop on Aspen and Grand back in Connecticut, but I could see Wild Things here too. I'm still not ready to expand. I don't know when I'll be, or if I'll ever be. And Timothy can't keep fixing my life. I'm already too dependent on him, what will happen when we end? "I can't rely on you to always be there."

"Yes, you can." Hurt fills his voice. "Because I am always going to be here for you, Mina. This is what relationships are."

I cross my arms. "Until they aren't."

"What's that supposed to mean?"

My throat is burning and I swallow. "Things ended with your musician boyfriend. And when your ex-girlfriend wanted to move out East, you broke up."

His face pinches. "If you don't like this shop and you want to move back East, *ask me to come with you.*"

The anguish in his voice makes tears well up in my eyes. I should've told him about Charlotte's offer. Of course, he found out. I probably left a tab open on my laptop, or he overheard one of Charlotte's calls.

"Mina. Ask me."

"What if you say no?" My voice comes out like a whispered squeak and I hate it.

"I'm not going to say no to you. Not ever." His gaze is too much and I drop mine to the smooth hardwood floors.

"I haven't decided what I want to do, and all this—" I wave my arms around the shop, but I don't just mean this place. It's everything that's happened since that house party. "It's too much right now."

Timothy edges closer to me and I don't move away. Then he's next to me. "It's the perfect time to jump."

I sniffle and wipe a tear away. "So you bring me to the edge and push me off before I'm ready?" How can he not see I need time to build up to making these leaps? I need to be certain.

He reaches toward me with a tentative smile. "I hold my hands out to you and ask you to trust me and jump with me. I won't let you crash."

Unless it takes me so long to jump that something else catches his attention. I'm never going to be enough for him. I don't think I'm enough for myself right now. Wild Things hits its first major hiccup and I crumple. "I need to think about this."

Timothy nods but I can feel his disappointment in me, and suddenly I can't do tonight. I can't go to a party and pretend everything's okay because it's very much not okay.

He locks the shop and we go back to his house. When he helps me out of the car, I'm numb. "You go to the party," I tell him when he goes to follow me inside. "I need some space."

He looks crushed, his shoulders drooping, but he nods. When he holds out his arms, I walk into them and he holds me tight. His hugs really do help, but this is bigger than one hug.

"I love you," he whispers. "Please remember that."

"I love you, too," I say back. "Have fun tonight. Be careful."

He promises he will.

Chapter Twenty-Seven

Timothy

The whole private room at the venue goes silent when I walk in, then erupts in wild applause.

I grin, but I'm gritting my teeth to keep the scream inside.

When it goes on and on like a standing ovation, I take a quick bow and walk straight to the bar hoping to make it stop.

It's going to be a long night of having my accident and retirement shoved into my face. If I didn't feel obligated to be here, I'd be home trying to fix this mess I've made with Mina.

Nic is at the bar with his costar Greta Wilson, nursing a whiskey and looking like he wants to be anywhere else. Tonight, I'm going to attach myself to his side and use him like a shield.

Very Important People stop to talk to me, dancing around asking me not to sue. Since the only person to blame is me, I politely ignore their hints and openly take zero responsibility.

The cast and crew are better, but everyone wants a piece of me and I don't have that much to give. Nic leaves me for Stella—the way my night's going, I'm not surprised. They met years ago, before Addison. There was a spark between them, but Stella being a stunt driver was a hard limit.

They're out on the balcony with the rest of the stunt crew and a few of the rowdier actors. Instead of taking a seat beside Nic, I drop into the one next to

Stella before I realize the whole table is re-living my greatest hits.

Once I would have jumped in and told the stories myself. But I'm not that guy anymore, so I do my best to look more abashed than depressed as Curtis talks about the time I leaped across a series of crumbling rooftops—attached to a wire but I still had to make those jumps. Danny pipes in with a skydiving stunt. Stella talks about one where I clung to the truck she was driving. A few stories get silly—the time Danny wouldn't lower me off a wire until I admitted Armando's food truck was Arturo's after a rebrand. It's not, he's wrong, but I hung in an uncomfortable-ass harness for a while before I decided losing blood flow to key parts of my anatomy wasn't worth a slice of greasy pizza.

My colleagues are going to go out and make more movies and do more cool things and I'm not and Christ I miss it. I won't be setting any new records. I'll never be the Greatest Of All Time. What I've already accomplished will be topped by guys like Dex.

My skin is too tight, pent-up energy ready to burst out. I've never been still for this many weeks in my life and a future full of this crawly, itchy feeling stretches for an eternity. I can't do it. Deep down, I know I can't.

When they start talking about how I've inspired them, I can't take it anymore. I get up. I'm not dead and this shit belongs at the after-party of my funeral when I can't hear it.

Stella springs to her feet, pushing me back into my seat before walking around to grab two chairs from an empty table. Everyone watches as she places them about four feet apart.

My heart kicks up a notch.

"The Floor is Lava, friends," she says with a smile. "The throne is empty. You can judge, Timothy."

That chafes. I am undefeated at this game. I cross my arms and pretend her challenge doesn't sting. "Might as well, since none of you could beat me anyway."

Stella goes first, with an aerial twist. Simple and clean, she lands it easily. She's been practicing, but what she did I could do blindfolded.

Danny is light on his feet but his size is against him in this game and while he lands a simple flip on the second chair, he wobbles too much, jumping into the lava before he can fall.

With me out of the game, my money's on Curtis, but he passes on account of a pulled hamstring.

Dex steps up. He's been so quiet I forgot he was here. He rubs his hands on his pants, rolls his shoulders then perfectly executes the exact maneuver I did last year.

He shouldn't be a sore spot because I got the girl. But he got my job and I guess I'm still pissed I can't have both. I'm on my feet before I can help it, grabbing a third chair and placing it on the other side of a low gas fire fixture. The chairs are of the sturdy outdoor type and if they could take Danny, they can take me.

There's silence and I'm sure everyone is watching me, but I'm thinking this through. Studying the distance. Considering how much recovery will have set me back. I move the chair a few inches closer.

"Timothy," Nic grabs my arm, his voice low and firm. "Don't do this."

I shake him off. "Relax. This is kids' stuff."

"You promised."

"Not to do stunts. This isn't a stunt." It's very clearly Floor is Lava, which is not a stunt.

Nic gets up in my face. "I'll call her."

"Pfft." I'm not scared of my mother when we have the whole of the continental US between us. "Use my phone if you want. Tell her I say hi."

"Timothy."

I grab both of Nic's biceps and physically move him aside. "I've got this."

And I do. Easy. I climb onto the first chair, do an aerial cartwheel onto the second, and backflip over the fire onto the third. Perfect landing.

My friends all jump to their feet and hug me, clapping and cheering. *Timothy's back.*

I'm not back. I can never be back, why the fuck can't they see that?

Nic looks pissed, and when Stella takes his arm, he pulls away from her and storms off. She doesn't follow.

Danny brings me a beer, I'm declared victor. It's the shittiest-tasting victory I've ever had. Dex is good-natured about it, at least on the surface, and frankly, the surface is all I care about tonight.

I laugh, joke, drink, and honestly, I should win an Oscar for this because I'm a mess inside. Danny, Curtis, Stella, the hundreds of people I've worked with over the years—none of them will be my colleagues anymore.

It's bittersweet, heavy on the bitter.

I spy Dex all by himself, leaning against the rail and staring out at the city. Guess I'm not the only one feeling shitty. I try really hard not to care, but...I do. What happened on the bus wasn't his fault and I don't want to walk out tonight without resolving this.

Sighing, I grab two cold beers and walk over.

"Hey kid," I say, handing him one.

"Not a kid." He takes the beer but doesn't look at me.

"I was a bratty punk once, too," I say dryly.

Dex laughs but I can tell by the edge in it he's offended.

"You're good." I tip my beer toward him. "One day you might even be great. Maybe as good as me." I am mostly, slightly, joking.

He exhales slowly, his eyes tracking across the view. I imagine he wants to throttle me. "Right."

We stand in silence for a while, drinking beer and staring at the city and it's almost companionable except for the thick tension. "I was hers since the moment I saw her," I finally tell him. "She was mine sometime after that. Doesn't excuse the way I treated you on set that day. I'm sorry."

Dex nods and swigs his beer.

I frown, staring out at the city as I take a deep drink. I could've walked away. Fallen back on my professionalism. It's my fault. Not his, not Mina's.

My beer tastes bitter. I set the bottle in a nearby potted plant. "I was frustrated," I tell him. "With myself, with her. With you, for somehow getting her to agree to a date when she'd been turning me down for five years. I let it get in my head and took it out on you, and I'm sorry."

The silence stretches again and I'm about to clap him on the shoulder, say

"Good talk," and walk away, when he says, "I don't think she was saying yes to me when I asked her out."

I cock my head and squint, but nope. I don't see it.

"I saw the two of you at the bar when we arrived. Before you saw us. When I asked for her number later, she told me she hadn't dated in a long time. I think when she said yes to me, she was signaling she was ready. To you. I was never going to get more than a drink with her."

Huh.

Nah. He doesn't know Mina. She doesn't do subtle well. If she'd wanted me to know she was open to us, she would've done something.

Unless she was scared. Because as much as I love this woman, she's a chicken. If she was scared, she wouldn't make a move. She'd stand there, waiting and hoping I'd figure it out, like…

Wait a second.

Like at the bowling alley. When I almost kissed her. If she hadn't wanted me, she'd have smacked me for being handsy and presumptive.

Danny interrupted us.

Dammit, things might have worked out differently. I could've had Mina and my job, maybe. No accident. No retirement. Beer roils in my stomach as I imagine everything I lost in that one moment of hesitation.

I should've jumped, not waited.

I want to hit something. And that something is my old boss.

Already looking around the room for my target, I clap Dex on the shoulder. "I have to murder Danny. All the best, Dex." I mean it. The *all the best* part, not the murder part. Dex reminds me enough of me that I hope he can reach the top, even if it means he erases me.

That lasts all of ten seconds before I admit to myself those hopes are lies. I don't hope he'll be better than me, but I do accept he might be, or someone else will.

I'm halfway through the restaurant, headed toward Danny when Nic steps directly into my path.

"I have to say it," he says in his most authoritative voice.

I'm tempted to blow past him, but might as well get whatever this is over with now. "Say it."

"You didn't train to be a stunt driver because I asked you not to."

Okay...not what I was expecting. I narrow my eyes at him. "Yeah, and the whole wide world of every other stunt was there for me at the time. What's your point?"

"I'm asking you. As your friend and as the person who doesn't want to be blamed for your death by your twin sister, who will look up the most painful ways to end me—don't ever do the type of shit you did tonight again."

I laugh it off. "That wasn't a stunt. And Jessie—"

"Doing acrobatics between wobbly restaurant chairs on a concrete balcony does not prove dick size," Nic snaps, interrupting me.

I shake my head. "You don't know that, though. Have you seen Danny naked? More inches than the internet attributes to you."

Nic doesn't laugh. "If you won't do this for me, do it for Mina."

"You don't know a thing about Mina."

"I was worried she'd hurt you," he says, "but you're going to hurt her."

I'm never going to hurt her. That he would even suggest it pisses me off. And how dare he assume she'd be on his side? She knows me. She trusts me.

"I'm only going to say this once," I say to him through gritted teeth. "I'm going to live my life and that might involve jumping off my balcony into the pool, or doing some backflips off a chair, or fucking Mina on a poorly installed sex swing."

A muscle in Nic's jaw ticks and he looks five seconds from violence. "Timothy, you almost *died*."

"You need to trust that I know what I can safely do, and that I've judged a situation to be low-risk. If you can't do that, mind your own fucking business."

He mutters something under his breath and walks away.

Great. I'm fighting with both my best friends and I don't even remember what I was doing before Nic interrupted me.

Doesn't matter, because the noise falls away, the entire room dims, and time slows the moment my eyes catch her.

Mina.

I take off at a run—or as much of one as I can in this crowd—and she braces just before I tackle her into a wall.

"You came." I am not going to start sobbing into her hair because I've missed her. Maybe a sniffle.

"You have no respect for this dress," she complains and I laugh because she might be mad at me about buying that building, but she came for me. She's still choosing me.

"That's why you're here, isn't it?" I joke. "To show off that hot as hell dress some thoughtful, sexy man bought you."

Her fingers are cool on my heated skin, sweeping over my cheeks. Her eyes are so tender I think I am going to cry a bit, because how did I get this lucky?

"I'm here to take you home," she says softly.

"You aren't mad at me?"

"I'm overwhelmed," she admits. "I thought I needed some space to sort it all out and make some decisions, but I don't want to do it alone. I need my best friend. I want to talk it over with you, without you fixing everything for me. Then maybe tacos and porn."

This woman speaks my language. I will put that damn ring on her finger if it's the last thing I do. But right now, I grab her hand and pull her toward the door. "We can be home in...way too long. I'm going to have to do things to you in the car, it can't be helped. Might want to take your panties off right now."

Mina laughs and I feel a million pounds lighter. We're going to be okay. We're going to talk out her problem and my impulsive gift, find a solution, and do it together.

Chapter Twenty-Eight

Mina

"Whatever you decide, I'm keeping the property as an investment," Timothy announces as he flips a strip of bacon the next morning.

He's wearing nothing but the jockey shorts I made him and a pink polka dot apron he found in a drawer, his mom's name embroidered over the chest. Every splatter of grease that manages to hit flesh makes him go "ow" in a quiet but gravely offended voice and I am not-so-secretly enjoying that he's tolerating the pain to give me a view.

"I made some promises to Soraya and Eric," he continues, "and it'll get Mom off my back about jobs for a little while. Plus, Nic will give me shit for putting him through a PowerPoint presentation for nothing if I bail."

My jaw drops. "You made a PowerPoint presentation?"

He grins at me over his shoulder. "It was all slides of models wearing Mioe dresses or standing around naked holding Eric's handbags. Don't get too excited."

I laugh, but I'm relieved. I don't want Soraya and Eric to lose out if I can't jump. I still don't know what to do about...well, any of my problems. Including his shop. "I'm still impressed."

"Yeah, you are." He winks at me and returns his attention to the bacon. "So the way I understand it, we have two separate but potentially related decisions to make."

"Yeah." Last night we cuddled, and cuddling turned into the softest, slowest, most intense sex of my life, and this morning I've been filling him in on all the things I hadn't told him about.

He's approaching this in a calm, rational manner, and it's making me feel better. We're tackling it as a team.

Timothy pokes at the bacon in the pan with the spatula, wincing when some grease spatters his hand. "Do we move to Connecticut so you can take on a lease your friend is offering, or do we stay here? If we stay here, do you want to have space in my shop to sell your product?"

That's the big decision.

"And the second—*ow*, stupid bacon—is what to do about your supply-demand problem."

I groan. That is the pressing one that could make the big problem moot if I fail. It's the one I don't want to deal with.

"So the big one." Either he's drawn to big or he doesn't want to solve my immediate problem either. "We have more connections here, but I'm not sure that matters. If you want to go home, we'll make new connections." Timothy stops, spatula midair, and turns to look at me. The look in his eyes...it's not hurt, exactly. But close. "Are you going to ask me to come with you, or do I need to invite myself? You didn't ask last night."

He's coming, whether I ask or not, and that makes me smile. "If I decide to go, I'll ask you to come with me. But it's a lot, asking you to uproot your whole life to move with me."

"I'm retired and my family is out there. I wouldn't call it uprooting my whole life."

"Your friends are here."

He points the spatula at me. "Believe it or not, I have friends back home too."

"Nic's here," I point out. I don't need to say more.

"Yeah..." He goes back to the bacon. "I have a plan for that."

I take a sip of my coffee. "You have a plan."

"I do." His voice is full of glee. "And I can't tell you," he adds, "because we aren't married and if it all goes wrong, I'm going to need you to claim spousal privilege."

I arch a brow at him. "What, are you committing a crime?"

He grins. "Worse."

I set my coffee on the table. "Okay, now I need to know."

He points the spatula at me again. "Not until you husband me."

"Timothy. Tell me. Right now."

He mimes zipping his lips and starts taking bacon out of the pan.

"Fine," I say, picking up my coffee and preparing for a little psychological warfare.

"Fine, you'll marry me?" he asks casually, reaching for a bowl.

I watch the way his muscles move from the simple task of picking up a bowl. The way the Kraken tattoo moves. "Fine, you can keep your secret plans secret. Besides, I already know what they are."

He dumps the beaten eggs into the pan and turns to me with an alarmed look on his face. "You do?"

"Of course I do." I grin and sip my coffee. "It's obvious."

"It's not obvious," he grumbles at the pan as he scrambles the eggs. "There isn't a plan yet."

A-ha! Knew it.

"I could help you with the plan."

He flashes me a quick wink as he whips the apron off. "You could help me with something else."

I take a pointed sip of my coffee and bring us back to the problems at hand. "So I can't make three thousand panties by the end of August. My options are to piss off clients by canceling a bunch of orders, hire some help and hope the quality doesn't take a dive, or sell my brand to the highest bidder and let them tank everything I've worked for while I start from scratch with a pile of money." The pile of money is the only appealing part of that option. I don't want to start over.

"Hiring help is your best option," Timothy says, and we agree. But that starts the next chain of problems.

"Then I have people who depend on me for their job and livelihood. What happens if I can't pay them? I'm not even sure I could pay them, plus the cost of all the materials I need. What about dental insurance? I'm sure there are papers I'd need to file." Panic has already wrapped a fist around my chest and started to squeeze, and when Timothy sets a plate heaped with fruit, eggs, bacon, and toast in front of me, I nearly dry heave. My plan was always to go to business school before trying to expand. So I'd know this shit.

"I can take care of it." Timothy sits next to me, smiling and shoveling a forkful of eggs into his mouth.

"What part of it?"

He swallows and elbows me. "All of it."

"No."

"Come on. Hire me. I need a job, apparently, so hire me and I'll make all these problems go away. Then we can have hot but forbidden boss-employee sex and I won't report you to HR."

I stare at him. "Do you listen to yourself?"

He glances down at his lap and nods with a comically impressed look on his face. "Yeah, obviously I do when I'm talking about banging you on the desk in your office. Hey, let's go desk shopping today."

Why am I with this overgrown man-child? I'm smiling into my coffee, though, and that's why. He makes me laugh. Drags me out of my head where I'm spiraling and makes everything feel possible.

"Between the two of us," Timothy says, his voice serious again, "we must know enough out-of-work costume crew. People in between jobs or looking to make a little extra money on the side. Maybe some fashion school students. What if we offer a one-time contract, pay well, drop off supplies, pick up the finished product, and you do quality control, giving bonuses based on that? Then you do the embroidery and we have a few friends over to help pack everything and ship it out."

I give him a hard look at that last suggestion, given this all started because he had a few friends over, but maybe it's not a bad idea.

We talk over details while we eat, and make a plan. By the end of the day, we've found twelve people willing to take on about thirty hours of sewing over three weeks for well above the minimum wage. It's going to eat into my profits, but I think it will work. Since it's a part-time, one-off gig and everyone can work from home, I don't need to worry about dental or trying to set up a workspace or anything like that.

Though I might take Timothy up on the desk sex.

It's a little harder to get enough off-cast fabric that will be cohesive with the line and I have some decisions to make, so I spend the afternoon collecting scraps and hanging out in my storage unit with my swatch book and fabric hoard. It takes all day, but I come up with something I'm happy with.

Thanks to the money I've made hanging out with my best friend and keeping him out of trouble, I can afford this. I have time. Thanks to Timothy, we have a plan.

"Tell me I'm the fucking greatest," he says when we're in bed later that night, pulling my leg up his hip as he thrusts into me.

I can't even laugh because I'm so close, but I kiss him and claw him as close to me as possible because I can't get enough of him. And when we drift off to sleep, tangled in each other, I finally feel like I'm enough.

Chapter Twenty-Nine

Mina

Now that we have a plan, I'm less panicked. I'm a little excited, even. Timothy and I bundle fabric, delivering it to the wardrobe people who were interested in the extra work, along with instructions for what I need from each of them.

I'm still terrified it won't work. My brain enjoys conjuring up all the ways I'm going to fail, but Timothy does his best to help me when I'm sewing and distract me when I'm not. Watching him carefully pin elastic to the fabric, his tongue sticking out as he concentrates, makes my heart all full and happy. He rubs my shoulders when I take a break and massages the stiffness from my fingers at night. He makes sure I'm eating and drinking enough water and threatens to carry me away from my machines when I refuse to finish by 8 p.m.

I need to be done with my part before the product starts coming in from the people I've contracted work out to, but he has a point and I'm grateful he's looking after me because right now, I can't. Not when I still have hundreds of panties to sew. Thousands to embroider.

Timothy left with Jax a while ago for a light workout, making me promise to stop for a small break every hour. I'm drinking a hazelnut latte and looking over the piles of work I have to get done today when my phone rings.

I glance at the screen—I'm getting calls about Wild Things and I'm not in the mood to talk to anyone trying to buy me out or add their name to the list—but when I see it's Celia, I answer.

"Mina."

Something in the way she says my name makes the little hairs on the back of my neck rise.

"We're paying you to stop Timothy from doing dangerous shit. What happened?"

Timothy.

Fear throws me to my feet, ready to run to the door, but where the hell are my keys? I freeze and scan the surfaces around me. When I speak, it's around my heart, lodged and thumping in my throat. "Is he okay? He went to the gym with Jax, I don't—"

Her voice softens. "He's fine, he hung up on me a few minutes ago."

"Thank god," I whisper as I sink into my chair.

I think I'm going to be sick. As awful as that first phone call after his accident was, this is worse. The way my heart is slamming adrenaline through my body has me shaking. And for what? Timothy's fine, he fought with his mother, probably over something ridiculous. Maybe over the investments I'm still not comfortable with Timothy making in my life. "Is this about the panties?"

"The *what*?" Celia's stunned voice makes me cringe.

"His investment in them? Well, in a property that—"

"Honey, I have no clue what you're talking about and I don't give two shits what that boy does with his money so long as it's legal. I'm talking about the stunt he pulled at the wrap party and how I'm paying you to keep him from doing that shit. Talking him down, physically restraining him, I don't care what it takes—"

Stunt.

He...

No, he wouldn't.

He promised.

"What stunt?" I ask when I manage to find my voice. "I had a—thing, so I arrived late." I don't want her to know Timothy and I fought and she won't care about Wild Things, so I leave it at that. "We left after I arrived."

"I'll send you the video," she says. "It went viral enough for his older sister to see it and she sent it to me. You weren't there?"

Her tone sparks my anger, and I'm already primed by the adrenaline I can't handle. "No, you said I didn't have to be with him all the time."

"I said to use your judgment," she snaps. "Timothy went to a party where his colleagues—other stunt professionals—would be, where there was alcohol, where he might feel the need to prove himself. No offense, honey, but I'm starting to think your judgment might not be the best."

"*My* judgment?" My voice rises sharply. I might not be loud and brash but I am not a pushover. I don't care if she is Celia Foley—she's not talking to me that way. "You hired someone you didn't know to babysit your son, who, by the way, is an adult and can make his own choices."

God, she's right, though. I should've been there.

I turn around and Timothy's standing two feet away, beaming at me. I jump, clutching my chest and glaring at him. How long has he been standing there?

Celia's reply is immediate and barbed. "I thought if Nic got him to stay away from stunt driving, the woman he wants to marry can keep him from the rest. Clearly, I was wrong."

"I'll return your money," I say coolly, though I have no idea how when I've spent a lot of it. I end the call and throw my phone onto the sofa.

I'm going to scream. After I throw up.

"That," Timothy says with a smile, walking toward me, "was hot. You stood up to Celia Foley. Nobody does that."

"You hung up on her," I point out. My phone chimes. Incoming message. I walk over to it to avoid Timothy. I need a moment. This can't be happening. He wouldn't.

"Yeah, but I'm her son. She expects it from me." He sinks onto the sofa and pats the cushion next to him. "Thank you for taking my side. I was questioning whether I was an adult allowed to make choices. I'm almost thirty-four, for Christ's sake—"

Timothy's talking, but I'm not listening. Celia's sent the video with a message that says 4:05. I skip ahead to that spot and press play.

In the video, Timothy jumps onto a chair. I'm sure there's some technical gymnastic-related word for what he does next, but I don't know it. And though I do know he makes it safely—he's alive and uninjured on the sofa in front of me—my heart still goes berserk. When he flips over a fire, I forget how to breathe. Even when he's safely on the ground, I still stare at the screen, waiting for something, anything, to go wrong.

"See?" Timothy takes the phone out of my hands and rewinds it, sinking back on the couch to watch. "She's overreacting. No one dies from The Floor is Lava."

Probably someone has. Timothy easily could've, if he'd hit his head. My brain barely touches that thought and the effect is like touching an electric fence.

Timothy's a fucking tiger and I'm holding his tail.

I jolt into action, and that action is flight.

"Mina!"

I'm already taking the stairs two at a time. I pull the suitcase out from under the bed in my old room, open it, and start throwing clothes in.

"You can't be serious," Timothy says, incredulous, from my doorway.

"You broke your promise to me!" I'm not sure where that shout comes from. Some deep part of my splintering heart.

"That wasn't a stunt," he says, sounding annoyed. "A stunt is like…jumping out of a helicopter or getting tugged around on wires or—"

"I know what stunts are, Timothy," I snap, throwing a T-shirt into my suitcase.

"My point is," he says, forcing some calm back into his voice. "Jumping from chair to chair isn't a stunt. Backflips and cartwheels and all that shit? Not stunts. They don't count."

Of course, he thinks they don't count. Somehow, I've forgotten who this man is. I let him lull me into a false sense of security when I should've known better.

Goddammit, I'm a dumbass.

The leggings in my hand drop into my suitcase as I sink to my knees. It was a mistake to get involved with Timothy. Despite all the ways I was wrong about him—the casual dating and lack of real relationships—I was right about this. Timothy is a wild creature, and those can't be tamed. Not by a serious head injury. Not, it turns out, by me.

I wonder what else doesn't count, and suddenly, I know. "The snowboard? The climbing gear? The motorcycle? You were never going to give those up, were you?"

He doesn't deny it. "I'm giving up the career I love at a time when I'm at the top. That's a lot."

"It's not enough," I say, my voice wavering as I stare at him. I'm not enough. Like Celia said. "You gave up stunt driving for Nic because his parents died in a car crash, didn't you? You loved him enough to make that sacrifice. Why can't you do this for me?"

He sighs and leans against the door frame. "Because when I gave up stunt driving, I still had everything else. It was a small thing I wasn't as interested in. I love you, Mina. More than anyone else. But I can't stop being who I am. You wouldn't love me if I were someone else."

He can't stop being himself, and I can't be with someone like him. I'm not strong enough. The worry and the fear will gnaw away at me until I snap. Or I'll hold him back until he resents me. Either way, we'll never make it.

"You are more than what you do," I say, sniffling. "If the most exciting, daring thing you ever did was run to the grocery store on Christmas Eve to pick something up for me, I would still love you."

Timothy steps closer, crouching next to me, to brush the tear away. "Baby, it was a flip off of a chair. I was careful."

"You were careless with me." Anger pushes the words out, but they don't sound angry. They sound sad. The effect they have on Timothy is devastating. His eyes drop, his face going pale. His shoulders shake when he draws a breath and if I stay any longer, I'm going to wrap my arms around him and forgive him. We'll move on and things will be great until the next time. And the time after. Because Timothy will never change.

I can't let myself love him anymore. I need to let go before it's too late.

"I have to go," I mumble, pushing to my feet and yanking the suitcase with me. "I'll come back for the rest of my stuff in a couple of days."

"So that's it?" He's already on his feet, blocking my way to the door. "Can't we talk about this?"

"Why?" I push a tear off my face. "We'll never find something acceptable to both of us."

"We could try."

"I can't do this. I don't think you can either." I push past him. He doesn't stop me and that hurts too. "You've given up a lot like you've said. You aren't willing to give up any more. I get that, and I hate it, but I'm not going to live my life terrified every time my phone rings. Wondering whenever you aren't with me if you're going to decide today is the day to climb the...the..." Why can't I think of a single tall building in all of California? I give up and make an irritated motion with my hand that I hope he understands. "...just to prove you're better than everyone."

Timothy follows me out onto the stairs. "Is that who you think I am?"

"Isn't it?"

When he stares at me with a hurt look on his face, I continue down the steps, my suitcase thumping loudly on each one. He's still standing on the stairs when I make it to the door.

Our eyes meet. I don't want it to end like this. I don't want it to end at all. Unshed tears fill his eyes and his usual confident posture droops like it's taking all the strength he has to stay on his feet.

I don't know what to say. Goodbye is too final and even though I need to say it, I can't. Timothy was my best friend for so long. I hope we can find our way back to that place again one day, but right now I need to take care of my heart.

I open the door and jump. Nic's standing there, hand reaching for the doorknob. He looks upset. Guess Celia called him too.

"You should've stopped him," I growl because I'm pissed at Timothy and every person who was with him that night who stood by and did nothing.

"I know," Nic admits, looking at my suitcase and frowning.

"Can you get me out of here?" I can't handle LA traffic right now and it's the least he can do for doing nothing. I shove past him and head toward his car.

Chapter Thirty

Timothy

When Nic looks up at me, I nod. I still have Mina's phone. I hold it out until he comes into the house so I can drop it into his hands. "Take care of her?"

"Go talk to her," Nic hisses.

I can't. She won't listen. "You're my best friend, but so is she. Just…be there for her. She needs somewhere to stay and she'll be safe at your house from everything except hideous concept art and your random hookups." I can't pull off the light tone I'm going for and it comes out sounding mean.

Nic points a finger at me in warning, but I think we've both had our fill. He doesn't bust my nuts again over the harmless little chair gymnastics and I don't ask him to put Mina in a hotel so she won't have to suffer through the purgatory aesthetic of his house.

The door closes with a finality that makes my skin itch. I don't know what to do with myself, but I need to move. Something grabs hold of me and I march out onto my balcony. The rail is cold under my hands. It would be easy to swing my legs over and cannonball into the pool. Simply because I want to. Because I know I can do it and I won't hurt myself and I'm so fucking angry.

Instead, I take a deep breath and let it out in a scream loud enough I'll probably get a police check-in courtesy of the neighbors.

I go back into the house, but I can't stay in this room. Not when my pillows smell like Mina's shampoo and her dirty clothes are in my hamper. I go downstairs, but I can't look at the couch without remembering our first time.

My house is hers. My heart is hers. I don't know what to do with either now that she doesn't want them.

I stomp down to the basement. I don't bother to turn on the lights, just wrap a throw blanket around my shoulders and flop on the couch.

She's gone. She's my best friend, and she walked out and I have never once in the five years I've known her thought she could do that to me. Not Mina.

Does no one on this planet understand me? I'm not complicated.

I thought Mina could see through everything everyone thinks they know about me, into my gooey center where she found something worthwhile. She told me I'm more than my old job, more than the things I do for fun.

All I am to her is a walking risk. She never saw me at all.

I wake disoriented and alone in the dark, my phone buzzing in my pocket.

There's one moment of breathing space before reality crashes in on me and I remember Mina's gone, probably forever. My mom's pissed at me. Nic too.

I have no job. No life.

Everything sucks the big one.

When I see Nic's number on the screen, I greedily swipe to accept the call. My voice fails when I answer, coming out in a croak. "How is she?"

"Crying in her room. I'm assuming your mom told her about your stupid Floor is Lava bullshit," he says.

Even alone in the dark, I wince. "Yeah."

"And did you learn your lesson?"

That sounds snarky and condescending, and it pisses me off. "Yeah. The love of my life left me. Turns out she never really knew me."

"Yeah, sounds about right." Nic's voice is so thick with sarcasm I want to reach through the phone and hit him.

"She wants me to be someone else."

"No, she wants you to be yourself. You can do that without trying to prove you're indestructible."

I grab the nearest throw pillow and put it over my head. "You don't get it either." It's not about proving myself or having something to brag about. Those are perks—can't deny it—but they aren't why I do things.

"Explain it."

The demand catches me by surprise, and for about thirty seconds I toy with whether to answer it. Finally, I sigh and decide to go with the truth. "I get twitchy."

"You get twitchy," he repeats, his voice flat.

I blow out a frustrated breath. Why am I bothering? He still won't understand. "Certain activities help me focus and find a sense of calm, making me feel better. More relaxed."

Not sure, but I think I hear him grinding his teeth over the phone. "Run a fucking marathon and take up meditation. You don't need to hurtle yourself through the air to get some exercise."

"A marathon doesn't sound fun." It sounds like chafed nipples.

"Then I guess you have to ask yourself if the fun you want to have is worth losing the woman you've spent the last five years in love with."

God, that's not what this is. It's not a choice I can make. "I can't be someone I'm not."

"You aren't what you do," Nic counters, probably thinking he's winning.

"Exactly! And Mina said the same, but that's all she sees me as. I'm some reckless guy, impulsively going through life without a thought or a care in the world." I retired for her, can't she see that? The doctors and my parents might have been able to dissuade me for a while, but the only thing keeping me from trying to sneak back into my career is Mina.

"Mina didn't want to talk about it, so I can't speak for her, but you're wrong."

I make a dismissive sound. "I'm not worth the risk. That's what this is."

"She took a chance on you, and you betrayed her trust for a game of The Floor is Lava."

"She's going to need her stuff," I say, changing the subject because I'm tired of not being understood, of having two different conversations. "Her sewing equipment, especially. I'm going to bring it over." I don't want her to lose even a minute of the time she needs.

Nic sighs. "Why don't you come to talk to her? I'd rather you two work shit out."

Same, but she didn't think it was possible. She's already made up her mind and I need to respect that.

Chapter Thirty-One

Mina

I WAKE IN A halo of tissues, clutching the box to my chest.

I left Timothy.

That's all it takes to wring a few thousand more tears from my eyes. I'm in one of Nic's guest bedrooms, still wearing my clothes from yesterday, and my heart is mashed to a pulp.

I miss Timothy. I want him to hold me and tell me he'll make everything better. I want to believe he can.

On some level, I knew this would happen—it was the reason I wanted to keep him in the friend zone, even after I realized my attraction. Keeping my heart safe and keeping myself a functioning adult...those things were important to me.

They need to be important to me now. Even though I don't want to get up, I have to find it in me to go back to Timothy's for my sewing stuff. I can't lose him and my business. I won't survive.

I throw on some yoga pants and a T-shirt and go looking for Nic. I'm going to need him to drop me off.

Every surface in Nic's house is shiny and reflective, white on white with the occasional startling slab of charcoal gray. None of the furniture looks welcoming. I don't know how he stands it.

That it fits my state of mind makes it worse. Every thought is a reflection of what went wrong and I can't escape it into some cozy corner because there aren't any.

I've lost my best friend and the man I love.

I stop short at a glass wall. Nic has a home gym.

This house might be the physical manifestation of my pain, but there's a place for me to work through it and fight. This is what I need right now. I'll go to Timothy's for my stuff after.

I hit the gym hard. Maybe too hard. A couple of minutes in and the seam bursts on the punching bag, spilling sand onto the floor like a broken hourglass while I gape at it, trying to catch my breath.

I feel Nic in the doorway before I look up. "It was poorly made," I say.

He doesn't look convinced.

When I move to clean it up, he tells me not to, but something in my eyes makes him reconsider. He brings me a broom and dustpan before he disappears again.

I think he's scared of me.

The door of the guest bedroom next to mine is wide open when I head back to my room to shower, so I stop and stick my head in.

All my sewing stuff from Timothy's place is here, the plastic tubs lined next to the bed, the workstation set up below a window with a view to the backyard. My machines are still in their cases, but everything looks organized.

I open a tub at random and pull out a pair of teal period panties waiting to be embroidered, and my heart tears in half. Maybe my entire being tears in half.

It's over, then.

He's not going to try to get me back.

I expected...I don't know. It's unfair, but I expected him to fight for us, to realize that I'm what he really wants, and throw himself at my feet, begging me to reconsider.

I love him so damn much and yeah, I walked out, but deep down I wasn't ready for this to be over. How can he let it be over when he spent five years waiting for me?

Tears fall down my face as I close the door and sink to the floor to cry. He must have realized I'm not worth it. He's made his choice, and it's not me. It's the adrenaline. I should've kept my stupid heart to myself. Buried my feelings for him. At least then we'd still be friends.

I can't cry all day, but I give myself some time to let it out before I push back to my feet and return to my room to shower. When I return to my new sewing room, I'm empty and numb.

My movements are automatic as I set up my sewing machines. My serger is on the left, my coverstitch machine on the right. I'll set the embroidery machine up later, but right now I need something that will force me to focus. I grab the next bundle of unfinished panties and sit down to work.

My grandmother used to sew while we waited for my parents to come home. I was too young to remember, but she told me how we'd wait, trying not to watch the clock, and the memory of her sad eyes bubbles up now. The steady rhythm of her machine filled the space where she held her breath, waiting for them. I absorbed her dread like a sponge. I still feel it.

Years passed, and I was the one promising her I'd be back. From my first summer job, from a date, from a night with my friends. She'd be up sewing until I came home. One night, when I stayed out too late, she told me if she could smash every mountain, every cliff face, to bits with a hammer to stop my parents from climbing, she would in a heartbeat. I never stayed out too late again.

I get it. If I could smash all the shit Timothy loves...

That would make me an awful person. He loves it and he deserves to have it and I need to accept Timothy isn't for me.

I miss him anyway.

Everything about him. His smile, his laugh, the way he touches me, his cocky attitude. I miss his quiet moments when he just holds me and sighs happily. The way he challenges me and pushes me outside my comfort zones. I miss him as a friend, as the person I turn to first, as the one who is always there for me.

I want to run back to him, but I don't see a way through this for us and I don't want to be there when...when...

When he miscalculates.

I couldn't live with the guilt of knowing I wasn't enough for him to stop. I wasn't enough for my parents and they left me an orphan. If they had loved me more. If Timothy loved me more.

It's hopeless. Sooner rather than later I'm going to have to figure out how to live with this massive gap in my life. I'll have to move on. Make decisions about Wild Things and my future.

That day is not today. Today, all I can do is sew.

Chapter Thirty-Two

Timothy

THE NEXT TIME I wake, it sounds like someone is pounding on my door with a jackhammer. They don't go away, so I stumble upstairs and open the door. Bright morning sunshine assaults my eyes and I move to block it with my forearm, but Danny shoves a duffle bag into my hands, followed by a My Little Pony backpack and a brown paper bag from a French patisserie.

"The fuck?" I ask, blinking.

"Language," he hisses, clapping his hands on the shoulders of his mini-me. His five-year-old daughter beams at me with the most adorable smile. Freya is exactly like her dad, but has the good sense to dote on me.

"Sorry, kiddo," I say, arranging my load so I can get a fist bump. Then she's off like a shot to explore my house. "Stay out of the bedroom at the top of the stairs!" I holler after her. I doubt Danny would appreciate Freya wielding a dildo sword. Or holding it to her forehead pretending to be a unicorn.

Danny pushes past me. "Heard you had a room," he says simply. "Thought we might take a mini-vacation to Uncle Timbo's house to swim in his pool and eat all his food."

Great. I pinch the bridge of my nose. "Is my mother paying you?"

He turns a grim look at me. "Remember when Linnea and I were going through the divorce and she was in Sweden on business and I broke my leg? You came over every day to play with Freya and walk the dogs. You made sure Freya had something other than Spaghetti-O's or frozen waffles for dinner. But even if you hadn't done any of that, we're here to look after you now. Would've been after the accident, if we were needed."

I don't know what to say to that or how to feel about it. Gratitude, embarrassment, and a whole lot of self-pity.

Danny heads straight to my kitchen. I drop the food on the table, drop Danny and Freya's bags in the room next to Mina's, and head to my room to shower. When I come back down, Danny and Freya are eating croissants.

We talk about movies for a while, because Freya has questions and opinions, but when our conversation turns to industry gossip, she gets bored and wanders off.

"Mina left you?" Danny finally asks in a gentle tone at odds with the sheer size of his tattooed ass. It isn't a question. He's heard everything from someone. Possibly from Mina.

I nod.

"That sucks," Danny says with a shake of his head. "You two were good together."

We were. It sucks. I thought losing my job was the worst thing that could happen to me. Turns out my imagination was lacking. Now I get the fun part of learning how to live without her.

"It's for the best," I say even though I don't believe it, getting up to refill our coffees.

"Are you fucking kidding me?" Danny asks, twisting in his chair to gape at me.

"Language!" Freya calls out in a sing-song voice. When I look up—and up and up—and see her clinging to the rail of my staircase, my heart leaps into my throat.

"What is she doing up there?" I hiss at Danny.

He glances her way and shrugs. "Climbing."

"If she falls—" The open stairwell goes from the basement to the second floor. Waist-high metal railings wrap around the stairs, but where Freya's climbing—up on the second floor—if she falls, she's small enough she might go through the gap straight down to the basement. My ceilings are high and my room is half a floor above the rest of the second floor, so it's a nearly four-story fall on a body only three and a half feet tall.

Danny brushes croissant crumbs off his chest. "I've been watching her climb since before she could walk. Thousands and thousands of mini-heart attacks, man. I know what she's capable of, but more importantly, she knows what she's capable of."

I trust Danny's assessment of his kid, but it's like a bucket of ice water dumped over my head. He gets it about his spawn and lets her go, trusting her capabilities. Why can't Mina—or my mom or Nic or my twin—get it about me?

"You know," Danny says after a moment where we both watch Freya climb back down to the landing, "sometimes she goes too high. She gets herself into unfamiliar territory and she gets scared. The fear sticks her in place and I have to remind her she can handle it. Sometimes I have to climb up and show her how. Other times, she works it out herself."

I take a sip of coffee. "She's lucky to have you."

"When was the last time you were so scared you got stuck?" Danny asks.

I shrug because I can't remember. I like the thrill. It doesn't scare me—it invigorates me. It pushes aside everything else and for a few blessed moments, there is a calm focus in my head.

The last time I felt fear? Real fear? Probably the day my homemade zip line came apart and Jessie landed on Nic. The metal pipe I'd found for a handle hit him near the eye and there was so much blood. Jessie was screaming, and I didn't know if she was hurt or scared for Nic. I froze up. Didn't know what to do.

Nothing since.

Yeah, I was scared to tell Mina how I felt for years, but that's a different kind of fear. Not what Danny's talking about. Right?

"Think about it," Danny says, tapping his temple like I'm missing something.

My phone rings and any hopes that it's Mina die when I see who it is.

If I don't answer, I run the risk of Mom hopping on the next flight to LA and I'll be in even bigger trouble for messing up her schedule.

"I'd better take this," I say.

I go to my room and flop across my bed. It smells like Mina and sex and all things good that now make me incredibly sad. "Hey, Mom," I say flatly, putting the phone on speaker and pulling a pillow over my head. Might as well take a nap while she yells at me.

Over the next twenty-four hours, the following texts appear on my phone:

> I swear to god Timbo, do not make me come to LA

JESSIE (EVIL TWIN)

> You need to call Mina and work this stuff out. Better yet, come over.

NIC

> Hey dickhead, if you don't respond to my texts I am going to book the next flight and you'd better go into hiding because when I get my hands on you . . .

JESSIE (EVIL TWIN)

> Mina can have my house. Can I move back in with you?

NIC

> You can't ignore me forever. When you're ready to talk, to me or Mina, let me know.

NIC

> She broke my gym. Timothy, she's SCARY.

Nic

I toss both Jessie and Nic into a group chat with me titled TIMOTHY FOLEY FAN CLUB. Jessie immediately leaves the chat. Nic doesn't see it. Or is too scared to look.

One day, when I can figure out how to get back on my feet, I'm going to get those two together.

Who am I kidding? Mina's hit me with a knockout and I am not getting back up. Nic and Jessie are on their own.

"Daddy says you're dumber than a brick wall," Freya says after bouncing a beachball off my head. We're in the pool, with this little piranha-child standing in the shallows and me out deeper. It's been a week since Mina left. I think. Time doesn't matter right now, but a million years feels about right.

"Does he?" I ask, pulling myself out of the pool to get the ball. "Did your daddy ever tell you about the time he ran headfirst into an actual brick wall instead of the fake one he was supposed to?"

Freya giggles. When I jump back in the pool and toss the ball to her, she hits it clear out of the pool. Again.

"That was on purpose," I grumble, getting back out. "I need a bigger pool, so you can't do that."

Pretty sure Danny told her to wear me out and trample my already destroyed soul. I love Freya, she's great, but children are vicious little shits.

"He also said you're a chicken."

Vicious.

"Yeah, well, he's a rooster." Closest I can get to calling him a dick and not getting yelled at for language by a five-year-old.

She laughs and I know she'll be calling him a rooster for a while, which makes me smile. Honestly, this smells like a setup. Danny and Freya were whispering over breakfast when I came downstairs this morning. I can hear them now:

Tell Timbo he's a chicken. Tell him he's a dumbass.

Language, Daddy!

Okay, tell him he's dumber than a brick wall. If we annoy him enough, he'll sort his shi—stuff out.

"He says you're scared," Freya continues. "He says you're stuck."

Yup. A setup. Danny is using his daughter to get me to think about what he said on the first day. And every day since. Climbing and fear and getting stuck.

I'm not scared. I'm not stuck.

I can crawl out of this wallow anytime I want.

Liar.

"Your daddy is full of it." I cannonball into the pool close enough to splash her.

"Full of what?" she asks, splashing me when I resurface.

Bullshit. Can't say that, though. "Silly ideas."

Fine. I'm stuck.

I feel like a caged zoo animal. I should be free, but my world has shrunk and I'm pacing and pacing.

Maybe I am scared. What if nothing compares to what I've lost? Both Mina and my job.

"Tell your daddy I get what he's saying," I tell Freya. "Tell him Uncle Timbo is scared he'll never be good at anything again in his life."

Goddammit, he's never going to let me live this down.

Freya laughs but does me a solid and tells me all the things I'm good at, which consists of making Kraft Dinner, making stuff glittery (getting that glitter out of my house is going to be harder than getting all the bodily fluids out), and darts. Oh, and smoothies.

Thanks, kid.

Unable to sleep later that night, I go back down to the pool. It's peaceful out here. I sit on the edge, letting my feet hang in the cool water.

I'm stuck. I've been existing in this limbo where I'm retired and without purpose. Even if Mina hadn't left, sooner or later, I'd have to face myself and figure out who I am now that I can't be who I was.

The problem is my life has been going in one direction since I could get into trouble—so since I could walk—and that brought me here, to stunt work. There was never any other option, which is why when I look back, there's no other path. No other way forward.

Maybe I'm not the only one who's stuck. Maybe Mina wasn't lying when she said she loved all of me. That stupid game of The Floor is Lava pushed her right back into being too scared to be with me.

That's ridiculous. A cartwheel won't kill me and she has to know that.

I stare at my feet and how the rippling water distorts them. Unless, to her, every cartwheel is potentially fatal.

Huh. Hadn't thought of it like that.

I guess, a simple cartwheel kind of...*could* kill me if I slipped and hit my head just right. I can't and won't live in Bubble Wrap, but I can see her point.

But again. I'm doing easy, low-risk stuff. She's overreacting.

I switch our places. Not with stunts, because my brain can't picture Mina doing anything like that. Instead, I imagine her boxing. Taking a blow to the head causing the kind of injury I had.

My heart kicks painfully and I go cold, my breath sticking in my lungs until I force it out. When I picture her in a hospital bed...no. I can't do this.

To almost lose her and have her want to get back in the ring, even though she's not a professional, and she's careful, would break my heart. It would terrify me.

I've put her through that fear. She's been living with it since the accident, dialed up to an eleven. No wonder she snapped over The Floor is Lava.

If I want a snowball's chance of getting her back, even as a friend, I need to fix this. And maybe I need to for myself, as well. It can't be healthy basing so much of who I am on what I can do. But how do I walk away when everyone expects me to jump?

I wish Nic was still here—this is a perfect whiskey-by-the-pool conversation. Waking Danny isn't an option. Might as well talk to a lounge chair since he'd be asleep in it after five minutes of listening to my problems.

I pull my phone out of my pocket and for a long moment my thumb hovers over her name. She's going to kill me.

Nah, she loves me.

I press the button and the phone rings. And rings. And rings.

The moment she answers, before she can hang up on me, I blurt out, "How did you give up painting?"

There's a long pause, followed by my twin's voice, thick with sleep. "Timothy?"

"It was your favorite thing, it was how you coped with the world, and you walked away. How?"

"You called me at…" She groans. "It's 5 a.m. My alarm goes off in an hour and you woke me up to talk about painting?" Her voice is wide awake and angry now. "Are you high?"

"I need a purpose, and I need to know how to walk away from something I love. You were drifting around aimlessly for a while and you stopped painting. How did you get your shit together?"

There's another long pause, but this time I think she's debating whether it would be worth it to fly out and murder me. "You wouldn't let me day drink and watch The Bachelor," she says dryly. "Don't recall you giving me a choice."

I might have got her a job, but she kept it. She stayed standing after I picked her up. "Want to come to LA and sort my life out?"

"No."

"Jessie," I whine. "I kinda need some wisdom from my sister."

"You have another sister."

I snort. Our older sister Amanda has the ruthlessness of Mom combined with the quiet efficiency of Dad. She'd sort my life out in five minutes with spreadsheets, but it wouldn't be my life—it would be hers. Plus, her wife Hazel would kill me if I called at 5 a.m. and woke up the kids.

Silence stretches and I'm about to ask Jessie if she's still awake when she speaks again.

"You need something to be passionate about, to pour your energy into. Try stuff out and see what sticks. Volunteer at an animal shelter, or find something that would allow you to work with kids, maybe teaching them some kind of—" Whatever she says gets lost in a yawn.

It can't be that easy, can it? Objectively, those are good ideas. I could play with dogs and goof off with kids. "Great...now how do I walk away from the stupid human tricks?" Mom calls them that. Not my favorite, but it's a convenient shorthand for my hobbies. "How did you do it with painting?"

Her voice picks up a bitter edge. "I heard how bad I was over and over until it hurt too much to try?"

Shit. Stepped on a landmine. My heart aches for my sis. I didn't realize this was still a sore point. I thought she'd moved on. What else is she holding on to? Or *who* else. I clear my throat. "Right, but make this about me." I'd rather she be annoyed with me than stuck dwelling on rejections. "How do I stop doing things I love?"

She thinks about it for a minute. "I still doodle," she says with another yawn. "Guess I didn't really quit."

She doodles. Little pieces of art just for her, no risk attached. I'm glad she was able to hold on to that, but I want more for her.

"Why don't you try running a marathon?" she suggests.

I laugh. If she knew Nic had the same idea, she'd backtrack so fast she'd get dizzy.

Jessie yawns again and this time it feels pointed and deliberate, a massive hint to me that she'd rather be sleeping. "You're going to be okay, Timothy. You don't need to jump around on chairs or fall out of the sky. You'll always be a big dumb Labrador puppy in human form, and we'll always love you anyway."

That. Right there. My entire body freezes as something warm pushes out from my chest. I'm stuck because I'm scared. I don't know what comes next and I'm terrified I will never be good at anything other than stunt work. That I'll spin out and lose control and leave a trail of destruction in my wake without some place to channel my energy. That I'll be too much for the people I love to stand by me.

I'm wrong. They ones who matter will always love me. Even Mina, even if she's too scared to be with me.

I am loved and my fear is pointless.

And my ego...

I'd told myself countless times that the cheers and admiration were a side perk, and I was doing the job for me, to find a sense of calm and banish the twitchy feelings. Maybe sometimes that's been true, but not always. Not even most of the time, and I can see that so clearly in this moment. When I asked my mom to get rid of the balloons and flowers in the hospital, it was because I couldn't face disappointing people who believed in me. When I couldn't bring myself to face Danny and the rest of the crew, it was because I felt like an impostor. When I got on that chair to play The Floor is Lava, I couldn't let Dex have the cheers I felt were mine.

My ego needs to take a backseat. I don't need to prove myself to anyone to be worthy of love.

"I am a hot dummy," I say absently into the phone.

"Not hot," Jessie replies instantly.

I laugh. God, I feel lighter than I have in days. "You give the best pep talks."

"You called me at five a.m., what do you expect?"

"Emergency existential crisis. Couldn't wait. Thanks, J. I'll let you go back to sleep."

She mumbles something about her alarm and fifteen minutes, but I end the call with a loud kissy noise and a "love you, J."

Everything feels clear now. Obvious, in retrospect. Seriously, I am a hot dummy. I absently kick my legs through the water, enjoying the feeling of moving through it, staring at the dark sky too full of light pollution to see the stars.

I'm done with hiding away and sulking, holding onto a past that's no longer my present. Time to be awesome at other things.

Not marathons, though.

I need to talk to Mina. I want to hold her and apologize for scaring her. I love her too much to lose her. If she'll have me back, I'm hers and we'll have an earnest discussion about her fears.

If she won't take me back, I want her friendship. Even if it hurts.

Boxes of finished panties started to arrive at my place the other day, and I need to bring them to Nic's for Mina to embroider anyway, so tomorrow morning I'll do that. And hand her my heart one last time.

Chapter Thirty-Three

Mina

Driving around LA collecting boxes of underwear is an exercise in anger management. As is discovering several people already finished and have dropped their boxes off at Timothy's house.

I'm not ready to see him yet, so I call Danny. Nic told me he's staying at Timothy's. He's still there and happy to drop my stuff off in the morning—Freya wants to see the Ugly House. I'm both relieved and disappointed. As much as I want to see Timothy, I'm not ready.

Charlotte calls. She gave me extra time to think about the shop on Grand and Aspen after I ended things with Timothy, and that time is up. I decline. Starting a new life out East where I can try to forget Timothy is appealing, but I'm not ready. She's understanding and careful with my broken heart.

I spend the rest of the night checking the quality of the product I collected and transferring the bonuses I promised for early delivery and high quality. I even manage to embroider little pumpkin spice lattes on several pairs of bikini briefs before I call it a night.

Falling asleep, I think about expanding Wild Things, but my dreams are all Timothy. We pummel each other with pillows, stray feathers falling around us like snow as we fall into a cloud of puffy blankets. Then he's inside me and the look in his light brown eyes makes me feel loved and safe. Everything is golden and soft, a wave rolling slowly into me while he watches from above. There's bittersweet knowledge that this is a dream. The time when I had Timothy is past. I don't want to wake up.

I do and I cry in the shower and spend way too long trying to cover my red and puffy eyes with cosmetics because Danny will be here soon. Timothy's going to ask him how I am. I want Danny to believe me when I tell him I'm okay, so that Timothy will believe him when he passes it on.

I'm not even a little okay.

I'm barely functioning.

Cute shorts, T-shirt, hair in a ponytail. It's all I can manage when staying in my pajamas is so tempting, but no. I'll treat myself to a handful of the cookies Nic baked last night as a reward for getting dressed. Then I'll spend the rest of the day embroidering and crying because that dream reminded me of what I walked away from.

I'm way too fragile already as I walk into the living room, stopping short at the sight of Timothy. My heart thumps in my chest, trying to break free.

He's standing next to a stack of boxes, his back to me, staring out the window, hands jammed in his pockets. The room even smells like him, light and citrusy. It makes this cold, harsh house a little more inviting. Timothy has that effect.

His slumped shoulders are the only sign that like me, he's not okay.

I need to glue my feet to the goddamn floor so I don't throw my arms around him and beg him to take me home. Going back won't solve the problem between us. We're too different to ever work.

His shoulders inch up and he's not breathing evenly anymore as he watches me in the reflection of the glass. Waiting for me to say something, or to run.

It's too late to run.

"I know you see me," I finally say. I hate how my voice falters.

Timothy turns, slowly. The smile on his face is fleeting. Nervous.

Oh my god. Timothy Foley is terrified right now.

My hand covers my mouth before I catch myself and let it drop. I clear my throat. "How are you?"

"Good," he says with forced cheer in his voice. He winces. "I'm not good."

"Me neither," I admit.

"Mina, I'm sorry," he says, taking a step toward me and stopping again. "Come home. Please."

I'm holding my breath, and when I say nothing, he continues. "We can work this out. I'm done with that stuff. I promise."

How many days have I been waiting for him to come here, to say this? I think he might even mean it, but..."It's not that simple."

His face falls. "I'm making changes. Please, give me another chance."

I want to believe him. I'm afraid to speak, in case it's my heart that comes out and not my head, so I bite my lip and shake my head.

Timothy stares at me and I can't stand to see the pain in his eyes. Like the coward I am, I look away.

"So that's it," he says after eons drag by.

I shrug, then nod because I'm being strong and Timothy deserves more than a shrug. He deserves more than me. He deserves someone who can love all of him fearlessly, without caging him. Tears fill my eyes.

He takes a few steps toward me, slow. I relax when I realize he has to walk by me to leave. Going around Nic's massively long couch would be awkwardly obvious.

Timothy stops just far enough that he can lightly brush my arm with the back of his knuckles. "Can we still be friends? I don't want to lose you from my life."

"I'd like that," I manage, but I can't meet his eyes. I'm staring at his T-shirt, flat over his stomach. "But I need a little space first."

Timothy's hand drops to his side. "You know where to find me."

I nod and watch his reflection in the glass as he walks away. I make it about twenty seconds before I crumble on the floor.

I don't know how long I'm there, sobbing on Nic's hard sofa before I realize I'm not alone. My first horrifying thought is Timothy, but it's not. Nic's sitting in a chair, watching me with a look I can't read. That's the real genius of Dominic Fontana—the broody, unreadable look that can sell everything from cologne to watches to underwear to a superhero franchise. I sniffle and wipe my eyes with the back of my hands.

Nic points to a tissue box sitting right in front of me. He must have put it there.

"Thanks," I sniff.

"You let him walk out the door."

I did. I had to. When I don't answer, Nic gets up. He returns with a bottle of whiskey and a couple of glasses. He hands me one and sits again. So far, he hasn't pressed me to talk about it. Mostly, he's left me alone.

He doesn't say anything. Doesn't ask a single probing question. Just sits and drinks and stares at the wall.

I sniffle and take a sip. I hate whiskey and it's not even 10 a.m. but I could use the fire in my belly to chase away the cold emptiness of not having Timothy here. "How do you do it?" I ask after a few minutes of silence.

His gray eyes slide my way. "Do what?"

"Care about him and not lose your mind over the shit he does."

"I grew up with him," Nic says after a bit. "Maybe that's part of it. He's family and his family is my family. They're all I've got. I can't—and won't—walk away from my friendship because Timothy is a walking death wish."

I flinch. Timothy's careless and impulsive, but I don't think he's a walking death wish. "How do you deal, though?"

"I get mad. I yell at him. Maybe some silent treatment." He takes a long drink and stares at his glass. "I have to remind myself he's spent thousands of hours training, he's got all this experience...and he's careful. I've seen him walk away from stuff he didn't feel good about, even on set, surrounded by people he wants to impress. Beneath all the flashy showing off, he's surprisingly analytical. Have you ever watched him work?"

Guilt nibbles at me. I've avoided it. He's been my best friend for five years, but I've put my fear first and Timothy accommodated me. We didn't talk about his job. I've seen movies he's worked in, but it's easy to tell myself that a lot of what happens on screen happens in post-production and the leap off an exploding building is no worse than jumping off something no higher than a kitchen counter. And Timothy's prone to exaggeration, so the stories I have heard, I've attributed to ego and creative embellishment.

"If you love him," Nic says, finishing his drink and getting to his feet, "you have to accept all of him. Love all of him. Including the parts you don't like."

I love all of him. I do. Even the parts that terrify me. That's what makes this so hard. But I can't and won't put myself in a place where I sit like my Nan, waiting while my worry eats me alive. I never want another heart-stopping call from the hospital, and with Timothy, any time he's not by my side is going to be filled with worry.

It's different for Nic. A different kind of love too. He's used to Timothy, and he has Timothy's family. He's not going to be left alone.

I'm so tired of being alone.

Chapter Thirty-Four

Timothy

There's no point owning a building if you can't use it, so I haul all my shit to my still-empty Robertson Boulevard shop to sell my life away.

Not that I'm selling it. It's all for charity. A silent auction for a crap ton of used and some unused gear. Everything from my snowboard to my surfboard, from wingsuits and parachutes and climbing gear. Even my motorcycle. I took a quiet moment, before everyone arrived, to say goodbye. These items took me on adventures. Let me grow as a person. Gave me so much joy.

They're a part of who I am—or rather, the memories are. Other people will get to make new memories with this stuff now, and that's kind of beautiful. I'll make new memories too.

Turn out is good, but I know enough people, Nic knows people, and the people we know know people. I've signed everything signable with a Sharpie like I'm a famous person. Kind of I am, but not really.

"Hey," I say quietly to Nic, slapping his arm when he doesn't immediately leave his conversation with some boring director to pay attention to me. "Gabriel Sinclair wants my motorcycle. Get in there, outbid him."

"I don't want your motorcycle," Nic says with a frown.

"Well, you'll never beat him for Sexiest Man in America without my motorcycle."

"That man doesn't ride a motorcycle." Nic glares at me and walks away.

He's probably right, but the motorcycle is a classic. Maybe Gabriel Sinclair is a collector. Maybe that Boy Scout has a bit of a bad boy trapped inside. I'm not going to judge.

There's a rock star looking at an old snowboard. Jessie drew a picture of me on it once, flying off a jump, grabbing the edge. It was cool as fuck. I've still got it somewhere.

A couple of guys from an outdoor TV show are squaring off over the dirt bike I haven't touched in years. That bike got me laid a lot, so I stroll by and casually mention this. It also was a gift from my parents on my eighteenth birthday. Riding it felt like freedom. I finally had their blessing to go out into the world and be myself. That bike and I had some adventures, but life got too busy, I guess, or I got too interested in other things. Always thought we'd have more time together.

An actor from Warwick runs his hands along my surfboard. After Nic's parents passed, we spent a couple of months surfing. That board was practically an extension of my body. I can still smell the wax and feel the weight of it under my arm and the crushing feeling of watching my best friend fall apart while I could do nothing except stand beside him.

Without Nic at my side, my collar is too tight and the room too warm. I grab a beer from where the counter has been turned into a bar and let myself into the backroom, where I hope Mina will work soon, despite what we've lost. I like thinking of her here, sewing with that cute, focused look on her face.

One deep breath. Two.

I can do this. It's my life and I want this. Besides, I'm selling physical things, not my memories. Those will always be mine. As hard as this is, it feels right.

Would Mina trust this? Would her answer be any different if she walked through those doors and saw me getting rid of all my stuff? I didn't tell Nic to tell her or not to tell her and he hasn't mentioned if he did. When I asked him how she was, he told me to call her if I wanted to know.

I'd call her, but she wanted space and I have to respect that.

There are no messages on my phone from Mina, but it doesn't stop me from checking again. Just in case.

The door opens and Nic pokes his head in. "Hey, Danny's looking for you. He has some questions about the motorcycle."

"Okay, but Gabriel has deeper pockets. Wanna hang out tonight?" I ask, tucking my phone away. "Shoot some pool?" Danny and Freya are gone—Freya to her mom's with lots of stories about Uncle Timbo that will land Danny in hot water, I hope, and Danny to his bachelor pad. I miss the noise of them. Living alone is the worst. It makes me wish I lived closer to my parents and sisters. God, how much fun would it be to randomly turn up at Jessie's place and annoy the shit out of her? Amanda and Hazel's place, too, so I could hang out with my favorite niece and nephew. Teach them my wisdom. Hand down my Nerf guns.

Today's been hard. Not as hard as Mina saying no, but still. I don't want to be alone tonight. There's no one to stop me from crying into the undies she made me. *Dude, your face is gonna smell like your balls* is permanently etched into my memory thanks to Danny. Freya's giggle too. And yes, they did catch me crying into my undies, and that's probably more embarrassing than Mina witnessing my masturbatory misfire, because yeah, those undies were from the hamper, not my drawer. And they did smell like balls.

"Yeah, let's hang out," Nic says. "If I can offload some baking onto you."

"Always."

We go back out front and I answer some questions from Danny about the motorcycle he's not going home with. Then I find Gabriel Sinclair and force him to take a selfie with me—which I send to the family group chat with the caption:

The Sexiest Man in America. And Gabriel Sinclair.

It's late out East, but the responses come quickly.

> oh thank god you're selling that motorcycle. Who's Gabriel Sinclair? He looks a bit like Nic.

Mom

No he doesn't—Gabriel Sinclair is sexy and he can act.

JESSIE

Jessie be nice.

MOM

Yeah, Jessie, be nice.

AMANDA

I want your skis. Please rig the auction so I win at an affordable but socially acceptable charity price so we can still have our Caribbean holiday.

HAZEL

Who's the guy bending over in the background? He's got a nice ass.

JESSIE

I can't help it, I guffaw. I haven't laughed like this in ages. I can't stop, either, and I don't care how many people are looking at me like I've lost my mind. Tears are leaking out of my eyes, I can't talk when Nic gives me a questioning look. This is too damn good.

Oh, he does!

MOM

Meh.

AMANDA

I know that ass. <smirking face emoji>

HAZEL

That ass belongs to the Second Hottest Man in America, Dominic Fontana.

ME

Sure does. <peach emoji, fire emoji>

HAZEL

Your wife is RIGHT HERE IN THE CHAT HAZEL. I can have you kicked out.

AMANDA

No you can't.

MOM

<laughing emoji> The bisexual alliance in this family is too strong, wifey.

HAZEL

It takes a few minutes and I know Jessie is zooming in and trying to decide whether I'm fucking with her or if that really is Nic. She'll be scouring the internet for other photos from the auction, comparing his pants to the pants in the picture. It is Nic, though. Don't know why he's bending over, but it's him.

Jessie admitted Nic has a nice ass to a chat Nic is a part of.

<barf emoji>

JESSIE

Dad leaves us all on read. So does Nic, which is hilarious.

The silent auction raises a respectable amount for charity, and I kick Nic's ass at pool. Three times in a row.

"Hey," I console Nic as he leaves my place. "At least Jessie admitted you have a nice ass."

He attempts to look confused and fails.

"I'm not sure how your purgatory house is connected to hell," I say, clapping him on the arm, "but you might want to pop in tonight, to make sure hell hasn't frozen over."

He walks away, flipping me off, but I catch the little huff of a laugh he tries to hide.

"Take the win, Fontana!" I shout after him. "And thanks for keeping me company."

Tonight was good, and it feels good, but it doesn't cover what's missing. I still feel hollow. I miss Mina so much...I want to tell her about tonight, as her friend.

I think she'd be proud of me. I'm proud of myself.

Chapter Thirty-Five

Mina

Celia Foley sends me a text.

I put my phone back on the bedside table without looking at the message. I haven't returned any of her money like I promised before I hung up on her. I've already spent most of it so she'll have to wait.

Another text comes in as I head to the bathroom to brush my teeth. I assume it's from her. I should block her, or at least turn my phone off.

My heart slams to a halt.

What if something happened to Timothy?

I dive for my phone, fumbling through the pin.

> I'm sorry I questioned your judgment and blamed you for Timothy's actions. What he did was never your fault.
>
> Celia

I'll never get used to my heart pinballing between fear and relief every time I think Timothy's hurt or worse. I sink onto my bed and take a moment to breathe through it, until the pain subsides, reassuring myself with a little mantra of *he's okay, he's okay, he's okay.*

He told me what happened. I'm sorry you broke up. He misses you. I hope the two of you can find your way to be friends again, at least. I think you're good for each other. But that's my opinion. You have to choose what you want for yourself. XX

Celia

One more text, but this time it's a picture. Timothy and Gabriel Sinclair standing in front of Timothy's motorcycle in the Robertson Boulevard shop that Timothy bought. There's a number on the motorcycle, people milling about. Pretty sure the man bending over in the background is Nic, which I guess explains where he is tonight. He left a note saying he'd be home late.

Charity auction, if you were wondering.

Celia

Huh.

I wander into Nic's kitchen, grab the first bottle I see—whiskey, unfortunately—and pour myself a finger.

Timothy got rid of his motorcycle. Other stuff, too, I assume.

He must be hurting right now. I know this is hard for him.

He said he was making changes, but I can't believe he's doing it.

Another finger of whiskey. I pull out a barstool, sit at the kitchen island, and stare at reflections in the huge glass windows.

Maybe it's for me, and he's going to ask to get back together again, but I don't think so, or he would've invited me tonight. No, he's doing this for him. Saying goodbye to risky shit.

I'm proud of him. Sad for him.

It doesn't change anything, though. He can afford to replace anything he's giving away. He's still Timothy. Tigers don't change their stripes and his feet will never stay on the ground, even if he promises.

Another finger of whiskey goes into my glass. It's slowly shredding my resistance. I want to call him. See how he's handling tonight. Ask him if I can come over. Take him back and hope he means it. Feel his body hard against mine.

My phone is in hand, but instead of calling Timothy I scroll up to the video his mom sent of The Floor is Lava. This is what I need—a heavy shot of reality.

I press play, and this time I watch the whole thing.

Stella, Danny, and Dex all take turns doing fancy tricks as they jump from chair to chair. It figures it would be Dex nailing it right before Timothy suddenly decides he's in. But the others all make it look easy. Like they've practiced hundreds of times.

Oh god. They probably have. At countless barbecues and parties. What did Nic say? Thousands of hours of practice and muscle memory?

The person taking the video keeps it close, and the quality is high enough that I can see Timothy's face as he stands on the chair, taking a moment to work out what he's going to do, calculating the distance between the chairs. He loosens up his body, stretching while he does it, so it's easy to miss the way his eyes move as he plans it out.

What happens next has to be magic. He goes into some kind of zone. Total concentration and yet...he looks relaxed as he executes his series of moves. And he's precise. It looks as easy as breathing.

There's other footage of him online, mostly from before we met, on set and off. I flip through at random. Some of it scares the shit out of me, but Timothy never looks surprised when he nails something.

He knows what he's doing, and he's good. So good.

My heart is full of him and I miss him more than ever, and maybe I can trust him to judge a situation accurately.

Accidents still happen. There are bloopers and I watch him fail too. Sometimes painfully. But something about watching him make mistakes and get back up soothes away my fears.

Eventually, I set my phone down, resting my head on my arms.

I told him I'd jump, but the moment I saw how far, I balked.

The thing is, I can live without Timothy. I can work myself to the bone and keep my heart to myself and endure day after day of meaningless, lonely grind because I did it before.

And I was stagnating, too scared to go on a date or take the next step with Wild Things.

I don't want to go back to that. I love Timothy more than I love the quiet little space I've made to keep my heart safe. I love how he challenges me and how he makes me braver. I want him more than I want safety. I want to work things out with him, talk about the changes he's making and the things he's not willing to budge on, and this time I want to listen without going into fight-or-flight mode.

I want him back.

It's time to take a risk. To jump all in, for real this time.

A groan comes from somewhere deep in my chest. My heart is already thumping. I don't know how to jump. I need to show him I'm ready to live with a little fear in my life...but how?

Footsteps on tile—Nic's home. He was with Timothy tonight, and I wasn't. I should've been there. I groan again.

"You okay?" he asks.

I lift my head. "I made a mistake."

Nic gives me a *no shit* look.

"What do I do?" I whisper.

He slides the bottle of whiskey toward himself. "Something big."

I groan and drop my head again. "Like what?"

"I have an idea," he says after a moment. "You aren't going to like it, but Timothy...it's going to work on him. Trust me. I'll even cover all the expenses."

I'm so desperate, I agree. Nic refuses to tell me what his plan is, but I don't care. Timothy's worth it.

Chapter Thirty-Six

Timothy

Nic is up to something. The surprise trip to Vegas already had my Spidey senses tingling, but the way he's grinning like a dick after checking his phone...

Suspicious.

Whatever. I can roll with anything he throws at me.

I didn't want to come. It feels shitty to leave Mina back in LA, even if we aren't anything at the moment. The idea I won't be there if she needs me is a hard one to digest, but Nic hit me with everything: we haven't done anything like this in years, he needs a change of scenery after dealing with the divorce, I need a change of scenery after having my heart and head broken, et cetera. Mina, he said, would be hanging out with Danny and Freya, so I wouldn't need to worry about her.

Still, it's not me with her.

So. Vegas.

No surprise, we're in the penthouse suite at the Palazzo.

Big surprise, Nic doesn't drag me to a strip club. We have dinner at the hotel and he's busy smirking at his phone, which is just plain weird.

"Who are you texting?" I ask.

"Nobody."

He looks gleeful. Nic never looks gleeful when he's talking to someone.

"You're up to something."

He puts his phone away and straightens. "I am not."

"You are."

"Excuse me," a young man says, a bit hesitantly.

"Oh, look, a fan!" Nic sounds delighted to sign an autograph.

He's *really* up to something. Either this is an elaborate surprise boys' night out on the strip and the boys have yet to show, or my whole family is about to descend on us.

Except that would mean Jessie, and Nic wouldn't be smiling if she were here. And he'd have to invite her with the rest of them or he'd be in deep shit with my mom...

My phone chimes and since Nic is chatting like someone gave him a new personality, I take a look.

> Hey, bro. Freya made you something.

Danny

A picture comes through, and it's Freya proudly holding up a paper crown. With Mina.

Mina.

She's there, in the picture, smiling for Danny, looking relaxed and happy and...

> Tell Freya I love it.

ME

This pain is never going to lessen.

We finish dinner and head out. My heart is too heavy to do anything other than follow Nic through the crowd. He has a car waiting, and we climb in. I barely notice the lights on the strip or the tourists out for a good night. Normally, I love this shit. The energy of the place. There's always something new to look at even though I've been here dozens of times.

The car ride is short. Or long, I don't know.

I miss Mina. I am going to love her as long as I breathe. A part of me doesn't exist without her. I know I need to move on, but I don't see much of a point.

I'm so lost in my misery I don't realize where we are until Nic stops us at a fence.

We're standing next to the landing pad at the Strat's SkyJump.

"Mr. Fontana," a woman with a pleasant voice, an earpiece, and a clipboard says as she joins us. "On behalf of Golden Entertainment, thank you for—"

I stop listening to the corporate spiel. A controlled descent would probably be okay for my head, but I don't want to do it and I know Nic sure as hell doesn't want to. Still, it was nice of him to try to cheer me up with this.

"Excuse me, one moment," Nic says the instant his phone rings. He swipes what must be a video call and grins. "Hey, Danny. Ready?"

Danny? He's supposedly in LA with Mina. I narrow my eyes at Nic.

"Ready and terrified. You?" Danny doesn't sound scared at all. But why would he? We've been skydiving a bunch of times and this is a controlled descent. This shit is child's play.

"We're here." Nic hands me the phone.

I take the phone slowly, suspecting a trap. An extreme close-up of Danny's face greets me. "You need to exfoliate," I tell him. "What's going on?"

"Someone here has something to say to you," Danny says, and the camera flips to someone in a brightly colored jumpsuit. Her dark hair lofts about her face in a breeze, obscuring it before she pushes it back.

Not that I don't recognize her the second I see her.

Mina.

What the fuck is she doing up there? My heart knocks around loud in my chest, in sympathy. She must be terrified.

"Timothy." Her voice is shaking. She's shaking. I don't think I've ever seen her look so pale. "Hi."

"Hey. What are you doing?" I know what she's doing, she's wearing the jumpsuit, but this doesn't make sense. Mina wouldn't do this. This is the opposite of child's play to her.

"Um, the last time I wore a harness was much more fun," she says with a nervous laugh.

I can't laugh. Can't do anything except stare at her and try to make sense of this.

"I made a huge mistake," she says in a high voice as they hook a cable to her harness. "I was scared and upset and I don't want to spend my entire life like that. I didn't listen to you, didn't give us a chance to work it out. I turned my back on you. I'll never do that again."

The woman on the platform asks her to turn. Mina does slowly, looking over her shoulder at the camera. "Except right now, I guess, because they needed me to turn, but you know what I mean." Another cable is attached, and the first one is removed. Danny must be strapped in to get a shot this close.

My throat goes tight. I want to race up there and wrap my arms around her, tell her everything is okay, but before I can tell her to hold tight and step away from the platform, she's talking again.

"I watched you, all the videos I could find, all the things I was too scared to look at before, and you're amazing. I love you, Timothy. All of you. Even the parts that scare me. And maybe I need to be scared sometimes, so I can learn how to live with it. I'll do that. For you."

The checks are happening in the background while Mina takes a deep, trembling breath.

"Baby," I finally manage to say. "Go inside and wait. I'll—"

"I know where to find you, Timothy Foley," she calls over her shoulder as the attendant instructs her to put her hands on the red part of the railing and her toes on the yellow line. The countdown begins. "I love you," she says, "and I'm coming for you."

There's the smallest pause when the attendant hits zero, then Mina's gone.

I look up and here she comes, screaming obscenities the entire way down, arms and legs flailing.

I can't stop the smile from stretching across my face.

She fucking did it. She jumped. Eight hundred fifty-five feet. For me.

Holy shit.

She loves me enough.

The descender slows her for landing, and before her feet touch the ground, I jump the fence.

She crumples, but I have her in my arms and I'm never going to let her go. I wrap her tight, burying my face in her neck as I fight back the sob trying to escape my chest. Her skin is cold and clammy and she tastes like the wind and her arms quiver, but she's holding me and everything is going to be all right.

"Holy shit." She finally breathes out, squeezing me tighter, bouncing like her body doesn't know what to do with the extra adrenaline. What I wouldn't give to have someplace private thirty seconds away to give her a few ideas.

"You're amazing," I tell her, pulling her back far enough to look into her eyes. "I love you."

"I love you, too," she whispers, then her lips are on mine and the world is perfect and beautiful.

The kiss doesn't end until Nic yells at us. We both flip him off.

I brush some of Mina's hair back. Color is returning to her face, and she looks happy and dazed. "You could've called or come over, you know," I say softly.

Her smile freezes. "What?"

I glance at the platform far above us. "You didn't have to jump off a building for me. I appreciate it because wow, you did something that scares you, and that's so incredibly hot, but...all I ever needed was to hear you say you love me enough to be with me."

Mina blinks twice and goes feral in my arms.

"I'm going to kill him," she growls as she twists.

Holy shit, it's like trying to hold a wildcat. "Whoa, hey, easy—"

"Nic Fontana, you're a dead man!" she shouts over my shoulder.

He feels safe enough to laugh, what with Mina still roped in and a fence between them and my arms around her.

The woman with the clipboard and earpiece taps his shoulder, smiling. "You're next Mr. Fontana."

Nic's laughter dies. "What?"

Mina stops struggling, and it's her turn to laugh. "Oh yeah, I forgot. I promised you'd do a promotional video."

"You what?" The color is gone from Nic's face.

"Look at it this way, Nic," I say with a laugh, "Either you go and jump while I distract Mina, or I let her go and you take your chances. What's it going to be? And remember what she did to your punching bag."

Nic swears, points threateningly at us, and grumbles, "I'll see you both at breakfast tomorrow." He disappears inside, and I finally notice the attendant trying to unhook Mina.

"Let's get you out of this," I murmur into her ear, "Then find someplace more private."

Mina grabs my face, kissing me long and hard, and finally, at the insistence of the impatient attendant, steps back.

The light blue sundress she's wearing underneath has me ready to grab her, throw her over my shoulder, and race her back to the hotel. But Mina has other plans.

"I'm petty enough we need to stay and watch Nic," she says. "This was his idea."

I laugh. My best friends are now best friends, whether they know it or not, and I love it. My life is pretty fucking perfect right now.

We take up spots in the viewing deck. It feels so good having her back in my arms and I can't stop touching her, kissing her.

Danny and Freya join us, and we get real PG, with Mina standing in front of me, leaning against me, my arms around her waist, my head resting on hers. Freya tells me, with all the delight of a five-year-old squirrel-child, how scared Mina was.

"She threw up when we first got here!" Freya says happily. "She had to go brush her teeth!"

Mina shudders. I'm so proud of her. I squeeze her and vow to protect her even from impertinent five-year-olds. "Where's that crown you made me, kiddo?" I demand.

"In your room," Freya sticks her tongue out at me and hangs off her dad's arm.

Danny hands me a key, then takes Freya's hands so she can walk up his legs and flip over. "You and Mina have an executive suite at the Palazzo. The kid and I will stay with Nic and make sure he doesn't have too much fun."

"No fun!" Freya declares.

Nic's not here to have that kind of fun. This was his gesture as much as Mina's. His *I'm sorry I was a dick who stayed away for five years, please forgive me, I helped get you and the woman you love back together*. He didn't need to, no more than Mina needed to actually jump, but I'm so glad they both did.

Nic jumps, and the footage is golden. The softly exhaled *fuck* upon landing is his best work. Of course, I send it to my family group chat.

> That's my boy!

Mom

> woo-hoo, go Nic!

Amanda

> How does he make that ugly jumpsuit look hot?

Hazel

> HAZEL.

Amanda

> <kissing face emoji>

Hazel

> Behave yourselves in Vegas, I'm too busy to bail you out.

Dad

Jessie leaves it on read.

Mina and I spend the next twenty-four hours in our room. Twenty-four blissful, sweaty, naked hours of giving each other all the pleasure we have to give. Whispering how much we missed each other, how much we love each other, all our hopes for the future, for the present.

"I don't regret doing it," Mina says in a languid voice. We're in the massive tub, bubbles spilling onto the floor, champagne on ice nearby. Mina's sitting between my legs, her back against my chest. My head is resting against the tub, my eyes closed as I enjoy the feel of Mina's tits in my hands, the way her nipples pebble as I play with them. When I can get it up again, I'm going to fuck her in this tub, water splashing all over the sides.

"Regret doing what?" I ask. We've done a lot of things in the last twenty-four hours, and she enjoyed all of them.

"Jumping off a building. It was scary, but...it was worth it. And every other terrifying thing you're going to put me through." Her hands reach back to my neck, water dripping off her skin all around me. "You're worth all of them."

I lean forward to nibble her ear. "You're the best thing to fall out of the sky."

Epilogue

ONE MONTH LATER: MINA

THE ROOM IS FULL of parcels waiting to go out, and the sight fills my chest with pride and something else. A little worry, sure. But I'm embracing the fear on this journey.

I got the lease from Charlotte's dad. He hadn't started advertising yet and after a conversation with Timothy, we decided to move back home. Timothy's going to help me set up and be my all-around handyman and fix-it guy until he figures out what he wants to do. Sexing me up on my future desk is in his job description, or so he tells me.

It's going to be hard leaving Nic behind, but Timothy has this crazy idea once Nic gets together with Jessie, Nic will leave LA. He might be right. Nic was in the room when Timothy put Jessie on speaker when she called on their birthday. As soon as she started singing, Nic got this look on his face. It turned into a scowl and he walked away, but I know what I saw. He feels something for her.

He's also refusing to spend Christmas with the Foleys, and while he won't say why, Timothy insists it's because he's afraid to see Jessie.

I haven't met her yet. I've met Amanda and Hazel and the kids on a video call, but Timothy wants to introduce me to his twin in person this holiday season, where she'll have no choice but to get to know me. Which is in no way intimidating.

But I trust him. We've had a lot of talks and worked out a lot of things that he can still do as long as he's careful. He's back to his old energy levels, back to his happy-go-lucky self, and if he gets a little sad watching an action movie…it doesn't last long.

It only takes me a moment to retrieve the ring case, tucked away in the drawer of the bedside table. Timothy left it there, sometime after he came back from the hospital, with a note, telling me it was mine and if I didn't want it, I should sell it and keep the money. I hadn't opened the drawer until last week after Danny called, looking for a butterfly barrette Freya had lost while they were staying here.

Timothy hasn't asked me again, but I know where he is. The proposal still stands, and it's an easy decision now.

He's still asleep when I slip back into bed, ring on my finger. He murmurs something that sounds a lot like my name when I cuddle up to his side, his arm immediately coming around me. I smile at the sleepy kiss he gives the top of my head and hold my hand in front of my face, watching the morning light dazzle across the diamond. I hadn't looked at it closely in the hospital, but now I can see how beautiful it is, how perfectly at home it looks on me.

I can tell the moment he opens his eyes and sees the ring on my finger. He holds his breath.

"I want to marry you," I say softly.

Timothy doesn't say a thing. He rolls us so he's on top of me, raining kisses everywhere. It's a full forty minutes before he finds words. Not until we're both lying sated and waiting for our heart rates to return to normal.

"How do you feel about a surprise Christmas wedding in Connecticut?" he asks with a grin.

"How long have you been planning this?" I ask, immediately suspicious.

He shrugs. "I might have looked into a few venues."

"All part of your evil plan to get Nic and Jessie together?" I'm fully on board with this plan. I want to see Nic get his ass kicked by love.

"Two birds, one stone," he says lightly, and I tickle him for that. When we've settled back down, he holds me close. "Marrying you is the important part. Doing Nic a solid is a perk. I'll need him to be the best man, so he'll have to come. But I want to surprise him too."

"What if you tell him we're announcing our engagement and you want him there?"

He nods slowly. "Might work."

"Lexi and Charlotte will fight over being maid of honor," I say, toying with Timothy's nipple piercing. "I could never choose between them."

"You could have another maid of honor," he suggests, kissing my forehead.

"I could. Got anyone in mind?" I ask with a laugh. This is going to be fun.

"Fuck, I love you, woman," Timothy growls, lifting me on top of him. I push myself up to sit straddling him so I can enjoy the view of the sexiest man in the world. Touch him too. I love touching him. The way he feels under my hands, the way he reacts to my touch...

I tug at the piercing, and he growls and I laugh again. "I bet they get together before the wedding."

Timothy shakes his head. "Hell no. After. How about a wager? Morning blowjobs for a week."

Like most of our days don't already start that way. "Oral sex in the morning AND if I win, you have to model my line of men's underwear."

His hands skate over my body and he's already hardening again between my legs. "Morning oral, I'll model for you, but if I win, you have to come skiing with me."

Shit. I'm going to have to make damn sure I win this. "And the winner gets one free elimination during house hunting, no questions asked, no reason needed."

"Baby, you can have whatever you want," Timothy says, grinning at me.

I'm so happy, I can't stop myself from smiling. "Only you. Again. Right now."

The End.

Sneak Peek! Holiday Vibes

Book Two in the Over the Top Love series

Curious about Nic's book? Want to see what happens when you get all/most of the Foley's under the same roof?

> *Working for a sex toy company after failing to make it in the art world, Jessie Foley knows a di—er, phallus—when she sees one. And her brother's best friend—the reason she can't paint—is definitely a phallus. She'd rather drink bad eggnog than stay under the same roof as the annoyingly hot celebrity for the holidays, but patching up her relationship with her brother means making nice with his friend.*

> *Nic Fontana's shirtless smolder rocketed him to the top of a massive superhero franchise even though he can't act. Reeling from a recent divorce, unhappy in Hollywood, and facing a challenging script and a new director, he needs the support of the closest thing he has to a family now more than ever. What he doesn't need is a dangerous attraction to his harshest critic, Jessie.*

When a pair of mistletoe underwear spark a sexy encounter and the start of a secret holiday fling, Nic and Jessie are forced to come to terms with their complicated past and deeply-buried feelings. But when the holidays end, they'll have to risk it all to find out if what they have is more than just vibes.

HOLIDAY VIBES is the second book in the Over the Top Love series. This enemies-with-benefits, brother's best friend romance features a grumpy hero and a snarky, unlikable heroine finding their Happily Ever After. It can be read as a standalone. It also contains explicit sex scenes and strong language. Content notes can be found on the author's website.

Keep reading for a look at Chapter One of Holiday Vibes!

Holiday Vibes Chapter One

JESSIE

"I'm a candy cane slut and it's my time to shine," I whisper as I hit the end of the family group chat. There's no mention, no suggestion, no hint *he's* going to be here.

From my rental car parked at the end of the long drive, my parents' crafts-man-style house is beautiful, glowing like a Thomas Kinkade painting in the sil-very-blue world of moonlit snow. Vintage lights are strung along the windows. Smaller lights twinkle through the bare branches of a couple of trees. And inside a warm welcome awaits me, along with hot chocolate laced with Bailey's, topped with whipped cream, and I want it bad.

Dominic Fontana won't be here losing at a board game or helping my mom in the kitchen or someone would have said something in the group chat. He hasn't been here for the last four Christmases, so why should this year be different?

Except he's my twin brother's best friend, and he's recently divorced, so where else would he be, with no other family to claim him? There's a high chance Mr. Big Sexy Movie Star *is* inside and I don't want to see him again. Ever.

Cold is creeping into my rental. I'm not going to scour the last four weeks of the family group chat for clues again, though I'm tempted. No, I'm going to march inside and spend the next two weeks enjoying my favorite time of year with the people I love, because no way in hell is Nic here.

As soon as I get out of my rental car.

Which I'm totally going to do. Any second now.

Oh, god, I'm stalling hard.

This is annoying. It's been five years since the last time I saw Nic and while I'm still a hot mess, I don't *look* like a hot mess. Tonight, I'm armored with my impractical but sexy-as-hell boots and my favorite lipstick in "heartless red". Battle-ready.

And honestly, apart from potential death by humiliation, a little low-intensity warfare would hardly ruin two weeks of booze and food. He's probably not even here, and I'm freezing my ass off for nothing.

The pull of a hot drink wins. I climb out of my car, retrieve my suitcase from the back—with a grunt because I've overpacked it—and start up the driveway.

In the dark, with only the lights of the house, I don't see the patch of ice.

One foot shoots forward, and the other follows. Pain blossoms across the side of my ass and for the first time in months, I'm on my back with my feet in the air, and not under the circumstances I prefer.

I scramble to my knees and scan the windows in case someone saw my fall. Mercifully, there are no witnesses.

Grabbing my suitcase, I slowly climb to my feet, wobbling, sliding each foot forward inch by inch until I can reach the other side of the ice. My ass hurts, but since no one saw me fall, I'm going to pretend this never happened. Because I'm an adult and my shit is together.

The effort it takes to lug my suitcase up the first step nearly puts me back on my ass. I've packed everything I need to ensure I won't look like a swamp hag at any point over the next two weeks. I'm not repeating the mistakes I made five years ago. I've also crammed this beast with gifts and vibrators.

Those have nothing to do with Nic. I do graphic design and social media for a family-owned sex toy company called Sploosh! and as a perk, I get more freebies than I can use, which I happily off-load onto various family members.

Okay, I also packed half a dozen of my favorites, in case I need them. Again, nothing to do with Nic and everything to do with a sudden and unfortunate lack of men worth my time.

A couple more heaves and grunts, and I make it up to the wreath-laden door.

The warm smell of apple, cinnamon, and cloves engulfs me when I push it open and I suck it into my lungs, sighing in contentment. My mother's kitchen is the birthplace of good aromas, but something about the holidays makes everything deeper. Better.

My mother is none other than the legendary Celia Foley, an on-air institution who single-handedly launched the Home Cooking Channel with the first of her many successful cooking shows. If food is her first calling, Christmas is her second and her ability to make the magic of the season last beyond childhood is nothing short of miraculous. Never mind that our family only steps foot in church for funerals or weddings, this is our holiday. It is food and drink and family.

'Family' sometimes being loosely defined.

I listen to the voices and laughter floating above the soft holiday music. I don't hear Nic and I'm pretty sure I can identify all the jackets in the foyer as belonging to various family members here for game night. Everything is reassuringly the same as it is every holiday, from the banister ringed in deep green garland to the massive wreath with gold and red baubles hanging on the wall.

He's not here. All that worry, for nothing.

I let out a huge sigh of relief, and when I draw my next breath, everything smells more Christmassy, more magical. I feel joyful and triumphant.

I leave my coat and scarf on a hook, abandoning my suitcase by the stairs, and head down the hallway to say a quick hello on my way to the booze.

My father is in his favorite chair by the fire, his nose in a book, oblivious to the noisy room around him. My sister Amanda, who's ten years older than me, is playing Scrabble with her gorgeous wife Hazel, my cousin Lauren, and Aunt Kimberly. A group of kids go down in a tangle of limbs at a game of Twister and a roar goes up from the dining room, where a card game is in progress.

Lauren sees me first, squealing even though we saw each other two days ago. We work together at Sploosh! and spend a lot of time hanging out and gossiping about family dramas—namely our cousin Ashley, who never comes to Christmas and has gotten herself on a reality TV show. I used to babysit Lauren when she was little. Now she babysits me when we go clubbing, so I don't make bad choices. It's the circle of life, the young taking care of the old. Nature is beautiful like that.

Games are momentarily forgotten as I'm swallowed into a sea of hugs, everyone talking without waiting for anyone else. The commotion manages to pull my father from his book long enough for a quick kiss on the cheek as he asks me about the drive.

My twin's voice rises above the din, loud and booming, from the direction of the kitchen. To find Timbo, follow the noise.

I haven't seen him since before the accident. The one that nearly killed him and cost him his career as a stunt performer. The one my family didn't tell me about for days after it happened because they didn't want to 'ruin' my holiday in Italy.

That accident.

I offered to fly out to LA to look after him, but he didn't need me or even want me there. Then he didn't come home for Thanksgiving, spending it in California with some girlfriend.

Which, okay, it hurt. A lot. I get it, we aren't that close anymore. We haven't been close since we were fourteen and Nic moved in across the street, replacing me as Timothy's best friend. But Timothy's accident scared the hell out of me, and I want us to get back to how things used to be. This holiday—the two weeks out of the year my entire family gets together under one roof—is the perfect opportunity. Nic's absence is going to make this easier.

Extricating myself from everyone, I head toward the kitchen and the sound of Timothy's voice. Doesn't matter what story he's telling—they're all the same. Huge explosions. Massive jumps. Impressive falls. Timbo the handsome stuntman, no fears. Certain death. A hot doctor or nurse if this is about one of the times he broke something or needed stitches.

I round the doorway into the kitchen and slam hard into someone headed out.

Dominic Fontana grabs my arms, stopping me from falling as my holiday cheer goes up like a Yule Log.

"You."

I might have growled that.

He stares at me with those damned silver-gray eyes of his. They're cold and aloof because he's cold and aloof. His lips press together in displeasure, and same, buddy.

He hasn't changed. His long dark lashes are proof the universe is an asshole, as are those cheekbones. Hair a shade lighter than black sets off the silvery undertones of his flawless porcelain skin and his resting dick face manages to come across as a broody smolder.

He's ruined pretty men for me.

"Jessie," he says in a rumble, barely moving those lips.

He glares, and I glare back. It's a battle of the wills I'm not losing.

Timothy coughs. Nic looks first, so I win.

My brother points up.

Nic and I look up.

Oh, hell no.

Mistletoe.

We shove at each other in our haste to escape and once again, I end up on my ass.

"Fuckstick," I mutter, getting to my feet, but Nic's long gone.

My brother is smirking at me. I'm about to march over and give him hell when my mother, kitchen goddess, queen of cookbooks and TV shows alike, sails out of the butler's pantry, crushing me into a hug that's three parts cinnamon, one part Dior.

She pulls back and squeezes my arms. "You made it. I was starting to worry."

"Mom, take the mistletoe down. Please."

"Oh, sweetie." Her light brown eyes search my face first, then look about the kitchen, noticing the sudden absence. Her smile widens. "Nic wouldn't kiss you?"

Neither mistletoe nor spinning bottles could make that happen.

Timothy snorts. "Jessie wishes he would."

My stomach swoops. "I do not."

He shrugs and knocks back his beer, which is more maddening than if he'd tried to argue with me.

My mother laughs on her way back to the butler's pantry. "Maybe next time, hon."

"I'll kill him. Bludgeon him to death with a dildo from the factory reject pile." No way am I wasting a perfectly good sex toy on him.

Timothy wraps me in a bone-crushing hug of muscle and cable-knit sweater until I shove him away, reaching to muss his shaggy honey-blonde hair because that stupid head injury nearly took him away from me. A second later, I'm in a headlock.

He has seventeen minutes on me, several inches, and probably seventy pounds. I haven't stood a chance against him since puberty. I slap my hand twice on the counter in surrender, squealing at him to let me go.

Releasing me, he laughs. "Whatever, J."

Timothy never figured out the protective brother role. He'd laugh his ass off if Nic had kissed me. Or he'd make gagging noises. Hopefully, he'd question Nic's state of mind. Or...

Wait, why am I thinking about this?

I elbow my twin. Hard. "What's *he* doing here, anyway? Shouldn't he be off celebrating his divorce by screwing his way through another modeling agency?" I can't judge him because glass houses and all. Except I'm not pulling men hot enough to have a career in modeling, which is wildly unfair. And I haven't had a hookup in months. So I will be judging him. Respectfully.

Timothy laughs. "He's gone through them all."

I grumble under my breath and my brother gives me an obnoxious smile, letting me know he's going to enjoy every minute of my suffering.

And I'm going to have to take it if I'm going to fix my relationship with my twin.

"Be nice," he says mildly. "He's had a rough year."

My first *be nice*. Hell, I should turn this holiday into a drinking game—drink every time someone tells me to *be nice* to Nic. Two drinks if they bring up sleeping with models like that defines a 'rough year.'

Nic is the favorite of everyone in this family, except for me. If they only loved him for being a moderating influence on Timothy—which I used to be—I might be okay with it. But they side with Nic, seem to enjoy his company more than mine, and shower him with attention.

The thing is, Nic hates me as much as I hate him, but no one else sees it. No one tells him to *be nice*. He can insult me and say things that hurt me, and no one blinks. We've never gotten along, and after the shitshow five years ago, we never will.

But, I need these two weeks to fix things with my twin.

"I'll try," I mutter. I'll pretend Nic is somewhere else. Far, far away. The moon, perhaps.

A horde thunders into the kitchen, kids clamoring about pie and ice cream, saving me from what would no doubt be a lecture from my brother on the merits of Nic Fontana. The kids gather around the island, jostling for the best barstools, while the adults file into the room, talking and laughing. Hazel catches Amanda in the doorway for a quick kiss under the mistletoe.

My mother catches the direction of my gaze in passing and stops, pointing. "It stays up."

She would never take it down anyway. The sheer delight she takes in other people's terror at getting caught beneath it is the reason it's there. With only family around tonight, I'm safe, but at the wild Christmas Eve Folly, with my mother's infamous punch flowing, and Nic lurking...

He walks back in on cue, through the dining room to avoid the mistletoe.

My face is on fire, and he hasn't even looked my way. I need a drink.

There's always mulled wine in a slow cooker over the holiday, mugs on the counter. My mug is bright pink, the words *Blow Me, I'm Hot* printed across it. Everyone has a unique mug, from my mother's *Boss B*tch* to Timbo's Christmas T. rex. Nic's *Festive as F*ck* mug is on the counter, pulled from the back of a shelf after four years of gathering dust.

My skin prickles as a phantom breath whispers across the nape of my neck. I can't see him, but I know he's watching me. He always does, trying to unnerve me. It's not going to work.

By the time my mug is full and I turn to glare at him, he's no longer looking at me. His shoulders are tense though. I hate the way his shirt pulls tight on his chest when he reaches back to rub the base of his skull as he pretends to listen to Lauren and Timothy. It's obvious he's pretending. He's a shitty actor.

I take a big drink and spit the wine back into the mug, along with ten thousand incinerated taste buds. *Dammit.*

Nic, of course, saw that. He raises one perfectly thick eyebrow as if to say *good move, genius.* With a hell of a lot more care, I take a sip, extending my middle finger in his direction. He pretends not to notice and looks away.

Two weeks. Why didn't anyone tell me? I could've booked a hotel. In another state.

Okay, that's exactly why no one told me and there wasn't a single mention of Nic in the family group chat.

There's a small chance Nic had similar thoughts. I elbow my way into a spot along the island next to Amanda, accepting the slice of apple blackberry pie from my mother before leaning close to my sister. "Is *he* staying here?"

"Yes." Amanda looks at me pointedly while she sips mulled wine from a floral *This Might Be Wine* mug. The mug is massive but true—it's always wine. "Be nice."

Oh, hey. *Be nice* number two.

"*Here* here?" I prompt. "In this house *here*?"

Amanda rolls her eyes, tucking a strand of light brown hair that's fallen free from her messy mom bun behind her ear. "Yeah. The kids all think it's cool."

I scoff. "The kids also eat their boogers."

"Not since they were three." She protests, but amusement turns up the corners of her mouth.

"Their uncle was a goddamn stunt performer. Why don't they find Timbo cool?" Kids who eat boogers are possibly the only people who would mistake my twin for cool.

Amanda laughs. "They do."

Timothy's talking animatedly at the other end of the island. He's only this excitable when he's about to blow something up. Or leap off the roof. Or jump a car on a snowboard while another car tows him down the street. And he can't do those things anymore.

Early retirement isn't killing him yet. In fact, he looks good. Genuinely happy.

Totally not suspicious at all.

I take a bite of the pie, forgetting about my obnoxious brother and his dick of a best friend. Even on my poor scalded tongue, it's perfect, the pastry buttery and light, the fruit tart and sweet.

My little involuntary moan at the deliciousness of what will be the first of many, many good things stuffed in my mouth over the holidays goes unnoticed by everyone.

Except for Nic, apparently. His eyes are wide and the faintest hint of a blush creeps up his neck.

He scowls at the *'what?'* look I shoot him, tugging at the collar of his expensive shirt before going back to his pie.

Timothy drops a massive paw on Nic's shoulder, whispering in his ear. Whatever he says deepens Nic's scowl.

I smirk.

Until Timothy passes behind me, his voice close to my ear. "I saw that."

Saw what? A glare? Plenty more where that came from.

And yet...watching all my boisterous family talking and laughing, I have to admit Nic's reserved silence adds something to the chaos. A quiet sturdiness in a sea of noise and motion. Now that he's back, I feel how much it had been missing.

Not by me, to be clear. I enjoyed the unbalanced, unhinged pandemonium, and I'll hold my grudge against Nic forever.

Acknowledgements

Sometimes a character comes to life and basically takes over. For me, that character was Timothy, who first appeared in his twin sister's book and demanded his own, even though he had his HEA already. He threw everything up in the air and took me on a wild ride when I needed one the most.

I would never have survived this ride without all the love and support of my critique partners. Alexandra Kiley and Maggie North laughed with me, held my hands, passed me tissues, and kicked my ass as needed throughout this entire journey. They helped me out when the plot wasn't working, when character arcs weren't arcing, and when imposter syndrome took over, they talked me down from the ledge (more than once). Without them, all I'd have is messy vibes and banging. Seriously.

Writing can be such a solitary experience and I'm grateful for the friendship of my fellow Pitch Wars 2020 romance mentees, Maggie North, Regina Black, Nikki Payne, Courtney Kae, and Ella Sinclair—watching you all take over the world has been a blast! Whether you're reading my early drafts or helping me with cover art, I appreciate all your help and friendship.

Feedback is incredibly important, especially for a fist-time self-publishing author. I'm fortunate enough to have a group of incredibly talented friends within the writing community who took the time to read an early copy of this book to let me know what was working and what wasn't. So thank you to Regina Black, Ella Sinclair, Laya Brusi, Michelle Cruz, and Mae Bennett. A special thanks to

Kathryn Ferrer, who not only provided thoughtful feedback but also gave me support and encouragement and let me vent in DMs when things got hard. And to Livy Hart—thank you for your kind words and support.

Thank you to everyone in the writing community who has liked and commented and cheered me on, and to the FridayKiss community. I've learned so much through you all.

Thank you to every reader who took a chance on an unknown author and to everyone who left a review. I appreciate you so much and I hope you'll pick up the next book in this series.

Finally, thanks to my husband and kids for making sure I had the time and space to chase this dream. I love the three of you so much!

About the Author

Sarah Brenton (she/her) writes steamy, sex positive romance with strong characters getting dropkicked by love. She lives in New Zealand with her husband and kids and wishes she had enough time to write all the stories in her head.

Want to know more? Visit www.sarahbrenton.com, sign-up for my newsletter, and follow me on Instagram!

Also By Sarah Brenton